Helen Black grew up in Pontefract, West Yorkshire. At eighteen she went to Hull University and left three years later with a tattoo on her shoulder and a law degree. She became a lawyer in Peckham, and soon had a loyal following of teenagers needing legal advice and bus fares. She ended up in Luton, working predominantly for children going through the care system.

Helen is married to a long-suffering lawyer and is the mother of twins.

Also by Helen Black

Blood Rush
Twenty Twelve
Dark Spaces
Friendless Lane
Taking Liberties
Bang to Rights

Playing Dirty

Helen Black

CONSTABLE

CONSTABLE

First published in Great Britain in 2019 by Constable

1 3 5 7 9 10 8 6 4 2

Copyright © Helen Black, 2019

Epigraph excerpt from *The Sea* by John Banville, published by Picador,
an imprint of Pan Macmillan Ltd, copyright © John Banville 2005.

The moral right of the author has been asserted.

A CIP catalogue record for this book
is available from the British Library.

ISBN: 978-1-47212-987-1

Typeset in Bembo by Initial Typesetting Services, Edinburgh
Printed and bound in Great Britain by Clays Ltd, Elcograf S.p.A.

Papers used by Constable are from well-managed forests and other responsible sources.

Constable
An imprint of
Little, Brown Book Group
Carmelite House
50 Victoria Embankment
London EC4Y 0DZ

An Hachette UK Company
www.hachette.co.uk

www.littlebrown.co.uk

'The past beats inside me like a second heart.'

The Sea by John Banville

Chapter 1

31 August 1990, Manchester

There's a funny smell of burning that wakes me up. Please God, Fat Rob hasn't set his sleeping bag on fire. Again.

I throw off my blanket and hurl myself at the hump at the end of the settee but he's not in it. I'm glad not to find him in a ball of flames but there's still smoke in the air.

'Rob?'

He pokes his head around the kitchen door, hair like an Afro perm gone wrong. 'What are you doing up?'

'Wondering if I should call nine-nine-nine,' I say.

He jerks his head towards the settee, and I roll my eyes. I mean, I can't go back to sleep now, can I? But Fat Rob doesn't move so I sigh and crawl under my covers. The PVC under me makes a farting sound.

When Fat Rob's satisfied, he comes into the main room. Well, it's the only other room, actually. We kip in it, eat in it, watch telly in it. The shower's down the hall, but more often than not we just have a wash in the kitchen sink. The landlord calls this a bedsit. Probably cos we can only sit on the bed. And when I say bed, I mean settee. Not that the landlord knows about me. If he found out I was living here, he'd have me and Fat Rob out.

With a grin on his face, wearing only a pair of red boxer shorts and his new England tattoo, Fat Rob carries a chipped saucer in both hands. It reminds me of the time our Jay was a king in the nativity. Only Jay did

1

a massive burp and made one of the shepherds wee his pants. There was a puddle under the crib and Mary tried to mop it up with the tea towel Joseph was wearing on his head.

Now I know what the bloody smell is. On the saucer is a Danish pastry with a sparkler stuck in it. White flecks of heat spray over the thick icing and glacé cherry. 'What the hell's going on?' I ask.

Fat Rob bursts out laughing, 'Happy birthday, Lib.'

We eat half each on the number thirty-six, though Fat Rob insists I get all the cherry.

'Sorry, I didn't get you a card or owt,' he says, lips all sticky.

I nudge him in the ribs a bit too hard. 'Shut up.'

We know there's no money to waste on cards and that. It's cash in hand for both of us at work. He did think about signing on as well, but a lot of people know who he is now, and some twat would dob him in. I can't do it for obvious reasons.

What I don't tell him is that it's a long time since anyone remembered my birthday. So many kids came and went in Orchard Grove that we hardly knew each other's names a lot of the time. The only two I bothered with at all were Imbo and Vicky. But they had a lorry load of problems to be getting on with and not enough head space to be thinking about birthdays. If I'd told them, they'd have gone out and nicked some ale, insist we all got pissed, but I never did.

Our Crystal and Frankie are too young to be buying cards, and I'm not allowed contact anyway. Our Jay's back in jail and I'm pretty sure they don't let him out to go to Smith's or whatever.

To be honest, a cake – well, half of it – with my best mate, it's enough. I don't like a fuss.

'D'you miss 'em?' he asks. 'On days like your birthday, you must do.'

I think about that. What would we be doing if we were all together? Our Jay would crack us up with some rubbish or other in ten seconds flat and our Frankie would laugh so much he'd probably wet himself. Our

Crystal would press her face into my jumper and giggle, curly hair boinging up and down.

'You got a shift tonight?' Rob asks.

I nod.

'Shame.'

But it's not. I like my job. I like the people. I like the cash.

'See you there,' he says, and gets up for his stop.

He leans over and kisses the top of my head. He smells of fags and icing sugar. When he gets to the top of the stairs, he calls out, so the whole top deck can hear, 'You don't look too bad for thirty-two.'

I laugh and shout back. 'Thanks, dickhead.'

Cos what else can you say to someone who's saved your life?

Present Day

Paul Hill was smart and sombre in a black cashmere overcoat. The wife, on the other hand, looked like DFS had exploded on bank-holiday weekend: brown leather jacket, pencil skirt and knee boots.

'Bunny.' Liberty smiled at her. 'How nice to see you.'

Bunny leaned in, every item she had on creaking like a ship. 'Bloody hate funerals, I do.'

Liberty wondered if she thought this made her stand out from the crowd. If she believed that the average punter lapped up the flowers and hymns.

'I mean, we barely knew Jackson,' said Bunny. She wrinkled her nose in the direction of the front row of the church, where assorted members of the Delaney clan hunched in their nylon ties, desperate to get this over with.

All of Jackson Delaney's big players were behind bars. The rag-taggle bunch here today might run some low-rent money-lending deals up in the schemes of Glasgow, but part of Jackson's organised-crime empire they were not.

'You know why we're here,' Hill muttered.

Bunny rolled her eyes and took a seat at the back, her skirt screeching against the polished wood. Hill nodded at Liberty and moved along towards his wife.

'Lib.'

She smelt Crystal before she saw her. Juicy Fruit and lip balm. 'Hey.'

Her sister wore a chunky black scarf wound twice around her white throat. Trademark ripped skinny jeans replaced with dark grey ones, no holes. Had she lost even more weight? Now was not the time to ask.

Bunny waved at Crystal. Crystal ignored Bunny.

'Where's Jay?' Liberty asked.

Crystal pointed her head towards the doors of the church and, bang on cue, Jay arrived, sexy as fuck in a black suit that must have been tailor-made to fit him.

'Oi, oi,' he said. Liberty reached for the sunglasses balanced on top of his head and slid them into his breast pocket. He winked. 'Got a surprise for you, sis.'

Liberty was about to point out that a funeral probably wasn't the time or place, when her baby brother waltzed into the church as if he owned the place. 'You have got to be shitting me,' said Liberty, but she couldn't suppress the grin as Frankie landed a smacker full on her lips.

'Lib,' he said.

'Are you well enough to do this?' she asked.

But Frankie's answer was drowned out as the organ struck up 'Abide With Me'.

Liberty pulled back the heavy velvet drape and entered the Black Cherry. Mel had made sure the cleaners had scrubbed the place to within an inch of its life, the smell of sweat and sex overlaid with Zoflora. Instead of the usual stomach-punching bass, classical music drifted from the speakers over the club.

Liberty was determined not to laugh as the violins of Vivaldi's *Four Seasons* sprang to life, but she nearly cracked when Frankie elbowed her in the side. 'Don't,' she said, but Frankie just elbowed her again, a snort escaping his mouth.

Liberty crooked her arm to retaliate but saw her brother had his hand pressed just under his ribcage. It was a habit he'd picked up. Underneath his crisp shirt was the mother of all scars, and although Frankie swore it no longer hurt, his fingers still sought it out as if to assure themselves that his insides weren't pouring onto the floor. She grabbed his other hand and squeezed.

On the far side of the club, Jay was already at the bar, eyeing up the trays of sandwiches laid out for the funeral guests. He took a bite of a brown triangle and frowned. 'Egg mayonnaise,' he said. 'When did folk stop using salad cream?'

Liberty snorted and took a cheese and pickle offering. Growing up, salad cream had been liberally applied to most sandwich fillings by their mother. When money had run low, which it often had, there was more salad cream than anything else.

Crystal ignored the food and waved over to Mel for a drink.

'Remind me why we're doing this,' said Liberty.

'You tell me,' Crystal replied.

Mel scuttled towards them, six-inch heels clicking. She collected a bottle of Jack Daniel's from under the bar. 'It's expected.'

'By who?' Liberty asked.

Mel slammed down the bottle and snatched up five glasses. 'Everyone.' She looked to Jay, who was hoovering down another sandwich. 'Explain it to her.'

'We're the Greenwoods,' he said.

'Exactly.' Mel sloshed bourbon into the glasses. 'Delaney was an old-school face. We're showing our respect.'

Liberty knocked back her drink as the first mourners arrived, and Mel sent over one of the girls to show them to a table. She was called Justina and was known for her ability to put both feet behind her head to display an impressively pierced snatch, masked today with a pair of black trousers presumably provided by Mel.

As more people spilled into the club, the other girls carried trays of food over to them and took orders for drinks.

'How much is this costing?' Crystal asked.

Mel pushed a glass at her. 'We'll be open tonight as per.'

Crystal rolled her eyes but took her JD and held it up. Mel clinked her own glass against it, then Jay followed suit. Frankie took his turn, but quickly replaced his untouched glass on the bar and reached over for a Diet Coke. He'd been on the wagon ever since he'd got out of hospital. No booze, no gear. He was even threatening to quit the fags. 'Cheers,' he said.

Several guests stood as a woman in her late fifties entered the Cherry. One made his way towards her and put a hand on her shoulder. Her face was tired and lined, grey roots visible in her parting. She nodded at the man, as if her head were full of stones, the weight registering in each movement.

'Who's that?' Liberty asked.

No one answered as the man led the woman towards them. Clearly, Liberty was about to find out.

The woman eyed the Greenwood clan over the rim of her cup.

'Can I get you anything stronger?' Liberty asked.

'No, thanks.' She nodded at Frankie's Diet Coke. 'Best to keep a clear head, eh?'

One of the girls passed by with a tray of sausage rolls and dipped her hip, exposing the lace of her bra strap, so the woman could take one.

Liberty tried a smile. 'So, you're a relative of Jackson?'

The woman placed the sausage roll on her saucer. 'His sister.' She held out a hand to Liberty. 'Innis Delaney.' The skin of her palm was warm from the cup.

Innis held Liberty's gaze. Not even a blink. Fair play. A shout from behind broke the spell. One of the lads was calling for a song, another already on his feet belting out a number. The kid had a voice like warm honey on a spoon. Shame he'd a face like a slapped arse.

'Sorry you had to wait so long for a funeral,' said Liberty.

'They had to wait for the trial.' Innis snorted. 'Polis. You know how they are.' As the lad broke into 'Flower of Scotland', she leaned towards Liberty. 'Can I ask a favour of you?'

'Depends what it is,' said Crystal.

Liberty sighed. 'Of course you can, Innis.'

'If you ever hear who was behind it, let me know.'

'Just some junkie in the nick, wasn't it?' asked Liberty.

Innis laughed, exposing big yellow teeth. 'We both know that's shite.' The lad finished his rendition, wiping his too-big nose with a mayonnaise-smeared paper napkin. The other men called for a fresh round of drinks. 'I need to get this lot out of here.' Innis rose to her feet. 'But keep me posted.'

'Sure,' Liberty replied.

'Then I can deal with things properly,' said Innis.

Liberty watched the last Delaney exit the Cherry, leaving behind plates strewn with tomatoes and lettuce. They'd eaten every sandwich in the house, including crusts, but no salad had touched a Glaswegian lip.

Liberty signalled for Mel to get the club back to normal, and in less than ten minutes the music was pumping, and Justina had taken to the stage in a transparent PVC minidress. Mel shook out five pairs of black nylon trousers and put them into a carrier, tags still intact.

'You're not actually going to return them?' said Liberty.

'Waste not, want not,' Mel replied, and slid the bag under the bar.

'Jacko's sister's in charge, don't you think?' Liberty asked.

'In charge of what?' Mel asked. 'A bunch of inbreds?'

'What if she knows?'

'She doesn't know shit,' Mel said.

Liberty shrugged and held out her glass for Mel to top up with Jack Daniel's. 'She might suspect.'

Harry crossed the club to the bar, a grin on his face as he waved at Liberty. She liked Crystal's husband, who was warm and funny. Christ only knew what he saw in her sister. Halfway over he tripped and had to steady himself against the back of a chair. Was he pissed?

When he reached the bar the smell of him told Liberty that he was. 'Had a few?' she asked. He swayed in front of her, so she pushed him onto a stool.

'A couple.' He reached over for Liberty's glass, took a drink but missed his mouth, pouring most of it down his shirt. 'Fuck a duck.'

Something was up. Getting plastered in the middle of the day wasn't Harry's style.

'Everything okay?' she asked.

Harry's breathing was heavy as he searched for Crystal in the club, but she was chewing Jay's ear off about something or other. 'Not here.'

Liberty grabbed his hand and led him to the office. In the confines of the windowless room at the back, the stench of alcohol poured off Harry. Liberty cleared a stack of boxes from one of the chairs. Five-speed vibrators. Five speeds! Like gears in a car. Next, they'd make them with cruise control. Harry flopped down, no longer smiling.

Liberty perched on the edge of the desk. 'What's up?'

'I need . . .'

Liberty waited but Harry put his face in his hands. At last she put a hand on his shoulder and he looked up, tears in his eyes. 'You can talk to me, Harry,' she told him. 'We're family.'

A crash came from the club beyond the office door. Then shouts. Liberty put up a finger to Harry and went to check on what was happening. Next to the stage, a table had been overturned and a man was on the floor, howling like a banshee. A small crowd gathered around him and Mel barged her way through. Likely a works do or birthday party. Mixed group all wearing T-shirts stating they were '*On it till we vomit*'.

'If you haven't got him up and in a chair in the next three seconds, you're all out,' Mel shouted. The group laughed and jeered. 'And if you lot think I'm joking, just try me.'

Two women in the group hauled their fallen friend to his feet, and a bloke with a Glo-Stick tucked behind his ear put the table back in its place.

Mel nodded at Liberty. Crisis averted. But when Liberty turned back to the office, Harry was already on his way out. She hurried after him.

'Got to go, Lib,' he said. 'Feel a bit rough, to be honest.'

'Not half as bad as you'll feel later.'

He tried a smile and failed as Crystal appeared at his side, face like thunder.

'Harry's had one too many,' said Liberty.

Crystal narrowed her eyes, grabbed her husband's sleeve and dragged him out of the Cherry. Liberty frowned as she watched them leave. Something was most definitely not right.

The kid was face down on the tarmac by the slide, eyes still open. A few uniforms kept the locals at bay while SOCO set up their forensic tent.

DI Rose Angel scanned the onlookers, who had congregated around the rusty swings. Mostly youngers working for the local crew. When she moved in their direction, they evaporated. No intention of talking to the police.

Behind her, Redman chuckled. Rose ignored him.

A woman stayed on in the park, watching the show. Age difficult to say. People round here didn't wear well.

'She won't talk to you,' said Redman.

'We'll see.'

Coppers like Redman annoyed her. All this-is-the-way-it-is schtick. A boy, not more than fifteen years old, was dead just feet from where they were standing. If that didn't make you want to do things differently, it was time to get another job.

As Rose approached, the woman looked off into the distance, but she didn't move.

'Know him?' Rose asked, with a jerk of the head towards the body.

The woman shrugged, still refusing to make eye contact. It was a windy night and a crisps packet blew across the park and landed at her feet. Cheese-and-onion. She ground down on it with the toe of her trainer, as if it were a cigarette.

'He's a younger, right?' said Rose.

'Suppose so,' said the woman.

'Any idea what happened?'

'Do you care?' the woman asked.

'Why wouldn't I?'

The woman zipped her fleece right up to the top, shoved her hands deep into her pockets. She still had the crisps packet trapped under her foot. 'I've got a lad his age,' she said. 'Wants to go to college next year.'

Rose nodded. 'Good for him.'

The woman lifted her foot and the packet flew away past the slide, eventually getting trapped in the trees at the perimeter.

'These kids.' She stopped and ran her thumb across her bottom lip. There was a heart tattoo on the knuckle. A blue DIY job. 'They don't think.'

Rose eyed the woman. It was all there in her face. Worry. Fear. Exhaustion. 'And what do you think?' she asked.

'Not much if I can help it.'

'Was this just an argument that got out of hand? Or is something else going on here?' asked Rose.

The woman buried her nose in the funnel of her fleece so that when she spoke, the words were muffled. 'This whole place is getting out of hand.' Then she moved away, head down, shoulders hunched against the cold. When she reached the gate, she went through it and turned right into the estate without a backward glance at the body.

Empire Rise was deserted, most of the houses in darkness, the occupants tucked up in bed, alarms set for half seven. When Liberty opened her front door, she was surprised to find Sol still up, stirring a pan of chilli at the stove. Wordlessly, he ladled a helping into a bowl and handed it to her. She grabbed a spoon from the drawer and began to eat still on her feet. 'Good day?' she asked.

He shrugged and poured them both a glass of red wine. She'd already had quite a few slugs of JD, but didn't say no. He didn't ask after her day. Never did. It wasn't that he didn't care, more that nothing good could come of it. He might have resigned from the force, but he was still a copper at heart.

Liberty put down her bowl and slid over to him. 'Tired?'

'Not really.'

She kissed him on the mouth. 'Good.'

'You need to brush your teeth,' he said.

'You need to shut up.'

11

She kissed him again when her mobile sprang to life.

'Saved by the bell,' said Sol.

They both knew she would check it. Caller ID read 'Frankie'.

As Sol headed for the stairs, Liberty called her brother back. He was doing well. Off the drugs. But these things could all slip in a second. He'd been clean before only to slide into a deeper and murkier pit of carnage.

'Lib.'

'It's late,' she said. 'You okay?'

'Yeah.' His voice sounded clear. No hint of a pill or a cheeky line. 'Bit of a problem up on the Crosshills.' Car lights flooded the kitchen from the street outside, the thump of drum and bass seeping from an open window. 'Kid got stabbed.'

Liberty's stomach flipped. 'Dead?'

'Yep.'

The music stopped, but the car still idled in the street. 'Who did it?'

'Dunno,' said Frankie. 'But don't assume it's some turf war, Lib.'

'I'm not.'

Frankie laughed. 'You always assume that.' Actually, she didn't always assume that, but she did always fear that. 'More than likely some row over a pair of trainers. You know how stupid these kids are.'

'Find out.'

'I will.'

She heard a shout and a laugh in the background. 'Where are you?'

'A crack house up on Carter Street.'

'Not funny.'

'You're so easy to wind up.' He snorted. 'It's the telly.'

'Ha-chuffing-ha,' she said, and hung up.

She knew she could trust Frankie to get to the bottom of what

12

was going on and willed herself not to stress about it before she had all the information.

Upstairs, the toilet flushed, and she pushed thoughts of the family business to one side and made for the stairs.

'Just so you know,' she shouted up to Sol, 'I'm taking out my dentures.'

Sol was like a dog. Never fully asleep. All those years on the job, keeping eyes and ears open had fucked with his adrenal glands.

His first wife had been the same and liked to knock them both into unconsciousness with sex and vodka. The second had tried to help him with lotions and candles and crystals (you'd think that people selling bits of purple rock would soon go out of business but, no, there were whole shops full of that sort of crap).

Liberty just accepted that sometimes sleep came and sometimes it didn't. Bad dreams plagued her because she'd seen her mother chucked off a fifth-floor balcony. Lavender oil wasn't going to fix that.

He watched her now, fast on, face buried in the pillow, and hoped she was somewhere far away from her childhood. He moved a dark tendril of hair from her shoulder with his finger. There was a round scar on her skin where she said she'd picked off a chickenpox scab. Jacqueline Greenwood wouldn't have been the type to bother using calamine on her kids, that was for sure.

He felt protective of Liberty, in a way he hadn't about Angie or Natasha. Which was bloody ridiculous, considering how capable Liberty was of looking after herself.

Sol sighed. He wasn't going to get back to sleep, and if he carried on, he'd wake Liberty too. Carefully, he slid out of bed, pulled on his discarded boxers and padded down to the kitchen. He fancied a coffee and a fag but knew both would only make matters worse. Fuck it. He flicked the kettle, grabbed a packet of Marlboro and unlocked the window.

Outside, a car was parked up, engine idling. A pain in the arse on a quiet street at this time of night. If they didn't shift soon, he'd go out there and tell them to bugger off. A couple of months ago, he'd have flashed his warrant card. Now, of course, he didn't have one.

He lit his fag and blew the smoke out of the window. Liberty wouldn't have complained either way, but he liked to show willing. After all, it was her house – or, at least, her name was on the lease. She'd given him a key without too much fanfare and he'd moved in with the few bits and bobs he had, but he didn't consider it 'home'. Maybe that would be their next move. Choose a flat together? Somewhere they both liked? Liberty never talked about the future. Then again, Sol hadn't brought it up either.

That damn car. How long was it going to stay out there?

He took another drag and made for the door. Could be that the hit of nicotine and lack of sleep was making him tetchy, but he was going out there to have a word. He dug his feet into the boots he'd left in the hallway and pulled a coat off the peg. Halfway down the path, with the wind whipping round his thighs, he wished he'd put on proper clothes. But then he stopped short.

The car hadn't moved, and the engine was still running, but the angle of the streetlamp meant he could see inside and, from where he was standing, the driver was holding a mobile up at Liberty's bedroom window.

'What the fuck?' he muttered.

He waited and watched for another moment. No doubt about it, the guy was filming.

Suddenly, there was a sound behind him and the hallway flooded with light. Liberty stood in the doorway, a satin kimono wrapped around her, a puzzled frown on her face. At the same time, the engine gunned and the car took off.

14

Liberty wagged a finger at Sol in pants, boots and Puffa. 'Now, that's a great look.'

'Thought I heard something,' he said.

'And?'

'Just kids.' He threw away his half-smoked fag and watched the orange tip bounce on the pavement. 'But since we're both awake . . .'

Chapter 2

31 August 1990

Mr Simms plonks a stack of books on the end table. 'Take one and pass them along.' Mansfield Park by Jane Austen. My copy is battered, the pages covered with pencil notes. 'I recommend you get your own copy. Other people's annotations will not help.'

I'll get down to WH Smith's tomorrow. After tonight's shift, I'll have the cash.

The girl sitting next to me doesn't touch hers but carries on scribbling graffiti on her pencil case. CND symbols, smiley faces and a few rainbows. Her nail varnish is black, just like all the clothes she's got on. Everything except a pair of bright red Converse that look new.

Mr Simms goes back to the front and smiles. He's got a friendly face and acts as if he wants to be here. Not like most teachers. Maybe it's because we're only here for an induction day. By mid-September he'll have the dog on, like all the rest of them.

'I just want to point out the obvious,' he says. He's got the Manchester accent that Fat Rob takes off all the time. 'This isn't school. I won't chase you for your assignments. If you don't do the work, that's your funeral.' A lad at the back laughs. 'But if you want a decent grade to go off to uni or whatever, then you'll need to put your back into it.'

Another teacher sticks his head in the door and Mr Simms pops out to speak to him.

'Why assume any of us want to go to fucking university?' says the girl next to me. 'I mean, what's the point?'

I don't answer. First off because she's not really asking me. She's doing that thing where people make a statement through a question. And, second, because going to university is exactly what I want. How else am I going to get a decent job and somewhere proper to live? I can't kip on Fat Rob's settee for ever, can I?

The girl rubs her stomach. 'Christ, I'm starving.' She's quite posh when she speaks. 'Hangover from hell.'

I laugh. Whenever Fat Rob and me are hung-over we'll eat anything. One time we had Pot Noodle sandwiches for breakfast.

'Fancy some lunch?' she asks, this time looking right at me.

I've got thirty-two pence in my pocket. 'Forgot my purse.'

'My shout,' she says. I must look dubious because she smiles. 'Honestly, you'd be doing me a favour. I'm Kitty by the way.'

The canteen is packed and the queue for the till is massive. Kitty's got a ton of food on her tray. Tuna sandwich, chips, chocolate muffin and a flapjack. Oh, and a can of Coke. I stick with a ham roll and a packet of Skips. I don't want to take the piss.

When we finally get sat down, she grabs a nearby ketchup bottle and squeezes a ton over her chips in a zigzag pattern. Then she starts shovelling them in with her fingers. Fat Rob eats like a dog, but Kitty's something else.

'I'm never drinking again,' she says, mouth full.

I unwrap my roll. 'Where did you go?'

'House party.' She rips the clingfilm off her sandwich. 'Old schoolmate.'

'Good, was it?'

'Nah. Completely shit.' Kitty takes half the sarnie in one bite. 'Probably why I got so wasted. It's the only way I can stand any of that lot.' She takes my Skips, opens them and pushes a handful into her gob. 'You're not from round here.'

'You are minging,' I say. She laughs and sprays food all over the table. 'I'll have to introduce you to my flatmate.'

'You don't live with your parents, then?'

Shit. I didn't mean to let that slip. No one's asked about Mam and Dad, really. When I filled in the form to join sixth-form college, there was a box for one of them to sign. I just got Fat Rob to do a scribble with his left hand. The last thing I want is folk knowing my business.

'You lucky bitch,' she says. 'I fucking hate mine.'

I'm trying to think of something to say when she sticks her hand into her bag and pulls out a pouch of Old Holborn and some skins. 'Let's go and pollute the fresh air of Manchester.'

She leaves behind her uneaten food and marches off to the door. When she's not looking, I grab the muffin and flapjack, slide them into my bag and follow her out into the sunshine.

Present Day

The junkies arrived one after another. All ages, shapes, sizes and colours. The only common themes: bad teeth and industrial need.

Rose had taken a few drugs in her time. There'd been a period after her stepfather had thrown her out when she'd surfed various sofas and lived off ketamine and energy drinks. And she still drank too much occasionally, waking up with a thumping head and a sinking feeling as she checked who she'd texted after midnight.

But she kept it all in separate containers.

At work, she avoided social gatherings altogether. Getting drunk in the pub with a load of sweaty police wasn't Rose's idea of a good time. It didn't make her popular, but she didn't give a damn. They could whisper about her behind her back, say she had a rod up her backside.

The latest addict shuffled towards the dealer. He took more than a rod up his backside by the looks of him. Rent-boy. Though *boy* was stretching it. Had to be thirty at least.

Rose watched him: his hands shook so badly he dropped his

money. The dealer just laughed. This was what Rose was after: someone already starting to cluck. Plus, he couldn't weigh more than seven stones. She'd be able to take him if he got difficult.

She let him get his drugs, then slipped out of her car and followed him towards a row of garages. She'd need to grab him before he got inside. There would be more zombies in there and she didn't need a row.

When he was twenty feet away from a metal door spray-painted with 'Anya is a skank', she overtook him and stood in his path. He moved to the left, but she moved with him.

'What?' he mumbled.

Rose whipped out her warrant card and gave a grim smile. The man looked around wildly for a means of escape.

'When did you actually last break into a run? Because I'm thinking that if you even try it, that'll be the end of you,' she said.

'Cunt,' he replied.

She prised the plastic baggie from his fist and slipped it into her pocket. 'Now that's not nice, is it?'

The man's forehead glistened. It was a cold day, but his body didn't know that.

'Look,' said Rose. 'If you answer a few questions, I'll let you go so you can do your thing. How does that sound?'

'Cunt,' the man repeated, but he didn't resist as she took his elbow and led him towards her car.

Once inside, the man hugged himself tightly. He smelt like the bottom drawer of a fridge left far too long. Rose opened her window.

'Got a fag?' he asked.

Rose shook her head and he sighed, sending a wave of stench towards her so pungent she had to turn her head.

'Who runs things on this estate?' she asked.

The man nodded in the general direction of where he'd scored. 'I don't know their names.'

'Not them,' said Rose. 'I'm asking you who's running things.' When the man didn't answer she gave an impatient groan. 'I can nick you now, if that's how you want it. You'll spend the night puking up in the cells and I'll have paperwork on a possession charge. Hardly win-win, is it?' The man clutched his stomach. Please God he wasn't going to throw up in the car. 'This is Greenwood territory, am I right?'

The man flicked a nervous glance at her. He wouldn't want to get into a discussion about the local movers and shakers, but he'd want to get that brown powder into his bloodstream even more.

'They say so.'

'They do indeed,' Rose replied. 'I'm wondering if a regime change is afoot.' The man frowned, clearly puzzled. 'Are the Greenwoods losing control?'

The light bulb went on. 'Nah. I mean, there's been stuff happening lately. Youngers not from here coming in and starting trouble.'

'Hill's people?'

The man breathed slimy-potato breath at her. 'That's the weird thing. After Jackson Delaney got shanked, things calmed right down.'

Rose thought about that for a second. According to Redman and his mates, Hill and the Greenwoods had carved up Delaney's area after his death. No one seemed to care. It was better than a turf war. But there'd been a recent rash of violent attacks on the estates. No one was talking, obviously. But they pointed to cracks in the peace process.

'What's your name?' Rose asked.

The man let his head fall forward. 'I need to get off.'

Rose retrieved the gear from her pocket, held it up between finger and thumb and shook it. The rattle of the plastic made him look up.

'Salty.' He rubbed his palms against his jeans. 'Everyone calls me Salty.'

20

'Well, Salty, I want you to keep your eyes and ears open for me.'

'I'm not a grass,' Salty replied.

Rose rolled her eyes. They both knew that he'd give evidence against his granny for the cost of a couple of Xanax. 'Just information on what's occurring,' said Rose. 'Gossip, rumours, doesn't matter.'

Salty stared at the bag that Rose still held at head height. 'Fine.'

Rose dropped it into Salty's lap. He snatched it with his right hand and opened the door with his left. The rush of frosted air was welcome.

'I fucking hate the police,' said Salty.

'So, who're you gonna call when you get your next beating?'

'Why would I bother?' Salty yanked up his hood. 'Probably one of your lot dishing it out.'

Liberty left Sol fast asleep, one leg flung on top of the duvet, and drove over to Frankie's flat. She pulled up the 911 outside and pressed the horn.

Seconds later he dived out, blue beanie pulled down over his ears, piece of toast clenched between his teeth. 'Morning,' he said, fastening his seatbelt. Liberty grabbed the toast and took a bite. 'Oi.' She rammed it back into his mouth and snapped on the radio. Listeners were ringing in with their best hangover cures. Everything from pie and mash to a mug of Lemsip was suggested.

'Having a wank,' Frankie shouted.

'Excuse me?'

'Works every time,' said Frankie. Liberty's eyes opened wide. 'Though sometimes it's better if you throw up first.'

Liberty indicated at the turning to the Black Cherry. 'Thanks for the tip.'

'You're very welcome,' he replied, swallowing the last of his breakfast.

'So, what do you know about the younger killed up on the Crosshills?'

'Nothing much. Some kid comes onto the estate and stabs him up.'

Liberty stopped the car. 'Not a row over a pair of Nikes, then?'

'No.' Frankie got out of the car, stretched his shoulders. 'But not a row over food either. No one even knew the kid that did it.'

Now that was surprising. On the tight-knit streets of the estates, everyone knew everyone. Where they worked and who for was common knowledge.

Crystal was at the bar, back turned to the door, already at full pelt.

Jay listened and nodded. Mel chewed her lip and ran a tea towel around some glasses.

'We need to talk to Hill, find out what the fuck's going on,' Crystal ranted.

'I'm pretty sure Lib will do that,' said Mel.

Red rag to a bull. Crystal pulled her tiny frame to its full height. 'Lib? Since when was Lib in charge?'

'Morning,' said Liberty.

Crystal spun around. Christ, she looked shocking. Liberty's little sister was a natural beauty. Where Liberty had always been the clever one, Crystal was the pretty one. But this morning her pale, flawless skin was dry and blotchy, her eyes crimson-rimmed. Had she been crying? Crystal never cried. Ever.

'Don't tell me,' said Crystal. 'You've already spoken to Hill and bought whatever crock of crap he's selling you.'

Liberty skirted around her to the back of the bar, fished in the fridge for a Diet Coke. The bottles felt warm to the touch. Presumably Mel had just restocked. As if reading her mind, Mel filled a glass with ice.

'Cat got your tongue?' Crystal hissed.

Liberty poured the Coke. She didn't want a row. Especially not with Crystal, who would cheerfully use any opportunity to dredge up the past. But sometimes there was no choice.

'I've asked around to get a feel for what happened,' said Frankie. Crystal fixed him with a glare. 'What? You don't think I should have done that?'

Crystal stuck her hands on her bony hips. Jay reached over and rubbed her elbow, but she shrugged him off. 'And when did you get so fucking reasonable?' She spat at her older brother. 'Six months ago, you'd have been baying for blood.'

'And where did that get us?' Liberty asked.

'We were doing just fine before you showed up.' Crystal jabbed her thumb in her chest. 'Don't think you came here and saved us.'

Liberty closed her eyes. The same arguments raged again and again. Six months ago, the family was on the brink: Frankie in hospital fighting for his life, Jay out of control shagging every dancer in the club, Crystal kneecapping folk with bottles. Someone had had to take control and calm everything down. Liberty had done that, hadn't she?

'Whatever,' Crystal said at last. 'Do what you like.' She grabbed her denim jacket from the table. 'But when it goes tits up, don't say I didn't warn you.'

When she was safely gone, Jay grabbed Liberty's now empty glass, fished out an ice cube and stuck it into his mouth. 'Well, I'd say that went better than expected.'

Rose scanned the shelves of food for inspiration. As far as police-station canteens went, this one was by no means the worst. On a stint in Liverpool it had been pre-packed ham rolls, packets of crisps and a few bananas by the till going slowly black as they waited for a buyer. At least here they tried to offer a bit of choice. At lunchtimes they were even giving a salad bar a whirl. But this morning Rose did not fancy anything on display.

An assistant with a name badge jiggling over her left boob that introduced her as 'Alison' scraped the last bits of the breakfast items into a metal tub. A couple of hardened rashers of bacon, a lone grilled tomato, a plop of scrambled egg adrift in a pool of milky liquid.

'Can I get you owt, love?' Alison asked.

Rose's stomach churned at the sight of the mangled leftovers. 'Coffee, please.'

She took her drink and holed up in the corner. Her shift wasn't due to start for another twenty minutes, but she always got in early. People who arrived at the nick with seconds to spare, doing up their buttons and ramming toast down their throats, irritated her. Why didn't they just sort out their lives? Get up half an hour earlier?

When Redman and his friends arrived, Rose grabbed her mobile and began to scroll. They'd ignore her if they thought she was busy. Probably relieved. None of them pretended to think much of her, but if any of the senior officers caught them actively excluding her, there'd be trouble, so from time to time they tried their best to chat to her.

She checked the newsfeed on Facebook. Someone she went to school with had just got married. The updated profile picture showed off beefy arms pouring out of a white dress that stuck out like a wigwam. Her son stood next to her, scowling in a pair of grey flannel knickerbockers.

'Morning.'

Rose's heart sank as Redman took the chair opposite. 'Hi, Joel.'

'I feel like we've got off on the wrong foot, Rose,' he said. 'Haven't given each other a chance.'

Rose shrugged. 'We don't need to be friends.'

His hair was an odd colour. A sort of uniform yellow, as if it had come out of a tube. But she was pretty certain that Joel

Redman wasn't the sort of man to dye his hair. She'd be surprised if he bothered to brush his teeth most mornings.

'True,' he said. 'But we do need to work together.' The coffee had gone cold, but Rose blew over the rim of her mug anyway. 'The guv wants us to look into the stabbing over on the Crosshills estate.'

'The one where no one will tell us anything?'

Redman scratched his chin, nails crackling over the stubble, which Rose noticed for the first time was dark. Maybe he did dye his hair. How about that?

They watched each other for a few seconds, neither speaking, blinking at each other in turn. At last Rose put down her still-full mug and pushed back her chair. 'Right,' she said. 'Let's get on over there.'

Jay and Frankie took hold of either end of a huge cardboard box and ferried it across the club.

'What's in there?' Liberty asked Mel.

'Cock rings,' Mel replied, clipping together a stack of till receipts. Mary Mother of God. Just how many cocks could need a ring? There must be thousands in that box. 'I hope you're sure about Hill, Lib.'

'Don't you start.'

A group of dancers arrived, clucking like chickens. In the centre of the huddle was Justina, head bent, clearly crying as the others rubbed her back. Mel groaned. Another day, another drama.

Justina was led over to the bar, like a prize cow, and presented to Liberty. A brunette, whose name escaped Liberty, grabbed her friend's chin and yanked upwards, so Liberty could see the problem. A split lip, a swollen cheek and livid purple marks around her throat. 'Boyfriend,' said the brunette.

Even the word brought on a fresh bout of sobs from Justina.

'Well, she can't work in that state,' said Mel.

The brunette shook her head. 'Make-up. Not an issue.' Liberty weighed up the poor girl's face. It was going to take foundation by the bucketful to cover that little lot. 'Issue is boyfriend. Still in her flat.'

'And what exactly do you expect me to do about that?' Mel demanded. The brunette raised a tadpole eyebrow at Liberty. 'Don't look to her, lady,' said Mel. The brunette didn't back down.

'Police?' Liberty asked.

The brunette burst out laughing and translated to the other girls, who all hooted in derision. Finally, with a half-smile, Liberty took a notebook and pen from her bag and held it out to Justina. 'Address.'

Justina scribbled with one hand and wiped her nose with the back of the other.

'If you take him back, that'll be an end to it,' said Liberty.

Justina nodded, and as the women scuttled off en masse to camouflage her injuries and get changed, Mel snatched up the notebook. 'Since when did we start getting involved in the private doings of this lot?'

'You saw her face, Mel.'

'She probably nicked his nan's pension book,' said Mel.

'Just send him packing,' said Liberty. 'No need for a Jacobean tragedy.'

Mel tore the sheet of paper from the notebook and slammed it on the bar into a puddle of spilled pop. 'A Jackie what?'

'Just sort it, eh?'

Mel waved the now soggy page in Liberty's face, with a what-do-you-think-I'm-doing scowl.

Liberty rolled her eyes. 'I don't want broken bones or dead bodies.'

'Speaking of which,' a voice boomed across the club.

Liberty turned to find Paul Hill walking towards her, face inscrutable. 'Broken bones?' she asked.

'The other one,' he replied.

She nudged a stool out for him to sit and gestured for Mel to pour him a drink. He shook his head and took his place.

'You think one of mine killed your kid,' he said.

'No.'

He watched her for a second, weighing up whether she was telling the truth. She couldn't blame him. She certainly didn't trust him as far as she could throw him.

'That's good news, because it wasn't anything to do with me,' he said. 'No one wants all that shit to start up again.'

'They don't,' Liberty replied.

Rose knelt beside the steps of the slide where a jumbled collection of cards, flowers and candles was growing into a shrine to the dead boy. Someone had tied a Leeds United scarf around one of the bars and spray-painted 'RIP Road Kill' on the tarmac.

'That his street name?' Rose asked Redman.

'Uh-huh.'

She read the tributes one by one. *Always in our hearts. Respect soldier. One of us.* Behind her, Redman bounced on his heels. Why had he suggested this when he clearly couldn't be bothered to check for any new evidence?

Rose got to her feet, brushed off the knees of her jeans and headed to the outer perimeter of the park. Slowly, she began a circuit, eyes down, scanning the weeds and shrubs, occasionally stopping to nudge a piece of rubbish with the toe of her boot.

'SOCO has swept the area,' said Redman.

Rose didn't answer but carried on with her search. A blue plastic bag, tied by its handles, swung from a low branch of a tree. Rose pulled a biro from her pocket and went to unhook it.

'It's shit,' said Redman.

Rose glared at him. A kid had been murdered and Redman couldn't have cared less.

'Dog shit.' Redman nodded at the bag. 'The owners scoop it up and then just leave it hanging about like bloody apples.'

Rose's hand was still in midair, pen poised, when she heard the whir of wheels behind her. She spun round to catch sight of a bike racing across the park, its rider dressed head to toe in black. Tracksuit bottoms, hoodie, trainers. A black baseball cap pulled low. At the slide, the bike slowed, and the rider took a foot off the pedal and kicked out at the shrine. Pictures of the dead boy, a small plant in a plastic pot and a yellow teddy scattered.

'Hey!' Rose yelled.

The rider looked up, took another swipe that sent candles across the tarmac, then hit the pedals. Redman launched himself after the bike, but he was no match for the pumping thighs of the rider.

Rose assessed the layout of the park. When the rider reached the gate, he might go left or right. Left led to the main road. Right led into the estate. Rose would bet he'd go right, then quickly get lost in the warren of flats. If she was correct, he'd pass by her on the other side of the trees and fence in seconds. She threw herself between the branches, her elbow knocking the bag of dog turds, twigs scratching her cheeks, then vaulted the fence in one.

As she landed on the other side, the bike almost crashed into her. But the rider stopped just in time, attempting to make a skidding U-turn. In the moment that the bike slid, Rose launched herself at it and brought it crashing to the ground, landing on a wheel, the rim digging into her stomach. The rider, thrown off to the side, thudded to the pavement with a whoosh of air. There was a yelp as he scrambled to his feet, but Rose hadn't finished yet: she grabbed for his legs, pulling him off balance. He fell forward onto his knees and, for a split-second, Rose saw his face. Or *her* face. The rider was a girl.

A strand of brown hair escaped from the baseball cap and traced her cheek. A gold stud above pink lips. Clear and angry eyes met Rose's.

Suddenly the sound of pounding feet filled the air and Redman hurtled towards them.

The girl looked at him, back at Rose, then jumped to her feet. She curled her finger and thumb into the shape of a C, laughed and ran. Redman chased after her, but Rose already knew there was no point.

Liberty threw open the door to the back office. It hit the wall behind it with a crash. Jay and Frankie looked up at her. She opened her mouth to speak, knew she was going to scream, put up a finger and took a breath.

'All right, Lib?' asked Frankie.

In one long stride she reached him and slapped his shoulder.

'Ow.'

She slapped him again, harder. Jay let out a bark of laughter, so she slapped him too.

'You knew he was here,' she said.

Jay pushed a pile of gimp masks to the side of the desk and perched. 'Who?'

'Paul Hill. Don't pretend you didn't know.' Jay and Frankie exchanged a glance. Incensed, Liberty gave them both another hard whack. 'Why did you leave him to me?'

Frankie sat next to Jay. 'He likes you, Lib.'

Liberty was finding it hard to keep her cool now. 'He says it had nothing to do with him.'

'Right,' said Frankie.

'Right? Of course it's not right, Frankie. For all I know he's a lying twat who's about to try and steal our area from us. And then what?' No one answered. 'Then we'll have to do something about

29

it, won't we? And that will lead somewhere we don't want to go.' She pointed at Frankie. 'Or did you like it in the hospital? Bed baths by pretty nurses and morphine on tap?'

She immediately regretted her words. Below the belt.

'Actually,' said Frankie, 'the nurses were all well past their sell-by dates. Over forty, most of them.'

'Most of 'em were forty-five, I'll bet,' said Jay, with an exaggerated grimace. 'Imagine someone that old washing your bollocks.'

Liberty, who had turned forty-six the previous summer, shook her head at the pair of them.

Frankie clawed his hand, like a crone's. 'Wrinkled fingers getting a flannel up the crack of your arse.'

'You were better off in the coma, pal,' said Jay.

'I'm going to kill you both,' said Liberty. The brothers roared with laughter. Liberty shut the door behind her with her foot and leaned her back against it. She slapped Frankie again for good measure.

'Ow.'

The salad drawer of the fridge had been stuck for a couple of weeks. Through the gap, Sol could see a layer of grey fuzz growing over an opened packet of heirloom tomatoes (what the actual fuck did heirlooms have to do with tomatoes anyway? Weren't heirlooms old coffee tables that rich folk inherited? Whereas tomatoes were red things you sliced over a ham sarnie to try to squeeze in one of your five a day). He crouched and gave the drawer a yank. Nothing. He jammed all eight fingers under the rim and pulled. Nothing. He vowed not to buy any more fancy stuff that neither he nor Liberty ever ate just because he was bored.

One last try.

He heaved at the drawer, heard the crack of splitting plastic and fell backwards onto his arse, a large piece of the front of the drawer in his hands. The sharp edge carved the underside of his thumb in two.

'Shit the bed.'

Sol tossed the plastic away, and dribbled blood all the way to the sink. He smacked on the cold tap and plunged his thumb into the stream of water. The sting ran up his wrist.

'Shit the bed.'

He needed to get a job. In twenty-five years on the force, he'd crammed shopping and cleaning into the cracks of his day. Or not at all. Mostly not at all. Takeaways were invented for a reason, and if you didn't buy proper food, the fridge was always spotless.

He reached for a clean tea towel (when had he become a man who washed tea towels?) and wrapped it around his thumb. He stood at the window with his makeshift bandage, surveying the street outside. There was no sign of the car he'd seen the previous night. And maybe he hadn't seen what he'd thought. It had been the middle of the night and pitch black, after all.

After what had happened with Amira, the police wouldn't mount another surveillance on the Greenwoods. Not until the memory of that disaster had faded.

As for another crew? Delaney was dead, and Paul Hill had done a deal. There were a few other bit players in the area, but no one who could mount a serious challenge.

Chances were the bloke in the car had been talking on his mobile. Or taking a selfie. That seemed to be most people's main hobby, these days. Still, who was he to criticise? He didn't have a job or a hobby. He'd threatened once to buy an exercise bike and Liberty had laughed.

He mooched into the hallway and fished in his coat pocket for his phone, then scrolled through his texts. When he'd left the job, various ex-coppers had been in touch, suggesting he might do this or that. At the time, he'd just wanted to put as much distance between his old and new life as possible, but maybe now was the time to renew those contacts.

He found the number he was looking for. Pressed call.

'Sol Connolly. How the devil are you?'

'Not so bad, Hutch,' he said.

'Keeping busy?'

Sol clocked the discarded plastic, the trail of blood across the tiles. 'I could squeeze in a coffee, if you pushed me.'

'Carter Street?'

'Give me half an hour.'

Chapter 3

31 August 1990

When I arrive for my shift, there's already a queue forming round the block. Mostly lads, as usual. Not that you can always tell because everybody dresses the same, really. Baggy jeans and hoodies and that.

I nod to somebody I've seen around a few times, all centre parting and Embassy Regal.

'Hey up, Lib,' he says. 'Get us in, will you?'

I laugh. He's only taking the piss. He knows he'll have to wait the same as all the other folk. As I get to the door, he shouts after me, 'How's about giving us your number?'

One of the bouncers, who calls himself Red, though I'm thinking his name's probably Brian or something, shouts back at the lad, 'It's nine-nine-nine.'

'You what?' says the lad.

'Her number. It's nine-nine-nine.' Red puts a massive arm around my shoulders. 'Ask for an ambulance cos that's what you'll be needing if you bother this one again.'

As Red lets me inside, I smile at him. 'He was just trying it on, you know? No harm done.'

'I was that age not so long ago, Lib.' He ruffles my hair and goes back to manning the door.

The club's filling up. Bodies on the dance floor bouncing to the track smashing out of the speakers. They move in time as if it's all agreed up

33

front, but it's not that at all. It's just that with this sort of music you can't help yourself. I mean, I'm already bouncing my head along in time and I've just walked in.

Steph waves at me. She supposedly runs the bar, but it's hardly what you'd call a full-time job. Not many punters buy anything except a bottle of water. On my first shift here, I was meant to be the potman, but there were hardly any pots to collect. So, I started doing anything else I could to help out. Not because I was worried they'd get rid of me. To be honest, I don't think anyone noticed that I didn't have owt to do, but I like to be busy anyway.

Steph runs a cloth along the counter but gets bored halfway and starts dancing instead.

I pass around a podium. Two lasses are already up there, arms above their heads. Later on, there'll be ten or fifteen dancers on each one. Folk regularly fall off. One time this lad split his lip and cracked his front tooth. I took him to the bogs, cleaned him up a bit with a wet tissue. He was too off his head to care. Bet he was in agony the next morning.

I knock on the office door but don't wait for an answer. If I did that, I could be stood here all night.

The smell of weed greets me as I step inside.

'Hello, my gorgeous girl,' says Tony.

'Hiya,' I say.

I like Tony a lot. He's quite posh but not a bit stuck-up.

'Who's this, then?' the bloke in the corner asks, spliff hanging out of his gob, cloud of smoke above his head.

'My Girl Friday,' says Tony. 'And Saturday and Sunday.' That makes me laugh. 'Rider.' He hands me a sheet of lined paper, pencil scribbles all over it. 'Could you check it for me, Lib?'

I nod. The bloke must be a guest DJ. They get to order a rider. Food and that mostly. And fags. Sometimes drugs. Occasionally something weird. There was this singer in a band who asked for a facial sauna. Apparently, it was for her voice box. Tony told me to just put some hot water in a bowl and give her a towel. Sometimes Rob does that when he wants to get rid of his blackheads.

PLAYING DIRTY

As I make my way to what Tony calls the 'visitors' enclosure', a group of girls arrives, screaming and babbling. It's rare to find big gangs of lasses in here. And this lot are a bit overdressed for it, to be honest.

Then I hear one of them shout, 'Oh, my God, is that you, Lib?' She comes charging over to me. 'It is you.'

'All right, Kitty?' I say.

Her mates come over now. One of them's got a handbag, for fuck's sake.

'This is the girl I was telling you about,' Kitty shouts, above the music, to her friends. Her voice is different. A bit more Manchester. 'My new bezzie mate at college.' She kisses me, all sticky lip gloss and cheap-wine breath. 'What the hell are you doing here?' she asks me.

'I work here.'

'No way,' says Kitty.

'Way,' I reply.

She turns to one of the other girls, who is fiddling with what looks suspiciously like a shoulder pad. 'Didn't I say she was cool? I mean, who doesn't even mention that they work at the fooking Hacienda?'

Present Day

The doctor wrinkled his nose, tapped his front tooth with the biro in his hand. 'How did you say this happened?'

'Bike wheel,' Rose replied.

The doctor peered closely at the slash across her stomach. She'd been waiting two long hours to be seen and now this moron was in slow motion. Wasn't there, like, a time limit medics had with each patient? A rule that stated they had to get you in and out of the cubicle in a minute? If there was, Doc Tooth Tapper hadn't heard of it.

'You were cycling?' he asked, voice drawn out like a drunk.

Rose's arm was beginning to ache from holding up her jumper and the gash was stinging like crazy. 'No. It wasn't my bike.'

'So, you were knocked over?' The doctor pulled a pair of plastic gloves from the cardboard box on the desk. 'Was the rider on the pavement?'

'Sort of.'

'Then you should call the police.'

Rose closed her eyes, then opened them at the sound of a huffing noise only to find the doctor blowing up a glove like a balloon, each finger inflating in turn. When it was full of air, he pinched the base and waved the hand at her. 'I am the police,' she said. 'Look, I explained what happened to the last person. I assumed the information would be passed on to you.'

The doctor let the glove deflate. 'Schoolboy error.'

'Are you going to stitch me up so I can go back and do something useful with my life?' Rose asked.

'Depends on whether this needs stitches.'

Rose looked down at the cut that stretched almost from one hip to the other. The bleeding had slowed but it was still wet and gaping. 'And do I need stitches?'

Another tooth tap. 'Good question.'

Rose had had enough. She yanked down her jumper and jumped from the bed, sending a dagger of pain through her body. She gasped and leaned heavily against the wall. The doctor looked puzzled and nodded at the filthy, blood-stained sweater sporting a clear tyre track. 'Shouldn't let that near an open wound.' He smiled. 'Germs.'

By the time a nurse had patched up Rose with glue and steri-strips, she was in the sort of mood that she usually reserved for Christmas Day. So, when she marched towards the exit, clutching a bottle of antibiotics, and bumped into Redman, she could cheerfully have knocked his head off his shoulders.

'Why did you wait?' she barked.

He threw a Styrofoam cup into a nearby bin. 'Thought you'd need a lift home.'

'I'm not going home,' she said, as the automatic doors swooshed open.

Redman trotted after her. What had he been doing for the last few hours? Just hanging around?

As Rose stepped onto the concourse in front of the hospital a couple hobbled towards her. It was hard to tell who was holding up whom. A couple of rough sleepers, she guessed, with so many cuts and bruises on their faces and hands. The woman looked at the man, a flash of concern across her face. When the man caught it, she swapped it for a big toothless grin. 'You'll be all right,' she told him.

They shuffled inside, leaving Rose and Redman alone for a second. He checked the time on his phone and, for some reason, this infuriated Rose. 'Do you care?' she demanded.

'About what?'

She noticed he wasn't wearing any socks. No, actually he was wearing those little trainer socks. Black, like his shoes, the tops just peeping out, leaving a gap for hairy skin to display itself proudly. What sort of person wore trainer socks to work? 'About what's happening on the Crosshills estate? About the fact that it's a decent place full of decent people but they're scared to even talk to us?' She knew she should shut up but couldn't. 'About the fact that a fifteen-year-old boy who should have been at home playing Football Manager was out selling drugs?'

'It's not that simple,' said Redman.

Rose threw out her arms and instantly regretted it as pain ricocheted across her abdomen. 'It's completely simple,' she roared. 'You either care or you don't.' She jabbed her chest. 'Me. I care. And I'm going to do something about it. But if you don't, you should just fuck off.'

So he did.

Rose sighed and limped towards the taxi rank.

In the café, Liberty ordered three teas and took a table at the window.

Jay sat with his back against the wall, a picture of a cupcake above his head. For some reason, the strawberry on top still had its stalk. 'Why didn't we go to Scottish Tony's?' he asked.

Liberty gave him a look. The last person she wanted to bump into was Sol. 'You know why.'

'Is that what he does all day?' Jay asked. 'Sit around in cafés?'

'Drink your tea,' said Liberty.

'He must be bored shitless,' said Jay. 'I almost feel sorry for him.'

'Almost?'

'Hard to feel much for a copper.'

'Ex-copper,' Liberty pointed out.

'Only because he couldn't carry on in the job *and* shag a Greenwood.'

A little girl, with a ponytail held in place by fourteen clips and a starched ribbon that wouldn't have looked out of place on a bouquet of flowers, stomped into the café. She hammered on the toilet door, like a plain-clothes copper.

'Come on, Reece,' she shouted. 'Mam says we'll miss the bus.'

When there was no answer, she pushed at the door, which opened to reveal a tiny lad on the pot, legs swinging, trousers round his ankles.

'You done?' the girl demanded.

He nodded happily, jumped down and bent forward. The girl sighed, ripped off some loo roll and did his wiping for him. Then she watched him wash his hands, using soap, with the hawk eye of a mother. Well, most mothers. Liberty couldn't remember her own giving a shit about such things.

The door opened, and Frankie arrived. 'Is that mine?' he asked. Liberty nodded, and Frankie fell on his tea, heaping in three sugars with a grin. 'Cheers.'

Liberty and Jay watched him slurp it, trying not to look at each other.

'Any news?' she asked Frankie.

'Not much. The youngers all knew the dead kid. Street name Road Kill.' Frankie eyed Jay's untouched cuppa.

'Tastes like piss,' said Jay. 'We should have gone to Scottish Tony's.'

Liberty groaned, spooned sugar into Jay's tea and pushed it over the table towards Frankie. 'And what do the other youngers think happened to this Road Kill?'

Frankie pulled off his beanie, scuffed his scalp. 'Lad turned up out of nowhere and shanked him.'

'What does Tia say?' Liberty asked.

'She's a total nightmare,' Frankie replied, droplets of liquid still on his lips. 'She'd argue black was white just to break up the day.'

'Who's this Tia, then?' Jay asked.

'A lass we've got running the flats,' said Frankie. 'I'd get shot of her, but for some reason Lib's got a soft spot for the lairy little bitch.'

'She in the usual place?' Liberty asked.

'Don't give her another chance to talk shit,' said Frankie.

But Liberty had already picked up her car keys.

Tia's spot wasn't exactly subtle: a square of scrubland slap-bang in the middle of the Crosshills surrounded by blocks of flats. And in the middle of it all a brown-leather sofa, stuffing sprouting like moss from a thousand tears. Tia was sprawled across it, right leg slung over the side. The King Harry on the corner had been burned out last year, and a chemist was the only sign of life in walking distance.

Close by, a couple of youngers played rock-paper-scissors, slapping each other hard when they won.

When Tia caught sight of Liberty she gave a lazy smile but didn't get up. 'Well, if it ain't the queen of all she surveys.'

Liberty didn't answer but sat on the free arm of the sofa, hands in her pockets.

Eventually, Tia lifted herself to a sitting position, pulled out a packet of Golden Virginia and built herself a rollie. 'You shouldn't come up here.'

'Why's that?'

'Too many feds.' Tia licked the edge of the cigarette paper with her tongue. 'You don't need them to see you.'

'And why are they sniffing around?' asked Liberty.

Tia lit up and blew smoke into the air. 'You know why.' She laughed a mouthful of smoke at the tip of the fag. Some customers arrived, already half dead. Tia put her fingers into her mouth and whistled at her youngers to stop messing and start serving. One took the cash and disappeared into the King Harry. 'Fucking useless this pair,' she said.

She shook her head at the younger standing with the junkies, pointed first and second fingers at her own eyes, then pointed them at him. He shrugged that he didn't have a Scooby what she was trying to say. 'See,' she said to Liberty. 'I swear I'd do better with a couple of Rotties.'

'Tell me about the dead kid,' said Liberty. Tia took a last drag on her fag and flicked it away into the grass. 'Tia?'

The girl turned towards her and looked her right in the eye. 'Maybe it's better if you don't know what happened.' Liberty stared right back until Tia gave a theatrical sigh. 'Fine. But you're not gonna like it.'

***

PLAYING DIRTY

There were ructions going off at Scottish Tony's.

A couple of working girls were squaring up to a third. By the look of her she'd just got out of the nick. A strappy vest and denim shorts that she must have been wearing when she got sent down last summer and a clear bag, marked HMP Styal, clutched to her chest.

'Don't come in here giving it all this,' the first shouted, making a beak with her hand that she opened and closed. 'You owe me a ton and you're not getting your stuff back until you pay up.'

The third woman dumped her bag on a sticky table. A balled-up blue sock tumbled out and landed on a half-eaten plate of chips.

'Now look what you've done.' The first pointed at the sock now rolling in a blob of ketchup. 'You owe for my dinner as well.'

The woman in the vest threw out her arms. 'How can I get any cash together without my gear?'

'You'll have to improvise,' said the first.

Sol wondered what the recent inmate felt she needed. Whips? Chains? Then again, he knew what sort of outfits got the punters riled up at the Black Cherry (the one that really did his head in was the schoolgirl outfits. Surely that was nonce territory). He skirted around the women and headed over to Hutch, who was watching, arms crossed. 'Enjoying the show?' he asked.

'Better than *Love Island*, this,' said Hutch.

The first woman dug her hand into the prison bag and dragged out a red top. 'Why can't you wear this?'

The third snatched it from her and pulled it over her head to display the Arsenal logo. 'Who do you think is going to pay for a blow job with me in this?' she roared.

'To be fair, they are on terrible form this season,' said Hutch.

They waited for Scottish Tony to kick the women to the kerb, and ordered, Sol a sausage and fried-egg sandwich, Hutch a double cheese burger with a side of onion rings.

'We won't make it to Christmas,' said Hutch.

In truth, Hutch looked good. Hair slightly grey around the

41

temples but cut short. The tops of his arms well defined through a black sweater that must have cost a few bob. When he reached for the brown sauce and Sol caught sight of the Rolex, it was more than obvious that whatever Hutch was doing these days paid better than the job.

'I was sorry to hear about Amira,' said Hutch, dipping the end of an onion ring into a puddle of sauce. 'No way to go.' Sol nodded. 'That why you left?'

Sol wondered how much Hutch knew. Took a bite of his buttie to avoid answering.

'Also heard you'd got yourself a new missus.' So, Hutch knew quite a lot. 'Gotta say, mate, I pissed my sides.' Hutch laughed now. A big belly laugh. 'You always did think with your dick.'

Sol felt like he should defend himself but had no idea how he'd even begin.

'But,' Hutch pointed the half-eaten onion ring at him, 'you were always a fantastic copper.' He let the idea hang in the air, then took another bite. 'And what I need right now in my business is people who know how to get a job done.'

Rose hammered her fist against the garage door. A cough came from inside, but the door didn't budge, so Rose hammered again.

At last it opened a foot from the bottom and a voice spoke: 'What d'you want?'

'I need to speak to Salty,' said Rose.

'He's not here.'

Rose bent from the waist, grabbed the bottom of the garage door and pulled it up and over. 'Of course he's in here. Where else would he be?'

She came face to face with a boy of around eighteen. Acne from chin to hair line. Eyes red and crusty. He smelt of the same decaying fridge drawer as Salty.

'I haven't shit myself,' he said.

'Good to know,' Rose replied.

She scanned the garage floor, littered with sleeping bags and bodies. At the back, underneath a dartboard, Salty was comatose. Rose picked her way through the human debris and stood at his head. Whoever had last played darts had done quite well. Two double twenties and a five.

She fished in her pocket, pulled out a bottle of water and unscrewed the lid. Took a quick swig and poured the rest over Salty's face.

Half an hour later, when Salty could finally walk, Rose dragged him from the garage towards the nearest shop. 'Let's get some food inside you,' she said.

'Eh?'

'Food. You know, what you put in your mouth that isn't a crack pipe.'

Salty shook his head, sending droplets of water from him, like a dog. 'If I eat, I'll throw up.'

It was true that junkies could live on class As and fresh air for years, but Rose needed Salty to concentrate. 'There must be something you can keep down.'

'Sometimes I can manage one of them jars of baby food,' he said. 'Chocolate pudding.'

Rose laughed, assuming it was a joke, but the look on Salty's face told her that he was deadly serious. 'Chocolate pudding it is,' she said.

'The organic one is best.'

Salty scooped the baby food from the jar with a dirty finger. Then he gingerly sucked off the brown gloop. After a second suck, he gave a sorrowful burp. 'I need to sit,' he said.

Rose nodded and led him to a low wall outside a pawnbroker's.

She noticed his trainers. Grey knitted Adidas running shoes. The type that cost a fortune. Salty's were splattered with stains, just like the rest of him. 'Have you ever considered rehab?' she asked.

Salty let out a bark of laughter. 'I've done rehab more times than Amy Winehouse.'

'I thought the point was that Amy Winehouse didn't go to re—'

But Rose was interrupted by Salty dropping his jar with a groan. Glass smashed and chocolate pudding splattered across the pavement. 'Are you going to be sick?' she asked, leaning out of the way.

Salty shook his head and let out a fart. 'Other end.'

He darted past the door to the pawnbroker's, narrowly missing a woman on a mobility scooter. A little white dog perched in the shopping basket on the handlebars yapped at him. 'Watch it!' shouted the woman.

Salty answered with another fart and dived into the gully between the pawn shop and the flat on the other side.

Rose gave him a minute, but when Salty didn't return she approached the top of the gully. 'Are you still alive?'

'Just about.' He released a bovine grunt. 'You got a tissue?'

Rose rummaged in her bag and found an unopened packet of Handy Andies. She threw them in Salty's general direction, determined not to catch sight of his bare arse.

Eventually he emerged, face ashen, walking with a limp. He offered Rose the remains of the pack of tissues. 'Keep them,' she replied.

They sat on the wall again, a few feet from the pudding. Salty reached deep into the front pocket of his jeans and pulled out a half-smoked roll-up. His hands shook violently as he lit it. Rose almost felt sorry for him, but experience had taught her that pity wouldn't help matters. Wherever she went she chose someone like

Salty for good reason. Getting emotionally invested in their awful lives was to be avoided.

'Can we just get on with this?' he muttered.

'Have you heard anything about the dead younger up on the Crosshills estate?'

Salty took a long drag. 'Not too much.'

'Do you know who killed him?'

'Isn't it your job to find that out? Bit of basic investigation?' Salty chuckled. But Rose didn't join in. 'No one knows who killed him.'

'Someone always knows something,' said Rose.

Salty shook his head. 'The kid that done it wasn't from round here.'

The look on Rose's face made Salty chuckle again. Then there was a gurgle from deep inside his bowels and he bent forward, the smile wiped from his face.

'Where was he from?' Rose asked.

Salty shrugged. 'Manchester, maybe. Seems like a lot of kids are coming from over there.'

His face told Rose she'd pushed him far enough. She pulled out a ten-pound note she'd rolled up earlier and offered it to him. He went to grab it with a speed that would have been comical had she not expected it. She held her end tightly.

'Good work,' she said. She hung on for a few more seconds, then let go. Salty jumped to his feet, letting go another fart. Or, at least, Rose prayed that was what it was. He kicked at the broken glass jar as he passed and shouted at Rose over his shoulder, 'I don't fucking work for you.'

Rose gave him a wave and watched him trot away. He was wrong about not working for her. But he was right about one thing: she did need to do some basic digging around.

***

45

Tia led Liberty through to the back of a kebab shop. A huge piece of meat slowly rotated on a metal pole, grease dripping like dirty tears. The smell almost made Liberty heave. Tia gave the owner a thumbs-up, and he waved a knife the size of a machete at her as a greeting.

Out the back, there was a storeroom piled high with boxes of pitta bread and vats of oil, then a doorway with hanging beads. Tia pushed her way through and headed up the stairs beyond. Liberty couldn't help but notice that her feet were sticking to the carpet. As they reached the top, the sound of a telly leached out towards them: the familiar voices of Chandler and Joey. There was a padlock on the outside of the door. Tia fished in her pocket, pulled out a key and undid it.

Inside, a small room was kitted out with a single bed and a sixty-five-inch flat-screen. Monica Geller danced at Liberty, a huge Christmas turkey on her head. Tia snatched up the remote and turned off the programme, eliciting a grunt from the girl who was sitting on the bed.

'What?' Tia snarled. 'You haven't already watched it, like, a million times?'

'I need the bog,' the girl huffed.

Tia groaned and moved to her. She pulled a different key from her pocket and knelt. Only at that point did Liberty notice that the girl was chained by her left foot to the bed.

Chapter 4

31 August 1990

The club's mobbed but most people aren't paying any attention to the band on the stage. I don't blame 'em. The lead singer's some ginger, bouncing around like a complete twat. He's dropped his mic at least twice.

A couple of lads from up Cheetham Hill are dealing pills. I remember when Connor used to do it, all secret, like. He'd shake a customer's hand and pass the stuff on. Or sometimes he'd slide it down the back of a girl's waistband. Didn't stop him getting nicked, though, did it? These lads don't bother with the charade. Everyone knows what they're here for. And there's about another thirty of them in the club, just keeping watch in case there's any trouble.

The band finishes their set and hardly anyone claps. I give a quick cheer cos I feel a bit sorry for them. But I've got to admit that the whole place livens up when Rob lays down his first track. He catches my eye and gives me a thumbs-up. I give him one back.

Kitty comes bounding over and throws her arms around me. She's a bit sticky, to be honest. 'Don't tell me you know the DJ,' she breathes into my ear.

I laugh. 'I live with him.'

'He's your boyfriend?' I'm about to explain that, no, we're just best mates, but she's not listening. 'Can he get us something?'

'What?' I ask.

Kitty rolls her eyes. 'Ecstasy.'

'Oh,' I say. 'Rob doesn't deal.'

Kitty gives a little pout. 'Anyone else serving up?'

I look around. There are lads openly selling their wares. I mean, is she blind or something?

Then I see a gang of lads arriving. All Kangol cricket hats and City tops. There's a cockiness to them as they stride across the dance floor. I notice that the Cheetham Hill lads have clocked them as well, on red alert now, circling.

Kitty follows my eye line to one of the new arrivals. 'Good spot.' She pulls out a twenty-quid note and grabs hold of one of her mates.

'I wouldn't,' I tell her.

'Don't be a misery,' she tells me, already on her way.

I watch her approach the lad and touch his arm. He nods at her, fag dangling out of the corner of his mouth. But before Kitty can say anything, one of the regular dealers barrels over and punches the lad in the face. His lips explode as he falls backwards, and Kitty screams when his blood splats into her face. The other newcomers jump in, but the Cheetham lot are already on it in numbers. Someone pulls a hammer out of their pocket and a kid hits the deck.

Pretty soon the new lads have been chased out of the club and most folk just carry on dancing. But Kitty's mates are all sobbing, mascara running down their silly little cheeks. Kitty's not crying but she's swiping at the blood on her nose with her sleeve.

'What the fuck?' one of her mates wails. 'You said this was a cool place, Kit-Kat.'

I catch Kitty's eye and mouth. 'Kit-Kat?'

She turns to her mate, face still smeared red. 'It is a cool place, Amanda, but it's not fucking Disneyland.'

I turn and laugh at that as Rob drops the first bars of 'Acid Thunder' and I start to dance.

Present Day

Liberty stared at the chain around the girl's foot. It was a heavy link thing, wrapped around her ankle twice. Then it snaked away from her to the metal bedframe where it was threaded through and fixed with a padlock. The girl couldn't get away unless she took the bed with her.

'I'm about to pee myself,' she said.

Tia shook her head in disgust and undid the lock. Then she slid the chain through the bedframe, holding the end like a lead.

'The way you watch me take a leak is perverted,' the girl said to Tia.

Tia flicked her free hand to tell the girl to get moving. As she took her first step, with a clink that Jacob Marley would have been proud of, Liberty could see she was around fifteen. Smaller than Tia in height, but fuller, her chubby cheeks giving her an almost angelic appearance.

'You should pay me,' said the girl.

'Shut. Up.'

The girl moved past Liberty, Tia following with the chain held loosely in her hand. Liberty recalled that Tia used to have a dog. A slobbery Staffie that dragged her around. What had happened to him?

Then, out of nowhere, as the girl reached the door, she stepped back into Tia.

'What the f—'

The girl threw her head towards Tia and connected with her nose. There was a crunch as bone smashed bone. Tia took a huge breath as blood spurted from her nose and the girl ran through the door. She was just at the landing, her hand outstretched to freedom, when the chain went taut and stopped her in her tracks. Tia might have blood dripping from her nostrils but she still had hold of her end of the chain.

With a snarl, Tia jumped towards her prey, throwing a length of chain around the girl's throat and dragging her backwards into the room. The girl fell to the floor, hitting her head against the

49

bare boards, her hands grabbing at the chain, which dug into her windpipe.

But Tia wasn't letting go. She pulled tighter until the girl's feet windmilled in the air and her face turned blue.

'Enough,' Liberty said.

Tia glanced up. Blood ran from her nose, covering her mouth and chin. She looked like she'd slaughtered a goat.

'I said enough,' Liberty repeated.

'Have you seen what she did to me?'

The girl made a slurpy choking sound and her eyes rolled back in her head. Then Tia released her hold and the chain relaxed enough for the girl to give a huge gasp. Tia took a great handful of the girl's hair and hauled her back to the bed. She threw her down and re-chained her. The girl didn't speak, just gulped air. Even when Tia spat blood at her, she concentrated on breathing. At last the girl calmed and closed her eyes.

Liberty crossed her arms. 'Now, do you want to tell me what in God's name is going on?'

Sol and Hutch left Scottish Tony's and headed to the pub. Not the Three Feathers: neither of them had any interest in bumping into any copper they knew. Wordlessly, they settled on the Roundhouse, which turned out to be pretty busy for a Tuesday afternoon. A bunch of workmen still in their hi-vis jackets had obviously finished early and were crowded around the fruity, knocking back pints.

Sol ordered two Amstels and took the table furthest away. He drank some, wiped the froth from his mouth and smiled. 'Want to tell me what I'm doing here?'

'Like I said, you were always a good copper.'

The lads at the fruity cheered in unison as one of them lost the money he'd been feeding the machine. They honked as if he'd just got married. (Why did all blokes do that? Greet a mate's mis-fortune like a win on the lottery? Didn't matter that they actually liked the bloke – in fact the more they liked him, the more they'd celebrate his bad luck. And if he did manage to get a pay rise, or get himself engaged to a nice-looking girl, they'd call him all the twats under the sun.)

'I'm not a copper any more,' said Sol.

Hutch took a long drink of his lager. 'Yeah, well, my client doesn't want anyone who's currently job.'

'Why not?'

'Why d'you think?'

Sol smiled. 'Most of them are straight.'

'And it's the "most" that's problematic.'

Sol ran a finger around the rim of his glass. 'So, who's the client?'

'CDU.'

Sol's eyes opened wide. He'd been expecting some private security firm, not the Central Drugs Unit.

'At this stage it's a gathering-intel operation,' said Hutch. Sol didn't answer. There must be something very sensitive about whatever they were doing, if a national police unit was employing outsiders. 'Come to a meeting and hear us out?'

Sol drained his glass. He was intrigued, no doubt about it, and he needed something to do that didn't involve the salad drawer of the fridge.

'Look.' Hutch banged his empty glass on the table. 'If you don't like the sound of it, you can go home. End of story.'

Back at the station, Rose's injuries were killing her. She lifted her jumper to check the damage and wrinkled her nose at the purple bruise seeping up towards her ribcage. 'Lovely.' She dry-swallowed two paracetamol and tried to get comfortable at her PC.

First up was the file on the dead boy. Aaron Mason, street name Road Kill, had been fifteen years old. He'd lived all his life on the Crosshills with his mother and two younger sisters, Charli and Kelly-Jayne. Social services had been involved with the family since Aaron's birth and had seen no reason to take them off their books, though none of the Mason children had ever been removed into foster care. Crosshills Community School had permanently excluded Aaron at fourteen and he'd been enrolled in a Pupil Referral Unit though his attendance was recorded as 'patchy'.

His previous was nothing out of the ordinary. Possession times four, ABH, a couple of TWOCs. He hadn't spent any time in custody, but a sentence was in the post. Someone had made a note that Aaron was a runner for the Greenwoods, but there was no accompanying evidence.

On the night in question, at around 9 p.m., he'd been stabbed, by a person or persons unknown, in the recreational ground just streets from his home. The blade had pierced his chest, entering the left ventricle of his heart. Aaron had died minutes later.

Rose stuck out her tongue. There was a bitter coating from the painkillers. She looked around for a drink, saw a half-finished bottle of Mountain Dew on one of the neighbouring desks. The thought of backwash was deeply unpleasant, but beggars couldn't be choosers.

Next, she uploaded the file for another boy who'd been stabbed recently. Elijah Hunter, street name Smash, had been seriously injured on the Peabody estate just a week ago. The sixteen-year-old had received two wounds to his gut, which had required extensive surgery to his lower intestines. No arrest had been made and Elijah claimed to have no idea who had attacked him.

His record was much like Aaron's, except for the addition of a six-week stretch in HMP Wetherby for a robbery. He was thought to work as a runner for Paul Hill.

Rose took another swig of the Mountain Dew. The fizz had long gone, but it was sweet and lemony.

The third kid on her list was interesting. Naz Aktar was only thirteen and had been hit on the back of his head with a claw hammer on the same night Elijah had been attacked. The incidents had taken place within half a mile of each other. There was no address for Naz, but the details of a social worker in the Moss Side area of Manchester were on his file and presumably she'd picked him up on his discharge from hospital.

Rose tapped in a search for any other young people from Moss Side coming across the bows of the local hospitals and police stations and smiled at what she found. A girl calling herself Madison had been arrested on the Crosshills estate for affray. During her time at the station, she'd seen the doctor on duty, who had noted down several injuries consistent with an attack by a blunt instrument. Madison, who had refused to give a surname, had eventually been released into the care of the local social services, who informed the desk sergeant that they'd contact the authorities in Moss Side the next morning. Follow-up notes confirmed that Madison had absconded.

Rose leaned back in her chair and instantly regretted it as pain shot through her body. She gripped the side of her desk with both hands and let out a long stream of air from her mouth. When the agony had subsided, she pushed herself to her feet as carefully as possible and set off to find Redman.

Liberty dragged Tia out of the bedroom and down the stairs.

'I haven't locked the door,' Tia shouted.

'You just strangled the life out of her and chained her to the bed,' Liberty spat back. 'Where do you think she's going?'

Tia huffed but followed Liberty out of the shop. If the owner was shocked at the sight of the teen's bloodied face, he didn't show it, just gave a wave with a metal kebab skewer.

Once outside, Tia yanked out her phone, spun around her camera function to check her reflection. She growled at what she saw.

'What the hell is going on?' Liberty demanded.

Tia lifted her chin to get a better angle. 'This had better not be broken.'

'I'll break it myself if you don't start talking,' said Liberty.

Tia rolled her eyes. 'Fine.' She took out her packet of tobacco and papers. Then a small baggie of weed. 'Sorry, but I'm shook up.'

'Talk.'

Tia licked three papers together and laid them in her left palm. 'Kids have been coming up the Crosshills and starting trouble.' She sprinkled a few pinches of tobacco across the papers, then a couple of pinches of weed. 'We thought we'd sorted it. Gave 'em a taste of their own medicine, like.'

Liberty could only imagine what that had entailed. 'Who did they work for? Paul Hill?' Tia shook her head as she rolled her joint, twisted the end and lit it. 'Then who?'

'Don't know.' Tia took a drag and pulled the blunt from her lips. The end was completely red with her blood. 'At first we thought maybe a crew from the Peabody.' Grey smoke poured from her scarlet lips. 'But then we started hearing rumours.'

'What rumours?'

Tia shrugged. 'Some kid said he'd heard them talking. That they weren't from round here at all. Said they'd come from Manchester.'

'And you believed that?'

'Course not.' Tia laughed. 'People talk shit, don't they? But then that one turned up.' She lifted the glowing tip of her blunt towards the girl in the bedroom. 'And I knew straight away that something was going off.'

'So, you did what?' Liberty demanded. 'Just kidnapped her?'

'Well, she wouldn't have exactly agreed to a nice chat over a brew, would she?'

Liberty rubbed her face. This was ridiculous. Tia was keeping a prisoner in a kebab shop for information. She'd laugh if it wasn't so fucking serious. 'We'll have to speak to Frankie,' she said.

'No way.' Tia threw away her blunt in disgust. 'He'll go off his nut.'

'Are you out of your tiny mind?'

Liberty jumped between Frankie and Tia, fearing he might throttle her. A customer came out of the kebab shop, mouth already wrapped around a large doner. He eyed the tableau coolly, took another chomp of greasy meat and went on his way.

'Told you he'd go off on one,' said Tia.

Frankie's mouth contorted in anger. 'We've got the feds all over the estate because of this dead younger, and you . . .' He lurched towards Tia. 'You've got a kid chained up?' His eyes sparked. 'In my fucking area?'

Liberty put up her hands. 'Calm down, Frankie.'

He took off his beanie, rubbed his scalp, then threw the hat across the street with a growl. Tia sighed, cocky as you like, but she kept at a safe distance behind Liberty, back pressed against the glass of the kebab shop window.

'To be fair, we do need to know what's going on,' said Liberty.

'Listen to your sister,' said Tia.

Frankie spun on his heel. 'Shut your mouth before I shut it for you permanently.'

'Charming.'

Liberty shot Tia a just-be-quiet look. 'Get your hat,' she told Frankie. 'And we'll talk to the girl.'

Frankie took a deep breath and stamped towards the beanie.

He scooped it out of a puddle and held it up, like a dead fox after a hunt, letting the dirty water drip from it. 'I'm going to kill her,' he said to Liberty.

'Yeah? I'll probably get there before you.'

Rose rang the doorbell. It gave a perky ding-dong, immediately followed by the sound of feet bouncing down the stairs. When the door opened, Redman didn't seem especially pleased to see her.

He'd changed out of his work clothes and was wearing a sage green hoodie and black skinny jeans. His hair seemed to make more sense in that outfit. Rose hadn't changed out of the clothes she'd been wearing all day, despite the bloodstains and tyre mark.

'I haven't come to apologise,' she said.

He held open the door and gestured for her to come in. 'How did you know where I lived?'

'I'm a detective.'

He gave a tight smile and led her through to the kitchen. Empty cardboard wrappers for two M&S prawn sandwiches lay on the counter.

'Healthy tea,' said Rose.

He nodded, went to the fridge and pulled out two cans of cider. Without asking, he pulled the rings on both and held one out to her. She took it, clinked his can with hers. He didn't say 'Cheers'.

'The dead boy, Aaron Mason, isn't a one-off,' she said, and took a swig.

He pointed to a chair and she lowered herself into it with a wince.

'Hurting?' he asked.

'So much.' Rose pressed her hand to the worst spot. Redman nodded but offered no sympathy, not that she wanted any. She dived straight in. 'I'm pretty sure there's always stuff happening on the estates. Trouble between the dealers.'

'You could say that.'

There was a framed photograph of a footballer on the wall. His hair was bleached too. Rose wondered if that was where Redman had got the idea from. 'But this is different, Joel. For one thing, not everyone involved is from these parts.'

'Go on.'

'At least two kids have been from Manchester.'

'Manchester?'

Rose took another gulp of cider. Drinking at teatime, after all the painkillers she'd gobbled down today, it would probably go straight to her head, but right now she didn't care. 'Moss Side, actually. And what's really weird is that one of my sources tells me the person who killed Aaron Mason was also from there.'

'You've got sources?' Redman put down his can. 'What sources?'

'Just people I talk to.'

'But you haven't been here ten minutes.'

She shook her can, realising she'd drunk most of it already. 'I like to get a feel for a place.'

Redman reached behind him, pushing his chair onto the back two legs, and opened the fridge. He pulled out another can of cider, opened it and shoved it towards Rose. 'And why do you think we've got people coming into our area from Manchester?' he asked.

'I can make an educated guess.'

'Come on, you know you're dying to tell me.'

Rose laughed, and it felt good. Christ, she realised she was a bit drunk. 'I think we're dealing with county lines.'

Chapter 5

7 September 1990

Mr Simms closes his copy of Mansfield Park *with a grin, grabs a marker and scribbles on the whiteboard. Kitty's beside me, cheek pressed into her desk. There's still a spot of dried blood on the toe of her Converse from last Friday. You'd think she'd have picked it off.*

When Mr Simms stands aside, we all cock our heads to try to read his writing. How does Jane Austen present social mobility in the chosen text? *'This,' he says, waggling the marker at us, 'is the title of your first essay this term. So those of you who haven't finished the novel had better do so sharpish.' There are groans all around the classroom. 'I want you to think about all the ways the characters change their stations in life.'*

Kitty yawns, not even covering her mouth.

'Keeping you up, are we, Miss Spencer?'

She doesn't lift her head at the sound of Mr Simms's voice. I mean, I know she's tired, but she doesn't need to be an arse-ache about it. Teachers usually have a right fit about stuff like this, but Mr Simms just carries on like he thinks it's funny.

'Go anywhere nice, Miss Spencer?'

Kitty pushes herself up onto her elbows and lets out another yawn. 'Hacienda,' she says, like she goes there all the time, no big deal. But that's all front. It was a week ago and I'm pretty sure it was her first time. 'Good night, wasn't it, Lib?'

I glare at her. First off, I don't want Mr Simms thinking I don't take

58

my subjects seriously, and second, I certainly don't want him or anyone else to get wind that I work there.

'What?' she asks me.

I shake my head and open my book.

After class, I take off without a word, but she chases after me down the corridor, grabbing my arm. 'What's up, Lib?'

'I can't have people knowing my business.'

'Why?' She rubs her eye sockets with her thumb. 'It's not against the law to work in a nightclub.'

Actually, it is at my age. Is she stupid or what?

'Do you want some pizza?' she says.

'Eh?'

There are dark circles under her eyes that make me wonder what she was up to last night.

'Mum put a load in the freezer. Mostly cheese and ham, but there might be a Hawaiian as well.' I stare at her for a few seconds. 'I don't know how many times I've told her I fucking hate pineapple.'

On the way over, I'm already wishing I hadn't agreed to come. It's two buses and I can well do without spending the fares. Plus it's taken us the best part of half an hour already. I'd been hoping to make a start on that Mansfield Park *essay before tonight's shift but, no, I'm on the thirty-six, halfway to Didsbury. And, to top it all off, Kitty's fallen asleep so I'm left staring at the graffiti on the back of the seat in front. 'The streets are our's.' That apostrophe shouldn't be there. Most folk don't know that, but it's true. I lick my finger and try to rub it out, but it won't shift. Probably been there too long.*

When we finally arrive, Kitty opens her eyes and frowns. 'Don't judge me, Lib.'

'About what?'

'This.'

She jumps off the bus without thanking the driver and turns left off the main road into a long, winding path. There's that crunchy gravel under my feet as I follow her to a gate at the end.

'Don't know why they bother.' She throws her rucksack over it, then climbs over. 'Not exactly high security, is it?'

I hop over, landing on both feet, and when I look up, I see it. The loveliest house I've ever laid eyes on. Honestly, it's like something off the telly. A big square house, with plants growing up the walls and a black door slap in the middle.

Kitty fishes in her pocket for a key and opens the door, letting it bang against the wall inside. 'Anyone home?' she shouts.

When no one replies she throws her keys into a wooden bowl on top of a set of drawers. 'Thank fuck for that.'

I traipse down the hall after her until we get to a kitchen. It's massive, with wooden cupboards, all matching. I once had a foster place in a house as big as this. The carer was the only one I ever really liked, but her home was cold and dark and creepy. The roof was always leaking. Kitty's house is all sunshine and yellow paint.

One of the cupboard doors turns out not to be a cupboard. It's just a fancy door on a freezer. Kitty drags open one of the shelves and roots around. 'Pepperoni?' she asks.

I nod. I'm not fussy like Kitty.

There's a door in the far corner that looks like it leads to the back garden. I peer outside and see miles of grass. I mean, bloody miles of it, and in the distance there's something blue.

'What's that?' I ask.

Kitty looks over my shoulder. 'What's what?'

'That blue square.'

'Oh.' She whacks a pizza into the oven. 'Pool.'

My eyes must be out on stalks because she laughs for the first time today. 'We never use it.'

'Why not?'

Kitty shrugs. 'Dunno, really.'

PLAYING DIRTY

Present Day

Frankie stared at the girl chained to the bed, both hands clenched into fists. She'd stopped gurgling and gasping, but was still flat on her back, face ashen, the marks around her throat still lurid.

Liberty scooted past her brother and helped the girl to a sitting position. She didn't resist. 'We need to ask you some questions.' The girl shook her head.

'Don't test us,' Tia shouted from the doorway.

Frankie spun on his heel, a balled fist already halfway to Tia's jaw. Liberty left her place by the girl and leaped between her brother and Tia.

'You.' Liberty pointed at Tia. 'Get a bottle of water.' When Tia didn't move, Liberty dropped her voice to a whisper. 'Now.'

Tia kissed her teeth, but left the room, slamming the door behind her.

'I want to squeeze the life out of her,' said Frankie. Liberty could well believe it. 'I don't get why you insist on having her on the crew.'

Liberty's eyes flicked to Frankie's hand, unthinkingly pressed against his scar. He didn't know about Tia's involvement in the shooting. How Dax had shot Frankie, thinking he needed to protect her. If he ever did find out, he would almost certainly carry out his threat to kill Tia. But for Liberty it was a lot less clear cut. Tia had no one. And while Liberty accepted that she couldn't help her lead a different life – she'd tried that with Dax and look how it had turned out – she could at least keep an eye on her. And it was a whole lot easier to do that with Tia on their pay roll rather than someone else's. Though the sight of this poor kid chained up and half strangled made it hard to think of Tia as anything but a liability.

'What do they call you?' Liberty asked the girl, but she didn't even look up. 'Street name will do.' Silence. Liberty glanced at Frankie. His temper was much more even than Jay's or Crystal's,

HELEN BLACK

but Tia had already pushed him hard today. 'Look at your situation, here,' she said to the girl. 'You're not exactly in a position to play silly buggers.'

The smell of frying onions rushed up the stairs to greet them and Liberty's guts rolled.

'Let's go,' said Frankie. Liberty frowned. They couldn't give up this easily. But Frankie shrugged and turned. 'If she won't talk to us Tia can just do what she likes with her. Not our problem.'

The girl stiffened, and Liberty had to hand it to Frankie: he knew how to play these situations. Ten years as an addict had made him a top manipulator.

'Fine,' Liberty said. 'Call her back in.'

Frankie moved to the door, but before his fingers reached the handle the girl gave a sound, a cross between a groan and a quiet scream.

'Something to say?' Liberty asked.

'They'll pop me,' the girl replied.

'Do *they* know where you are?'

'No.'

'Whereas Tia has you pinned down,' said Liberty. 'Literally.' The girl let out another whine. 'I know where I'd rather take my chances.'

Liberty leaned over and put her forefinger under the girl's chin. The skin was petal soft. God, she really was just a kid. She lifted up the girl's face and looked deep into her eyes. Fear, confusion, but also anger. Probably some aimed at herself for getting done over like this. 'Name.'

'Mad Bug,' the girl said. 'But mostly people just call me Mads.'

Hallelujah.

'And where are you from, Mads?' Liberty asked.

'Manchester.'

Liberty let go of the girl's chin, but she continued to meet her gaze. 'Specifically?'

62

'What?'

'Whereabouts in Manchester?'

'Moss Side.'

Liberty's eyes widened. A lifetime ago she'd lived in Moss Side. *It's not fucking Disneyland.* A girl had said that to her. What was her name? She gave a deliberate blink as she tried to remember. Red Converse trainers thrown into the corner of the room, the white rubber edges flecked with dried blood.

The sound of stamping up the stairs outside pulled Liberty from her memories and Tia appeared in the doorway, face like a flat pint. She thrust out a hand holding a plastic bottle of water. Liberty took it and gave it to the girl. 'This is Mads,' she said to Tia. 'From Moss Side.'

'Well, I could have told you that much.' Tia gave a huge sigh. 'Question is, what the hell's she doing here?'

The CDU's main office operated out of Birmingham, but it had unofficial satellites all over the UK. And Hutch's satellite looked a lot like a nail bar. A Vietnamese manicurist looked up from her work, mouth covered with a cloth mask, and nodded at Hutch as he made his way through.

Sol tried not to gag at the sight of a bloke in the far corner peeling off dead skin from a woman's feet. He'd assumed they'd use some sort of electronic equipment but no: the bloke was wielding what looked like a potato-peeler and raking off huge strips of white skin, which he let plop onto a piece of old newspaper.

In the corner, next to a little shrine containing a plastic Buddha, a bowl of fruit and a mechanical gold cat that waved its paw, was a door. Hutch unlocked it and ushered Sol inside. The smell of nail polish followed them, but the room itself was clean and sparse, except for one wall, which was plastered with photographs, maps and Post-it notes.

63

A bloke sat on a metal chair, laptop on his knees, looking up at the wall, then back down at his screen. Sol could tell he was job. Or ex-job. Something about the way he carried himself.

'Say hi to Gianni,' said Hutch.

Sol nodded and held out his hand. Gianni hung onto the laptop with one hand and offered the other. 'Good to meet you at last, Sol.'

Sol flicked a glance at Hutch, who shrugged. 'I might have mentioned you once or twice.'

All three men laughed at that as Hutch grabbed a chair from a stack in the corner and set it out next to Gianni. 'Take a load off.'

Sol did as he was told, thrust both hands into his pockets and stretched out his legs. Hutch shook his head at the state of Sol's boots. They were scuffed and a bit mucky but still in decent nick. He only ever owned one pair of boots at a time and wore them until they fell apart. Actually, the last pair had gone missing. Tan Timberlands. Natasha had huffed and puffed about them for weeks. True enough, they'd been minging. Stood on, rained on, puked on, pissed on. But the more his ex-wife had moaned about them, the more attached he'd become, until one morning they'd done a moonlight flit and in their place he'd found a pair of black leather deck shoes, which baffled him. (Did anyone need special shoes to wear on a boat? And if they did, why not something less ridiculous?) That same morning he'd bought this pair on the way to work and he'd worn them every day since, except for Amira's funeral.

'Right.' Hutch rubbed his hands together. 'Shall we kick off?' He stood at the evidence wall and pointed to a photograph of a chunky man in his early thirties. Pink cheeks and thinning hair, he was getting into a wrapped Range Rover. 'Ricky Vine. One of the main players in Manchester's Moss Side.' Hutch tapped a second photograph, in which Vine chatted with another man outside a barber's shop. 'And this is Caleb Clarke, his number two.'

'Cute couple,' said Sol.

'Drugs squad over the Pennines did a lot of work last year trying to put these two away.'

'We nearly managed it as well,' said Gianni.

'What happened?' Sol asked.

Gianni wrinkled his nose as if the bad smell of it all still hung around. 'Let's just say some vital evidence went walkabout.' Sol weighed that up. As ridiculous as it sounded, things did go missing. Documents, tapes, photographs. All easy to lose. Hell, he'd worked on one case where an entire box of blood-splattered clothes had never been found. Thank God the suspect pleaded before he'd had to 'fess up to that cluster-fuck. As if reading Sol's mind, Gianni added, 'And let's also say that one member of the team retired to Spain after he said his wife won on the bingo.'

Sol laughed, though it wasn't funny. Bent coppers were like bent nails, useless at their job and a risk to everyone around them.

'Did you have another crack at Pinky and Perky?' Sol asked.

Gianni shook his head. 'We watched them for a bit, but they knew the score and took steps.'

'Which leads us back here,' said Hutch, thumbing the wall. 'Imagine you're a drug-dealer and you know the feds have eyes on you. What's your next move?'

'Job in a call centre?' asked Sol.

Hutch rolled his eyes and went back to his wall. In the centre there was a map of the UK with three locations circled in red. 'Every copper in Manchester knows who you are so you move your business to a place where they don't know you.' He unpinned the map. 'But not just anywhere. I mean, you can't set up shop where someone just like you is already serving food, can you?'

'Not if you want to keep your bollocks,' said Sol.

'So, you're looking for a place where the locals aren't all that.' Hutch handed the map to Sol. 'Where you can take over without too much fuss.'

Sol checked the map. There were places highlighted and one jumped out at him. 'Are you telling me that Vine and Clarke have moved over here?'

'Nah.' Hutch retrieved his map and placed it back on his wall. 'They're still plotted back home in sunny Lancashire.' He moved to the next set of photographs – all mugshots of teenagers. 'They just send their minions to set up county lines.'

'Kids?'

'Yup. Pick them up in Moss Side, buy them a few pairs of Nikes and soon they're begging to go "up-country".'

'But how's a bunch of kids going to sort out the local dealers?' Sol asked.

'Most of 'em are fucking nutters from care and what-have-you,' Hutch replied. 'Vine assumes that a bit of bloodshed and the natives will roll over.'

Sol thought about the local faces. The Hills, the Delaneys and, of course, the Greenwoods. If Vine thought any of them would give up their territories without a fight, he was seriously mistaken.

Liberty and Frankie walked away from the kebab shop in silence. Dark had fallen, and a cold wind blew at them in angry little gusts. Frankie pulled his beanie from his pocket, remembered it was soaking and shoved it back in with a growl.

Lights flicked on across the estate. The boarded-up windows and graffiti-covered walls didn't look any more magical at night.

'Home, sweet home,' said Frankie.

Liberty gave a short laugh. This was the place the Greenwood kids had last lived together, but Frankie had been a toddler, still in nappies. 'There's no way you can remember living here.'

'Now you sound like Crystal,' he replied.

A few drops of rain smattered over Liberty, including a big fat one that landed on her cheek. She rubbed it off, her fingers coming away grimy. Not fresh rain, then, just droplets blowing off the roofs and trees.

When they passed Tia's usual spot Liberty was surprised to see a couple of kids on her sofa, necking as if their lives depended on it. That was sacred ground and Tia would batter anyone she found there. As if thinking the same thing, Frankie nodded that they should go over. When they were within a few feet, the slurpy kisses rang in her ears.

Frankie reached over with the toe of his trainer and kicked the lad harder than he needed to.

The kid looked up, immediately ready for a fight, but when he saw it was Frankie, he grabbed the girl's hand and pulled her away. Frankie watched them go, then plonked himself down and patted the seat next to him.

'Are you shitting me?' asked Liberty.

He just patted a second time. God, the sofa was minging, and Liberty's coat had cost the best part of five hundred quid. She ran her finger down the arm. Wet *and* sticky.

'For Christ's sake.' Frankie grabbed her hand and dragged her down. 'Look at you, with all your airs and graces.'

Liberty tried not to think about all the horrible things that might be stuck to her coat. 'I'm billing you for the dry-cleaning.'

They sat for a moment, side by side, taking in the view. Tia had actually chosen a smart vantage point from which she could keep an eye on all the roads with access to the square. If anyone arrived, she'd know and could be in the rabbit warren of narrow passages in seconds.

'Well,' she said at last, 'at least we know it's not Hill taking the piss.'

Frankie nodded. 'Might have been easier if it had.'

'How d'you work that one out?'

'We know who he is. We know where he is. A turf war wouldn't be ideal, but we'd easily win.'

'You can't be sure of that.'

Frankie laughed. 'Of course I'm sure. We're stronger than he is and a lot smarter. Well, you are, anyway.' He patted her shoulder. 'But this lot in Manchester, we know next to nothing at all about them.'

Liberty thought about Mads still chained up, terrified of Tia, who was in no mood to play nice. 'We'll have to get as much as we can out of the girl.'

'Torturing kids,' he replied. 'Did you ever think life would get this fun?'

A bag head appeared at the corner of the flats, eyes darting from left to right. He clocked the Greenwoods and shock rippled across his pockmarked face. But he wandered over anyway and held his hands in front of him, fingers darting up and down, like a tiny shoal of fish. 'Is Tia around?' he asked.

'Nope,' said Frankie.

'Right, right.' The man took out a mangled tenner from his pocket. 'Are you . . .'

'Mate. Do we look like we're serving up?' asked Frankie. 'Tia's not working tonight. Try Sweatsville.'

'Just come from there.'

Frankie shot Liberty a look. 'And?'

'No one about, just some kid handing out cards.'

'Cards for what?' Frankie asked.

The man shrugged but delved into the same filthy pocket where he'd kept his money. He handed over a small white card to Frankie who read it and handed it to Liberty. As a lawyer, she'd always carried bundles of these. 'Liberty Chapman LLB. Partner at Howell and May'. This card bore four words – *Peng Food Served Daily* – and a mobile number.

'Can I get that back?' the man asked.

Frankie leaned forward. 'Ring that number, pal, and it'll be the last time you use your fingers. Get me?'

The man nodded and ran away. Liberty read the card again. Things were not looking good and it was going to be down to her to sort it.

When Liberty and Frankie arrived at the Black Cherry, Mel was turfing someone out. Not a punter, though she often did that, no bother, but one of the dancers. The girl was still in her work gear: black PVC thong, studded thigh-length boots, and a top with more laces than Timpsons.

Mel threw a stuffed carrier bag at her. 'Sling your hook right now.'

'You cannot do this,' the girl screeched.

'I can and I am,' Mel replied.

The girl screamed and charged at Mel, head down, her crown connecting with Mel's chest, knocking her off balance. Mel tottered backwards, trying to regain her feet, and grabbed the velvet curtain drawn across the entrance to the club. As she plummeted to the floor, the curtain tore from its pole and fell on top of her.

Liberty raced towards the girl in the boots as she was about to pounce on Mel and grabbed a handful of hair at the back of her head. The girl gave out another banshee wail, but Liberty held her very tightly and whispered into her ear, 'One more peep out of you and your best mate will never recognise you again.'

The girl went limp and Liberty let go. She bent for the bag and shoved it at the girl. 'Don't want to see you around here again. Clear?'

The girl nodded and wobbled away into the wet night air.

'All right?' Liberty asked, and held out a hand to Mel, who was struggling to get to her feet.

Mel grasped it and allowed the younger woman to pull her upright. 'You should have battered the thieving little cow.' Liberty smoothed down Mel's red satin shirt, tucked the tangle of gold chains back into her crêpy cleavage. Mel rolled her eyes but didn't shove her away. 'Jay's already here.'

'Crystal?'

'Not picking up her phone.'

Mel kicked the curtain into the corner and stepped into the club. All eyes were on her, even the girl on stage had stopped halfway through chucking off her bra to stare. 'Get dancing, you,' Mel shouted at her. 'Show's over.'

Liberty turned to Frankie, who was wearing a smirk. 'Why didn't you help me?'

'And miss the poisoned dwarf getting planted on her arse?' he replied. 'Behave yourself.'

Rose had enough sense to know she shouldn't drive. She might still be under the limit, but cider plus painkillers plus bone-deep exhaustion were a recipe for disaster so she took an Uber. The driver fiddled with the radio dial until he found a station playing old-school jazz funk, then drove on in silence, head bobbing.

When they reached their destination he turned to Rose, face puzzled.

'It's fine,' she said, and got out into the rain.

He waited for a moment, as if she might realise she'd made a mistake, so she gave him a wave and he reversed away. Rose watched him disappear, then approached the garage door and hammered on it with her fist. 'Salty,' she shouted. Groans came from inside. 'Salty, open up right now.' She hammered again. 'Don't make me call the drugs squad.'

The garage door opened from the bottom and stopped halfway. Rose dipped her head and peered inside. 'Thank you.'

Salty scowled at her and then at the rain pouring from a broken gutter outside. 'I'm not going out in that.'

70

Rose moved inside. She knew she shouldn't. Alone, injured and tipsy, she wouldn't be able to defend herself if she needed to.

'Make yourself at home, why don't you?' said Salty, and dragged the door down behind her.

The space was lit by several candles dotted around the floor. A couple with their backs to the concrete far wall were using one to cook up a fix. The man smiled at Rose, one front tooth missing. The woman didn't look up from her work. Salty sank to the floor beside her and rolled up his sleeve. 'What do you want?' he asked Rose.

'These kids from Manchester, do you know where they're staying?'

The woman placed a ball of cotton wool on top of the bubbling brown, and when it had absorbed it all, she pushed the tip of a syringe into the dirty clump and sucked the liquid into the barrel of the works. Salty tied off his arm with a piece of rubber tubing and slapped the vein to make it swell. 'What? You think they've invited me for a sleepover?' he said.

'Just thought you might have heard on the grapevine.'

Salty didn't take his greedy eyes from the needle. 'Well, I haven't.'

'Nobody mentioned they've got guests?' asked Rose.

The woman pricked Salty's skin and a red bead of blood danced into the barrel. Then she plunged down and he gave an almost sexual groan of relief. Rose crossed the garage and knelt in front of him. 'Think hard, Salty.'

He smiled at that and blew a spit bubble. 'Think, Salty, think.' Rose put out a hand to give him a shake but decided she didn't want to touch him.

'It's all the thinking that gets us in this mess,' he said.

The woman nodded. 'Amen.' She was already back at work, burning a fresh pile of powder on her spoon, stirring it with a pair of nail scissors, adding juice from a plastic lemon-shaped bottle.

'Do you know Mad Brian?' It took a second before Rose worked out the woman was speaking to her, then she shook her head. 'Ask about. Everybody knows who he is.'

'Why?'

'Because he's mad,' said the woman.

'No. I mean why should I ask about him?'

The woman's heroin was ready, and she reached for the needle still in Salty's arm and plucked it out. She gave it a quick rinse in a cup of water by her feet and made her fix. 'He was on about having family to stay with him.' She unzipped her jeans and pushed aside her grey pants to reveal a bush of grey pubic hair. 'But it's the first he's ever mentioned 'em in the ten years I've known him.'

The woman dug the needle into her groin with an intake of breath. Then tried again. As her head fell forward Rose stood to leave, dropping a tenner into the woman's lap before she dragged open the rusty garage door.

Jay sipped from a bottle of beer while Liberty filled him in on what Mads had told them. When she'd finished, he blew across the rim, producing a mournful whistle.

'We're going to have to send a very strong message back to Moss Side,' said Frankie. 'Let them know how the land lies.'

'But we don't want to do anything rash,' said Liberty.

'We don't need to, with Tia on the pay roll,' Frankie replied.

Jay put down his bottle. 'Lib, you need to talk to Crystal.' Liberty sighed. 'This is serious. We can't do anything unless we're all on board.'

'Have you met her? She'll argue with anything I suggest on principle.'

Half an hour later, Liberty pressed the intercom to Crystal's flat. She'd only been there a couple of times, both at Harry's invitation. If it had been up to Crystal, she'd probably never have set foot inside.

Liberty had lost far too much sleep over Crystal's hostility. When she'd first come back to Yorkshire, it had seemed understandable. Liberty had abandoned her siblings years ago and Crystal couldn't forget or forgive. Didn't matter that Liberty had been a scared kid herself. Later it became about Liberty's reluctance to join the family business. If Liberty wanted to be part of their lives, then she had to shed her own. But even when she did that, gave up her legal career and everything she'd ever worked for, Crystal still resented her. Truth was that Crystal would never make peace with Liberty because she didn't want to.

She pressed the buzzer again, hoping no one was home.

'What do you want?' Crystal barked.

Liberty waved into the camera. 'Nice to see you too.'

'I mean it, Lib, what do you want?'

Liberty shivered. 'There's something going off on the Crosshills and we need to talk about it.'

Crystal let her sister spend another minute freezing her arse off, before buzzing her up without a word.

Crystal leaned her elbows against the huge island in the centre of her kitchen. Behind her was a vast bare-brick wall that housed a stainless-steel oven. Spotless, of course, possibly never used since Crystal didn't eat, let alone cook. Liberty wondered what Harry did about dinner.

She slid onto one of the black stools. It was hard and cold, as if Crystal had no desire for anyone to be comfy in her kitchen. 'Is Harry home?'

'Why?' Crystal snapped.

'Just asking.'

'Well, don't.' Crystal glowered across the black granite of the island. 'Just tell me what the problem is.'

'A crew from Moss Side are trying to take over on the estates,' said Liberty. 'That's who killed the lad the other night.'

Crystal moved to the American-style fridge in the corner and took out two cans of Diet Coke. She slid one across the island to Liberty. 'How do we know?'

'Remember Tia?' Crystal nodded. 'She took one of their youngers in for questioning. Let's just say it all adds up.'

Crystal tapped the top of her can twice and pulled the ring. She took a long drink that must have drained half of it. 'So, what are you going to do?'

'That's what we need to decide.'

'I thought you were in charge.'

Liberty pushed away her untouched can. 'Just for once, can we not do this?'

Crystal stared at her in silence over the top of her can. Then she went to a cupboard and grabbed a glass, moved back to the fridge and took out a bottle of wine. She poured a good measure into the glass then placed both it and the bottle in front of Liberty.

'Thank you.' Crystal didn't smile or respond but Liberty accepted the gesture for the olive branch it was. 'Frankie and Jay think we need to hit back hard.'

'But you're worried.'

Liberty drank some wine. It was an expensive one from Argentina. She wanted to tease Crystal about forgetting her roots but could guess that wouldn't go down as well as the wine. 'We don't know who these people are or what they've got,' Liberty said. 'Kicking off something we can't finish doesn't seem like a smart move.'

'Sounds like they're the ones kicking off.'

'Maybe we can do a deal,' Liberty said. 'It's not like we're short of addicts round here.'

74

Crystal snorted. 'Bagsy we keep the crackheads and they can have all the zombies on spice.'

'I was thinking we let them run things on the ground for a price,' Liberty replied. 'I mean, we've been looking for a way to get out of the drugs game.'

Crystal wagged her finger. 'You've been looking for a way.'

Liberty's plan had always been to steer the Greenwood business away from crime. Make everything legitimate in five years, and there was a chance they'd all get out alive and walking the streets. She'd just about managed to drag the Black Cherry and the rest of the clubs away from the dark side. Maybe now was the time to ditch the street dealing. 'One night in jail was enough for me,' she said.

'Lightweight,' Crystal replied.

'And you fancy getting banged up for a lump, do you?'

'I'm not scared of doing time,' Crystal said.

Liberty could well believe it. Give it a week and her sister would be the top dog of her wing. A month and she'd be running the place.

'Can we agree that we hold off just until we know a bit more about who they are?' Liberty asked.

Crystal nodded. 'Unless they do something we can't ignore.'

So far, the Moss Side crew had caused problems among the youngers. And, yeah, someone had died, and that was a definite act of aggression, but it wasn't yet a declaration of war. Liberty topped up her glass and was about to take another swig when her mobile rang. She checked the screen and saw Tia was calling.

'What's up?'

'They came to the shop,' she said, voice muffled and woozy.

'Who?'

'Moss Side.' Tia gave a groan. 'Kicked the door in and had away with Mads.'

Another groan and the line went dead.

Chapter 6

7 September 1990

The water's freezing but I don't care. I mean, how many times do you get to swim in your own private pool? Like never, that's how many. When I was in junior school, we went to the baths once a week. We used to have to line up and show the swimming teacher the bottom of our feet to check for verrucas. Then we'd do breadths, like a pack of wild dogs. After, we'd get sent into the showers, but the plugholes were always full of hair that made me gip.

I've had to borrow a bikini off Kitty, which doesn't fit because she's less than five foot with no boobs and I'm the opposite. The bottoms are right up the crack of my arse and the top barely covers my nipples.

I splash Kitty and she screams, 'Don't get my hair wet – it goes all frizzy!'

I ignore her and scoop up handfuls of water, literally pouring it onto her head. She screams again, her eyeliner running down her cheeks. I dive under and grab her foot. She yanks it away but I grab the other. I can hear her muffled laughs from above.

I let water fill my mouth and surface, then spit it all out in a stream at Kitty.

'Nice.'

At the edge of the pool two boys, one white, one black, are staring at me. I duck down so my chest is submerged.

Kitty's still giggling. 'This is Lib, a mate from college,' she tells them. 'Lib, this is Matt and Tobias.'

PLAYING DIRTY

The white one lifts a hand to me but the black one just stares. I sink deeper until my chin is touching the water. Both lads are wearing suits and ties, which is weird. The white one might be just about old enough for some kind of office job but there's no way the black one can be more than fifteen.

'Coming in?' Kitty asks.

I hear myself gasp. There's no way I'm staying in here with them, but then I'll have to get out in front of them.

'Nah,' says the white one. 'Bet it's bloody freezing.'

Kitty flicks her wet fingers at him. If our Jay were here, I'd have pulled him in in all his clothes. Probably wouldn't have needed to – the daft bugger would have jumped in, shoes and all.

'C'mon, Tobe.' He pats the black boy's shoulder. 'Let's leave the ladies in peace.'

Tobias doesn't want to go, but eventually Matt drags him away.

'Don't mind Tobias,' says Kitty. 'He's not all there.' She circles her finger round her temple. 'Clever as fuck but something missing.'

'Who is he?'

'My parents' conscience,' she replies. She laughs when she clocks my bewildered face. 'They adopted him.'

Now the coast's clear I haul myself from the pool and wrap a towel round me. 'I'd better get off.'

Kitty's bedroom is like a massive L shape. In the long bit there's a row of built-in wardrobes and a dressing table scattered with make-up. There are at least three black eyeliners surrounded by shavings where she's been sharpening them. In the bottom bit of the room a double bed has a continental quilt and four pillows with matching slips. Me and Fat Rob use rolled-up jumpers.

There's a knock at the door, then Matt strolls in.

'We could have been naked,' Kitty tells him.

He looks me up and down and nods at the big yellow hoodie I've got on, the words 'Feed Your Head' peeling off. 'Very retro,' he says.

I can't tell if he's taking the piss. I mean Vicky left it me last year and it wasn't new then.

'Do you want a toastie?' he asks. 'Tobe's on the job.'

'Fucking hell, Matt! He'll burn the house down!' Kitty shouts at him.

'Shut up, Kitty.' Matt turns to me. 'Fancy one, Lib? Guaranteed to be charred to a cinder.'

'I need to get the bus,' I say.

Kitty outlines her lips in blue. It looks strange but kind of good. 'Working?' I nod. 'Lib does shifts at the Hacienda,' she tells Matt.

I sigh. Is she going to tell everyone she bumps into?

'I'll drop you,' he says.

'I need to go home first,' I say.

Matt shrugs. 'I'll drop you there, then.'

It's all a bit weird cos he doesn't even know where I live, but I agree because that way I can save the bus fare.

Matt's car is a Mini that makes a grinding noise every time he changes gear. When we stop at some traffic lights, he reaches behind his seat with his left hand, grabs a cassette tape, reads the handwritten label and chucks it back.

I look over and see piles of them knocking about on the floor. The light changes so Matt pulls off with a sound like two metal bars being rubbed together. I grab a handful of tapes and read. Bummed. The La's. Gold Mother. I stick Bummed into the tape slot and press play. As soon as the music comes on Matt starts to nod his head. He's got funny hair, tight little curls, like pubes, and a hole in his earlobe where I suppose he's got it pierced but doesn't wear a stud.

'How's Kitty getting on at college?' he asks. I don't know what to say. I only see her in English, and she doesn't seem to have read any of the books. 'Actually, I don't care,' he says.

I laugh cos at least it's honest. 'What do you do?'

'French, German and maths,' he says.

'I meant for a job.'

He frowns. 'I haven't got a job.'

'So why were you wearing a suit?'

'That's the uniform,' he says. 'We can wear exactly what we like, provided it's a grey suit, shirt and tie.'

I laugh again. I mean, what sort of college makes people wear suits? But I don't get to ask because we're coming up to my street. Before the turning I tell Matt to pull over.

He nods at the row of shops. 'You live in Fast Chick Inn? Handy when you're hungry.' I roll my eyes at him and get out. 'See you around, Lib.'

'Thanks for the lift,' I say, and slam the door. When I'm sure he's out of the way, I turn down my street.

Present Day

Liberty dipped the end of a cotton bud into the bowl of water, then ran it under Tia's bottom lip.

'Ow.'

The kid's face was mashed. One eye closed up, lips split in several places. And a couple of fingers on her right hand looked broken. Crystal handed her a half-bottle of vodka, but Tia couldn't unscrew the top and dropped it.

Crystal picked it up, took off the top and held it to Tia's mouth. Tia tried to take a gulp but pulled away. 'It fucking burns.'

'Two seconds' pain for a world of gain,' said Crystal. 'Trust me.'

Tia tried again, this time letting the vodka pour down her throat with a moan. Next Crystal produced a couple of pills and shoved them into Tia's mouth. She swallowed them with another gulp of vodka. She grasped the end of the bloodstained bed with her one good hand, feet grinding the glass strewn across the floor from the smashed TV. The chain that had been used to keep Mads in place lay coiled in the corner like a snake.

'This needs a stitch,' said Liberty, lifting up a flap of skin at the corner of Tia's mouth with the cotton bud.

Crystal leaned over and examined the damage. 'It's fine.'

'We need antiseptic,' said Liberty.

Crystal held out the bottle of vodka. Liberty took it and dribbled some over the cotton bud. Tia squeezed her eyes shut, knowing this was going to hurt like hell. Liberty gritted her teeth and wiped the bud across the loose fold of skin. Tia yelled out in agony.

'That'll do,' said Crystal.

Liberty was convinced that Tia needed an X-ray, antibiotics and co-codamol, but acquiesced. 'What happened?'

'First thing I hear is the door flying off,' said Tia. All three turned to it, now only attached by one hinge, a hole where the outside lock had been. 'Then three of them march in and one smacks me in the face with a bat.'

'They say anything?' Liberty asked.

Tia shook her head.

'Didn't need to, did they?' said Crystal, and patted the top of the pulverised telly. 'We got the message loud and clear.'

When Liberty arrived home, she found Sol on his hands and knees, scrubbing the kitchen floor. 'Is that blood?'

He nodded and held up a thumb covered with plaster.

'What have I told you about playing with the big boys?' she said.

He lobbed the stained dishcloth into the bin and kissed her.

'Are you bored shitless, Sol?' she asked.

'Well, to be fair, I've had more exciting snogs.'

Liberty pushed his fringe from his eyes and traced the scar underneath. 'If you wanted to go back to the job, I wouldn't care.'

'We both know I can't do that.'

'But you want to?'

He gave a lopsided smile. 'Right now, I'd rather hit the sack.'

The next morning Rose crawled out of bed, picked up a packet of co-codamol from her dressing table and swallowed one. The muscles in her chest and stomach had seized up, and trying to straighten her back felt like ripping herself in two. The nurse who had patched her up had told her to keep the wound dry, but Rose could smell herself. She tried to work out a way to have a shower. Could she hold a plastic bag against the cut and prevent the steri-strips from getting soaked?

She shuffled downstairs, bent over like a geriatric, grabbed a Tesco carrier from the hall and plodded back to the bathroom, a wince with each step. In the cabinet, among the contact-lens cases and half-used cans of deodorant, was a packet of plasters. Rose took out four and peeled off the backing, attempting to stick the plastic bag to her greasy skin. The first two rolled in on themselves and she threw away the flesh-coloured mini sausages. She was down to the last plaster when there was a knock at her door, which she ignored. Naturally, the knocking came louder and more insistent.

If Redman was surprised to find Rose bent double, wearing only a grubby dressing gown and a 5p carrier, he didn't show it. 'Thought you might need a lift to work.' Between the pain and the painkiller, Rose's reply was wet word salad. She gave up on speech and nodded for him to make himself at home in the kitchen. 'Coffee?' he asked. She shrugged that she didn't mind and headed back to her bedroom.

Ten minutes, five squirts of Impulse and two bloodcurdling screams later, she found Redman riffling in her cupboards.

'You need something to eat,' he said.

Rose took a black coffee from him, the spoon still in the cup. She licked the metal, enjoying the burn to her tongue.

He found an opened packet of shortbread, handed her one. 'I've worked with people before who think they can ride into town and change everything.' Rose nibbled the edge of the stale biscuit. 'They act like they're the star of the show and the rest of us are just the sidekicks. Doesn't matter that we've walked these streets all our lives.' He glanced at her stomach. 'Doesn't usually end well.'

The biscuit was dry and tasteless in Rose's mouth. She swallowed some coffee to force it down. 'Have you ever heard of someone called Mad Brian?' she asked. Redman nodded. 'Right, well, we need to go and see him.'

She put down her cup and walked to the door. Redman mumbled something under his breath as he followed her out.

It turned out that Mad Brian lived a couple of streets away from Salty's garage in a grey block of flats surrounded by metal fences.

'Known locally as Sweatsville,' Redman told her. From the hum of Rose's armpits, she thought she'd fit right in. 'The town council keep threatening to knock it down, but where will they put everybody?'

Two women walked past, swinging nylon book bags, their kids clattering along on scooters, coats buttoned up to their chins. One noticed Redman and Rose getting out of their car and nudged her friend. 'Don't suppose you lot have come to do anything about number sixteen, have you?' she asked.

'Sorry,' said Redman.

The friend pulled out her phone and exhibited her cracked screen. 'Ten times I've called your lot.' The children carried on ahead, wheels bumping along the pavement. 'Look, I don't care how them lasses earn a few quid. They can shag the whole of Yorkshire, as far as I'm concerned. But setting up a knocking shop here's not on, not where there's little 'uns playing out and that.'

Rose pulled out her cards and handed one to each woman. 'Report this to me later, okay? I'll make sure someone looks into it.'

'We'll hold you to that,' said the first woman, and they moved off.

Redman gave Rose a withering look. 'What?' she said. 'Would you want it on your doorstep?' She took out her notebook and scribbled down the number sixteen. 'Now let's visit Mad Brian.'

The climb up to the flat almost killed Rose, so she let Redman knock on the door. When there was no answer, Redman shouted through the letterbox: 'Come on, mate, don't make us come back with a ram.'

There was muttering from behind the door and the sound of several bolts being opened. Then Mad Brian appeared. His shoulder-length hair frizzed out like a pom-pom, and he appeared to have thick brows tattooed above each eye. There was a burn down his left cheek that oozed fresh liquid.

'You on your own, Brian?' Redman asked. Brian looked behind him as if to check and smiled. 'You gonna invite us in, then?'

Redman didn't actually wait for an answer and pushed past Mad Brian into the dingy hallway. Rose followed him, boots crunching on the mountain of unopened post, trying not to breathe in the smell of urine.

She took her place next to Redman in what she assumed was the sitting room, but there was no furniture, just piles and piles of newspapers and paperback books.

'Brian likes reading, don't you, Brian?' said Redman. Brian nodded and his hands fluttered to his throat. At first, Rose thought there were tattoos inked all over them, then realised the designs were drawn on with a biro. Numbers, letters, symbols. 'So, we hear you've got some family visiting, Brian. Who's that?' Brian shrugged. 'Brother, maybe?'

Mad Brian shook his head. 'Not him. He used to kick the shit out of me. That's why I'm not scared of owt.'

'Who, then?' asked Redman.

'Just family.'

'Can you show us where they stay?' Rose asked.

Mad Brian hesitated a moment, checked the markings on his hands and walked out of the room. He led them to a bedroom packed with sleeping bags and clothes. Rose nudged a pair of high tops with her boot.

'Nice to have company,' said Redman.

'They bring me books sometimes,' said Mad Brian. 'And chips.'

Sol buttered a piece of toast and put it in front of Liberty.

'I'm knackered, not paralysed,' she said. He grabbed it back, took an enormous bite. 'Oi.' She tried to snatch the slice, but he stuffed it into his mouth.

Laughing, she put another slice into the toaster, stood over it while Sol chewed. When her toast popped, she buttered it, cut it in half and shared it with him. 'One of us has to have some manners, eh?'

He watched her eat and rub her tired eyes. She'd tossed and turned most of the night. It didn't matter: he hadn't been able to nod off either. Too busy working through the meeting with Hutch. 'You know you asked me whether I wanted to go back to work?' he said.

'Yeah.'

'Well, what about you? Do you ever miss being a lawyer?' he asked. Liberty stopped, mid-bite. 'It must have been interesting.'

'I drafted a lot of contracts, Sol.'

'But you were good at it?'

She swallowed, took a long drink of orange juice. 'I think so. Look, where are you going with this?'

Sol didn't know. First rule of a copper's playbook: start with the end in mind. If you want a suspect to confess, only pose questions that are going to lead to that eventuality. Never ask anything if you don't already have a good idea what the answer will be. One time, after a working girl had bled to death while they waited for an ambulance, the powers that be had insisted he see the counsellor. Now there was a woman with a narrow range of questions:

84

'How do you feel about that, Sol?' Maybe there were some folk who liked answering that, but he'd never met one in Yorkshire.

He stood and kissed Liberty on top of her head. 'Ignore me.'

'I will.'

Hutch was waiting for him in Scottish Tony's as Sol had expected, a plate of egg and bacon already scraped clean. 'You want food, or shall we crack on?'

'I haven't said I'm up for it yet,' Sol replied.

Hutch chuckled and waved a tenner at Tony.

The Greenwoods were sitting around a table in the Black Cherry when Mel arrived with Tia. There'd been some huffing and puffing when Liberty had dropped her round at Mel's last night, but here they both were. Tia's face was like a smashed-up melon. Her lips had swollen to twice their size, not that it stopped her sucking away on a roll-up.

'Put that out,' Liberty ordered.

Tia made a show of one last drag before rubbing the end with her finger and thumb.

'I'll bloody well kill her,' said Mel.

'Get in line,' said Frankie.

Next to arrive was Hill and some man-mountain straight out of Central Casting. Jay pushed a chair out for Hill and nodded at Mel to give the muscle a drink.

Hill hovered behind the chair and pointed at the wreck of Tia's face. 'Before anyone says a word, I'm not responsible for that.'

'We know,' Liberty replied.

Hill surveyed everyone's expressions in turn, nodded and took his seat. 'So what gives?'

'You ever hear of county lines?' Liberty asked. Hill shrugged and she pressed the card into his hand.

'"Peng food served daily",' said Hill. 'What the fuck does that mean?'

'It means we've got a problem, Paul.'

Hill examined the card, turning it over in his hand. 'Where are they from?'

'Moss Side.'

Hill threw down the card in disgust. 'Let's just end the lot of 'em.'

'We could do that, yes.' Liberty pocketed the card. 'But I'd rather find out who we're dealing with first.'

Hill jabbed his thumb at Tia. 'Ask Freddie Kruger.'

Tia jumped towards Hill. 'I don't know nothing.' The muscle slammed down his glass and grabbed Tia's arm. 'Don't touch me, dickhead.' When he didn't let go, Tia sank her teeth into his hand. He gave a surprisingly high-pitched yelp before Mel dragged Tia off by her hair.

'You need to control your staff, Liberty,' said Hill.

Liberty glared at Tia until she sloped off to the stairs up to the dancers' dressing room. 'Making out like I'm part of it,' she shouted, just before she disappeared.

'She's a good girl,' said Liberty. 'Took a bat to the face for us last night.'

'Every cloud,' said Frankie.

'Look, Paul, I'll get straight to the point. Have you still got coppers on your pay roll?' Hill nodded. 'Right, then, let's find out who these faces from Manchester are.'

'You're assuming they're faces, then?' he said. 'Could just be a bunch of no-marks trying their luck.'

'Let's hope you're right. Either way, I'd say their luck's just run out.'

★★★

When Hill and his goon had left, Mel stomped upstairs to deal with Tia. 'That kid needs stitches,' she yelled.

Liberty sighed at Crystal, but she just pulled out her mobile with a shrug. Jay laughed. Crystal's bad attitude was always a source of hilarity to him.

'How come you got Hill involved?' he asked. 'Crystal's got plenty of people.'

'I wanted to involve him,' said Liberty. 'Make sure he sticks to the plan. We don't need him doing anything stupid to prove he's Billy Big Bollocks.'

'He knows his days are numbered,' said Frankie.

'All the more reason for him to kick off,' Liberty replied.

'Can we trust him to give us the right information?' Crystal asked.

Jay leaned back, left foot on right knee, arms behind his head, elbows at right angles. 'Your faith in human nature is a joy to behold.'

Crystal gave him the finger without taking her eyes off her phone.

'She's right, though,' said Frankie.

Liberty nodded. 'Which is why Crystal's going to get her people to double check.'

As they waited outside the chief inspector's office, Rose watched Redman run his finger under the edge of his trainer sock. She wished she knew him well enough to tell him they looked daft. Then again, how great did she look today without a shower and barely able to stand up straight?

While Redman's head was bent to his foot, Rose took a quick sniff of her armpit. The smell of Impulse was far too sweet, like a cake with vanilla frosting. Better than the alternative, though.

When Redman was done scratching his bony ankle, he said, 'Can I make a suggestion?'

'Go ahead.'

'Don't mention the Greenwoods.'

'But they run the Crosshills estate,' she said.

He leaned against the wall. 'I know that, but him indoors will run a mile at the very mention of the name.' Rose waited for him to expand. 'There was an op last year, didn't end well. A good cop died and an even better one left under a cloud.'

Rose was about to ask for more details when the chief called them in.

They took a seat at the near side of his desk as he poured them both a coffee from a cafetière. Then he offered a tiny jug of milk but no sugar. He used the teeniest spoon Rose had ever seen to stir his drink, then checked a notepad, which was the only other thing on his desk.

'Officer Angel, how are you finding it here?' the chief asked. 'Are the natives treating you well?'

Rose didn't look at Redman but hoped he was blushing, given what a bunch of pricks he and his friends had been to her when she arrived. 'I'm settling in nicely, sir.'

'That's the spirit.' He turned to Redman. 'I hear we may have a problem with county lines.'

'Very possibly, sir,' said Redman.

'I'd say definitely,' Rose added. The chief opened a hand to indicate she should continue. 'Young people from the same part of Manchester have come to our attention recently. Some have been attacked, some have been the attacker. We also discovered a vulnerable person whose home has been cuckooed.'

'Speak English.'

'Taken over by the out-of-towners, sir.'

The chief was still stirring his coffee. 'And why do we care? One dealer is much the same as another, wherever he's from.'

'In my experience these situations can go two ways.' Rose leaned forward and instantly regretted it. She swallowed a groan. 'The locals lie down, and you now have a bunch of much more aggressive players on the patch. Or the locals fight tooth and nail and things get very violent. We've already had one child killed and my bet is there'll be more.'

The chief tapped his spoon against the side of his cup and took a small sip. 'And what do you propose we do?'

Rose took a deep breath. She knew the reaction her first suggestion would get. Redman lowered his head because he could see it coming too.

'We round up all the local dealers and keep them off the streets for thirty-six hours.'

The chief lowered his cup and frowned. 'I may be being very dim here, but how will that help rid us of our unwelcome guests?'

'Nature abhors a vacuum, sir. Cut off the usual pipeline and the addicts will seek out a fresh supply.' She smiled. 'We just have to follow the breadcrumbs as quickly as we can.'

The chief steepled his fingers gravely. 'And how would we organise this initial round-up?'

'We use the expertise of our friendly natives.' Rose smiled at Redman. 'Drugs squad, Vice, anyone with knowledge of what's happening on the streets, we pool them together.' She lifted her right hand and chopped the palm of her left. 'Then we hit them all together, and we hit them hard.'

Jay insisted he wanted to go to the Jade Garden for lunch. Crystal cried off, saying she needed to make calls about the Moss Side crew.

'Have you two noticed that she's eating even less than usual?' Liberty asked.

Frankie tried to pick up a prawn with chopsticks but missed

89

the food altogether, the sticks poking sideways like a baby giraffe's legs. He tried again, made it almost to his mouth before dropping the prawn in his lap. Liberty handed him a fork.

'If you're going to mention it to her, you're braver than I thought,' said Frankie.

Jay spooned some egg fried rice onto his place. 'Or you've got a frigging death wish.'

'You're not worried, then?' she asked.

'Sometimes,' said Frankie. 'We all have shit we have to work our way through.'

Liberty signalled for the waitress to bring another round of beers. The owner had got his girls wearing short black tunics over red and black trousers, presumably to give the place a more authentic feel. The waitress scratched at the skin under her mandarin collar, which probably itched like hell, and gave Liberty a thumbs-up.

'I'm not working my way through any shit,' said Jay. Liberty burst out laughing. 'What?'

'You've shagged every dancer in the Cherry,' she said.

'Except the one with the gold teeth,' said Frankie. 'That's one scary-looking lass.'

The waitress brought over the drinks with an uncomfortable smile. Liberty noticed she had a rash from her chin right down her throat.

'I'm a changed man,' said Jay, spearing a chicken ball. 'Been keeping my nose clean.'

'It's not your nose we're talking about,' Liberty said.

Jay picked up another chicken ball and brought it up to his mouth, but as it touched his lips, he grabbed it from the fork prongs and lobbed it at his sister. It hit her square in the forehead. When it plopped onto her plate, she grabbed it and chucked it back.

As all three creased up laughing, Liberty remembered how much she loved being with her family.

'Seriously, though,' said Jay, 'I've knocked all that on the head. Can't risk it now the lads are getting older. Got to stay out of trouble.'

Liberty smiled. It might have taken a long time, but the Greenwoods were finally putting the past behind them.

Chapter 7

7 September 1990

Fat Rob's sat on the settee, legs crossed, in just his pants. He's got a fag hanging out of the corner of his mouth and is squinting through the smoke at a needle he's trying to thread. I sit next to him as he has another attempt at getting a tiny bit of cotton through the eye.

'Lick the end,' I tell him.

He gives the thread a suck and this time manages to pass it through. 'Get in.' He's got a red sweatshirt in his lap and at his feet a denim jacket and some kitchen scissors. I pick up the jacket and give it a sniff. 'Bought it in Help the Aged,' he says. I can tell. 'And I'm thinking I can customise it.'

'Customise it how?'

'You know how baseball jackets have different colour arms?' he says.

'Yeah.'

He plucks the fag from his mouth and taps the ash on a saucer he's got balanced on the arm of the settee. 'So, I'm gonna take the arms off this,' he nods at the red sweatshirt, 'and sew 'em on the jacket.'

'Can you sew?' I ask.

'How hard can it be?'

I'm thinking it's probably quite hard, but I just smile and wander off to make us a brew. I try not to laugh when Rob swears as he pricks his finger.

'I've just been swimming,' I tell him.

'Where?'

I check the fridge for milk. Fat Rob's girlfriend must have been round because there's nearly a full bottle. She sometimes calls in on her lunch break for a cuppa and a shag. 'That lass I met at college has got a pool in her garden.'

'Are they millionaires or what?'

I think they must be. The house and everything. One day when I've done all my exams, and I've got a good job as a solicitor, I'm going to buy a house like that. But I'll use the swimming pool every day. I mean, it'd be a waste not to.

I pass Rob a tea. 'You should see her bedroom. It's bigger than this. And she doesn't even share.'

'All right for some,' he says, takes a drink and smacks his lips. 'Do you think I can get this jacket done in time for tonight's shift?'

I kiss his forehead. 'To be honest, I think it's going to be a bit tight.'

Present Day

In the room at the back of the nail bar, Ricky Vinc and Caleb Clarke's faces stared out from the wall. Sol, Hutch and Gianni sat side by side staring back at them.

'So, this pair's still the target?' Sol asked.

'They're responsible for a whole ton of misery,' Hutch replied. 'And they think they're untouchable.'

'No one's untouchable,' said Sol.

'Amen,' said Gianni.

The sound of laughter filtered under the door. Then someone spoke in excited Vietnamese. Sol wondered how you stayed so cheerful when your job was to peel people's feet. 'I'm assuming there's a plan,' he said.

'We know they won't put a foot wrong in Manchester,' said Hutch. 'But they're less cautious in their outposts. Show him,' Hutch instructed Gianni.

The younger man slid into the files on his laptop and opened one saved as VINE 26. The screen sprang to life with a black-and-white image of two women at a kitchen table, working side by side. At first glance it looked like they might be preparing food, but on closer inspection Sol could see the drugs. Lots and lots of drugs, which the women were spooning onto electric weighing scales and then packaging up.

Gianni turned up the volume.

'What really pisses me off is that he got his sister to lie for him,' said the first woman.

'Thought she was meant to be your friend,' said the second.

'Oh, yeah, she was all over me in the beginning.' The first woman sealed the top of the baggie she was working on and chucked it on top of a huge pile. 'Liking my posts on Facebook and all that.'

'But she still lied to you.'

'To my face. I'm telling you, she's a basic bitch. All the while her brother's having it away with some skank up Cheetham way.'

The second woman nodded. 'Blood's thicker than water, though, eh?'

Gianni's thumb hit pause. Sol noticed a red spot on the nail, like something had whacked it. The first woman froze mid-rant. 'It goes on like that for a bit, until . . .' He moved the video along, then pressed play. The two women were still weighing out when a mobile on the kitchen table vibrated.

The first woman checked it. 'He's here.'

The second nodded and began placing the filled baggies into an empty shoebox. Then she looked almost directly into the camera and said, 'Get the door.'

The camera moved away from the table and out of the kitchen, along a hallway to a door. A hand appeared on the screen and pulled several bolts. When the door opened, a man's figure filled the screen. A bulky torso at first, wearing what looked like a grey jumper. Then an arm with the Stone Island logo visible.

As that man moved past the camera, another stood in the doorway, on his phone. His face was obscured by the angle and the fact that he wore a baseball cap pulled down low. Sol watched as his hand slid his mobile into his jacket pocket.

'All right, Jaz?' he said.

'Yeah,' said a voice. A young woman. Neither of those in the kitchen.

'Sound,' said the man.

Then the hand re-bolted all the locks.

'Better pray there's not a fire,' said the man, with a laugh.

And then the camera turned and caught him properly. Gianni pressed pause and Sol looked from the screen to the wall and back to the screen. Same cocky smile, same fat pink face. It was Ricky Vine. Absolutely no doubt about it.

They watched the video twice, listening carefully, until they heard the smash of a bottle in the nail bar, a squeal, lots of shouting, followed by a wave of polish remover evaporating under the door. Barely able to breathe in the tiny windowless room, Hutch suggested a bite to eat and some fresh air.

'There's enough evidence on that video file to nick Vine for something,' said Sol, as they queued at a burger van.

The man in front produced a long, scribbled list. It was going to be a wait, so Sol lit a fag, protecting the lighter flame with his hand.

'If we could use it, we wouldn't be here now,' said Hutch.

Sol took a drag, blew smoke up to the sky, but the strong wind caught it and swirled it at Gianni. Politely, he didn't cough.

'You got deep inside the lion's den,' said Sol.

'Yes, we did.'

The smell of bacon filled the air, as the burger guy threw six or seven rashers onto his griddle for the man in front. With his free hand, he filled a row of polystyrene cups from a metal urn. The tea was the colour of teak.

'Couldn't the undie give you a heads-up for a raid?' asked Sol.

Surveillance evidence was rarely enough to secure a conviction on its own. Far better to use it to catch the perps red-handed. Hutch glanced at Gianni, but the younger man studiously avoided his eyes.

'Hutch?' asked Sol.

'We lost contact with our informant.'

'For how long?' With his order ready and filling the counter, the man in front began counting out pound coins. Hutch watched the shrapnel pile up. 'How long?' Sol demanded.

Hutch didn't take his eyes from the coins. 'Three months.' Three months? An undercover copper couldn't go on the missing list for three months. The alert went up if they didn't contact their handler every forty-eight hours. This made no sense at all. As the guy in front moved away, arms full of paper bags and cups, Hutch gave the burger guy a grin. 'Three bacon rolls, mate.'

Sol turned to Gianni. 'You gonna fill me in?'

Gianni watched a couple of kids ride by on their BMX bikes, shouting and pulling wheelies. 'She wasn't police.'

The room was packed with sweaty coppers. Someone had turned up the heating and no one knew how to reset it. Rose used the side of her fist to wipe off the condensation on the window in a circular motion that made a porthole to the car park beyond.

Redman was upfront, covering the clear boards with a marker pen. Much of what he wrote was undecipherable.

There was an excitement in the air that Rose could taste. So much of the job involved reacting to whatever crap the day could throw at them. Ducking from it sometimes, occasionally catching it, but more often than not getting splattered full in the face with it. An operation in which they took the fight out to the streets was something everyone relished.

'Right,' Redman shouted. 'These are the places where we can be pretty sure to find who we're looking for.' The cuff of his shirt was covered with black ink. 'Where they live, where they deal. If you think we're missing anyone obvious, speak now or for ever hold your peace.'

An officer put up her hand. Her curly hair was held on top of her head in a bun, but much of the back wasn't long enough to reach and was held in place by a barbed-wire fence of clips. Redman nodded at her. 'What about the scrubland by the flats? There's always some girl out there. Sits on a sofa, like she owns the place.'

'Good shout,' said Redman. 'Do we know her name?' The officer shook her head. 'Never mind,' he said. 'We all know who we mean. Gob on legs.'

A laugh rippled around the room. If this had been an op to secure convictions, Rose would have insisted on much more intel beforehand, but today's purpose was unambiguous: pick up as many local dealers as possible. Clear the streets. If they found anything to charge them with, that was a bonus.

'DI Angel is in charge today,' said Redman, holding out a hand to Rose. 'She'll be coordinating us.'

Rose smiled. 'It's important we act at the same time. Once word starts spreading, they'll go to ground.'

'Quicker than Ronaldo,' said Redman, and everyone laughed.

'So, we get in place and we wait,' said Rose. 'Then, on my word, we go in and we go in hard.' A few whoops and a whistle. 'We're not knocking on doors today, people.'

Liberty couldn't hear herself think. The music in the Black Cherry was always loud but the current track was ear-shattering. Mel was at the controls, smacking a button with the heel of her shoe.

'Where the hell's Tia?' Frankie yelled in her ear. 'She'd better not be doing anything stupid.'

Liberty thought that wasn't an option she'd put much money on. When another song ramped up, even louder than the last, the dancer on stage blocked her ears.

Mel limped over, still brandishing one shoe. 'The volume's stuck.'

'You think?'

'What?' Mel screamed.

Liberty grabbed Mel's shoe and went to attack the control panel herself. When Sol had asked her if she ever missed her old job, she'd thought it a daft question, but right now she'd have given anything for her secretary Tina to waltz in and just fix her life like she did in the old days. Room too hot? Sorted. PC frozen? Sorted. Coffee gone cold? Another one is already on the way. She twiddled the knob, but it wouldn't budge so she whacked it with the shoe. No joy. Another whack. She didn't hear the crack – frankly, she couldn't hear anything – but she felt it. The heel was broken, the two pieces held together by a shred of gold plastic.

When Harry made his way across the club towards her and shouted, 'Everything okay?' she didn't know whether to laugh or cry. Instead, she grabbed him by the elbow and dragged him outside.

The wind had got up and was blowing rubbish across the car park. Liberty wrapped her arms around herself. Harry took off his scarf and draped it around her shoulders. 'Sorry,' she said. 'It's all going a bit Pete Tong in there.'

Harry laughed. 'You know the other day when you said I could talk to you if I needed to.' Liberty nodded. 'Well, I do. I mean I need to talk to you. If I could tell anyone else I would.'

'Just spit it out, Harry.' He didn't. He screwed up his face as if he couldn't think of anything else he'd like to do less. 'Come on. Just get it over with,' she said.

A black shape scuttled past the base of the skips near the back door. A rat. And it wasn't even dark. It circled back, nose twitching, long tail like a foul fat black worm. Where there was one there was bound to be another. She'd need to call someone about it.

'Crystal's pregnant,' said Harry.

Liberty stared at him. 'And is this good news?'

'I'm a bit shocked,' he said. 'The doctors told us it would never happen.'

Liberty's mouth fell open. She'd always assumed Crystal didn't want kids. And she couldn't blame her. They hadn't had a role model in that department, had they?

'How does she feel about it?' Liberty asked.

'She won't discuss it.' Harry closed his eyes. 'I only know because I found a pregnancy test in the bin. Do you think you could . . .'

He let his words trail away, but Liberty shook her head. 'Me and Crystal.' She shivered. 'I'm not someone she confides in. You know that.'

'I know that she needs you.' Liberty almost laughed. Crystal Greenwood did not need anyone, least of all her older sister. 'She hates you because of it,' he said.

'She hates me because I left her twenty-five years ago.'

Harry grabbed Liberty's hand. 'Why do you think she insisted you join the family business?'

'To torture me.'

'Think about it, Lib.' He squeezed her fingers. 'She wants you around every bit as much as your brothers.'

Rose and the officer with the bun were in an unmarked car at the end of the alley. Dusk had fallen and the addicts were out like cockroaches, scuttling in the cold and dark. One at a time, they approached a metal fence at the end. It was impossible to see what lay behind as someone had smashed the streetlamp, but things were being passed back and forth, which confirmed that the dealers were working.

Rose picked up her radio. 'You in place, Redman?'

There was some static, then Redman's voice rang out. 'Yeah. We can't see much, but there's activity for definite.'

'Once I give the order, we'll push from this end, you from the other,' said Rose. 'One of us will get them.'

More static, then laughter.

The woman officer attracted Rose's attention and pointed to a scuffle that had broken out at the fence. There was a roar, then someone started swinging with what looked like a cricket bat. More shouts and then a deranged laugh. The person with the bat was obviously off his head and didn't connect with anyone. Eventually another addict landed a flying kick in his back and he went down on top of his weapon.

'It'll calm down in a second,' said the policewoman. 'They'll wanna get off as soon as they've hands on their gear.'

She was right. After a few more screams and kicks aimed at the man on the ground, the alley cleared as the addicts rushed off to do what addicts do.

Rose changed the channel on the radio so that all units could hear her. 'Everyone wait for my word.' She checked her watch, waited, checked again. 'All units ready.' She spoke clearly, no hint of nerves. 'And go. All units go. Go, go, go.'

The policewoman dived from the car, pepper spray in one hand, torch in the other. She ran down the alley, boots slapping the puddles. Rose ran after her, baton already drawn, stab vest making movement hard, digging painfully into her already knackered body. But there was no way she'd go without. Dealers rarely went quietly.

When the policewoman was within a foot of the fence, someone appeared at the top. Then someone else. They'd obviously heard Redman's team and made a run for it. As the first body dropped into the alley, the officer was already on him, hooking her foot around his leg, bringing him crashing to the ground.

'Stay down, stay down,' she ordered.

The second man landed and rushed at Rose. She took out his legs with her baton.

'Don't move,' the officer shouted at her perp. Then a scream rang out. She must have sprayed him. 'I said don't move.'

Redman and another officer dived over the fence, Redman yelling, 'Police.' He was at Rose's side in a second, cuffing the man she'd detained.

'Is this your thing?' she asked.

'What thing?'

'Hurdling fences,' she answered. 'Did you win medals in school?'

He frisked the man and pulled out a flick knife and a roll of money. 'You're a proper comedian, Rose.' She gave a small curtsy and they pulled the man to his feet. 'I'm arresting you on possession with intent to supply class-A drugs. You do not have to say anything . . .'

Liberty found Tia on her sofa. 'Are you shitting me?'

'What?'

Liberty flopped down next to her. Today's coat had cost even more than the last, but she was too knackered to care. What with the bloody music in the Black Cherry and Harry's news, her head was breaking in two. 'You're back out here with your face in that state.'

Tia laughed. 'You think the punters care what I look like?'

'I mean you should be indoors,' said Liberty. 'Having a rest.'

Tia rolled her eyes. 'Where?'

Liberty sighed. Obviously, Tia couldn't go back to the kebab shop. And Mel probably wouldn't want her for another night. 'I'll sort something.'

'Why?' Tia asked.

'God only knows.'

Then, out of nowhere, a van spilled up the street and screeched to a halt. Police in helmets jumped out and raced towards them. The youngers had it away on their bikes. Tia leaped to her feet, growled in frustration as she realised she wasn't going to be able to run fast enough.

'Oh, shit,' said Tia, and tossed a fag packet over her head into a pile of rubbish.

Liberty put up her hands. One of the coppers grabbed her, dragged her from the sofa to the ground, pushed her face into the mud. Tia was soon lying next to her, spitting out grass, laughing.

'You think it's funny?' screamed a copper.

'Yeah,' she said. He took a handful of her hair and lifted her head back. 'You've really messed up, pal.' She swivelled her eyes at Liberty. 'You know who that is, right?'

'I don't care if it's the Queen of fucking Sheba,' the copper shouted in Tia's face.

'You will, though.' Tia's battered face was lit with laughter. 'I promise you that you will.'

Chapter 8

8 September 1990

I wear the red sweatshirt to Kitty's. Of course Fat Rob didn't manage to use the arms to make his new jacket. He tried unpicking the seams on the denim one, but they'd been done with a proper machine and wouldn't budge.

She's asked me to come and help her with the Mansfield Park *essay. To be honest, I don't think she's even read the chuffing book yet, so I don't know how much help I can be. But Rob spends Saturdays sleeping or playing records because his girlfriend works in Dorothy Perkins so it'll be nice to get out.*

Kitty answers the door and shoos me into the kitchen. 'Mother insists on meeting you. Sorry.'

At the counter, Kitty's mum is rolling out dough with a wooden rolling pin. She waves a floury hand and smiles.

'Hi, Mrs Spencer,' I say.

'Call me Rochelle.'

'Fuck's sake,' Kitty whispers, under her breath.

'I'm not deaf,' says Rochelle, laughing.

Kitty sighs, takes two cans of Pepsi from the fridge and drags me away to her bedroom. I go to her desk but there's no sign of her college books. Instead it's covered with pencil drawings of monsters, most of them half finished. 'These are good,' I say.

She flops onto her bed and turns on the telly with a remote control.

It doesn't look like we're going to do much homework. 'I might give up college and become a tattoo artist,' she says. 'Apparently people pay loads for really great ink.'

I glance at the drawings. I wasn't lying, they are good, but I'm pretty sure you have to train to do tattoos. There's noise on the landing outside Kitty's room, voices and banging about.

'The return of the Brothers Grimm,' says Kitty.

Her door opens and Matt walks in. He's wearing a rugby kit, both knees muddy. When he sees me standing in his sister's bedroom, he nods.

'How was school?' Kitty asks. I laugh at that because no one goes to school on Saturdays, but Matt doesn't laugh, just plonks himself down on Kitty's bed. 'Fucking hell,' she shouts. 'You're filthy.'

Next, Tobias arrives wearing the same kit, though his is clean. Maybe the lads really have been to school. Like a detention or something. Maybe playing rugby is a punishment. Tobias stands right in front of me and stares.

'Tobias,' Kitty says, 'not polite.'

Matt leans over, grabs Tobias's hand and pulls him to the bed. The younger boy lets himself be guided but doesn't take his eyes off me. I feel stupid, now, all three of them on the bed and me on my own, like I'm about to do a turn or something. I pull out the chair at Kitty's desk and sit on that. A repeat of some police show comes on the telly.

'Hey, you like this one, don't you, Tobe?' says Matt.

Tobias drags his eyes from me finally and I realise I'm sweating. It's hot in Kitty's room, but if I take off the sweatshirt, I bet there'll be damp patches under the arms of my T-shirt. I drink some of my Pepsi and try to concentrate on the telly. The main copper is questioning some bloke about robbing a shop and he's trying to explain that it had nowt to do with him. Kitty snorts as the bloke's account gets more and more daft. I laugh too. Then suddenly the bloke bows his head. 'Sorry,' he says. 'I just wanted to get something nice for my sister.'

And I'm thinking then about our Jay and the time he nicked a Madonna single for me at Christmas. And I didn't even like Madonna. But Jay didn't know that because the social workers never let us see each other, did they? Then I'm thinking about our Crystal and how she used to like the Smurfs, but I can't be sure that she does now, can I?

'Lib?'

I look from the telly to Matt who says my name again. 'Lib? Are you all right?'

My cheeks feel hot and wet and I realise I'm crying. I wipe the tears away with the sleeve of my smelly sweatshirt and stand. 'I need to go.'

Present Day

The police at the station were all as high as kites. Buzzing from their operation, chatting six to the dozen, voices just that bit too loud.

Liberty sat on a bench in the custody suite, waiting to be processed with all the other suspects. Tia took it all in, hands cuffed in front of her. 'You packing?' she whispered.

'Don't be ridiculous,' Liberty muttered back. 'I'm not a bloody gangster.'

Tia held her gaze for a fraction of a second too long. 'Lot of familiar faces here.' She nodded at the man being booked in by the custody sergeant who, no great surprise, was the only copper in the room not delighted by the evening's turn of events. 'Tee Pee. He runs a couple of streets on the Peabody.'

'Name,' barked the sarge.

'Fuck you.'

'Your mam must have spent ages thinking that one up.'

Tee Pee kissed his teeth as someone searched his pockets and slapped down three mobile phones onto the counter.

'Popular fella,' said the sarge. He held out a pen. 'I don't suppose you want to sign for your belongings?' Tee Pee looked away in disgust. 'Fine.' The sarge called out to the group of officers now sharing a bag of chips, grabbing at them like starving fledglings. 'Who does this one belong to?' A PC put up his hand, mouth open around a hot chip. 'Cell number six,' the sarge ordered, and pointed to the whiteboard. 'Write him up.' The PC picked up a marker pen and stood poised at the board. 'Mr Fuck You charged with fuck-all. Next.'

Liberty walked to the desk. She could feel dried mud at the corner of her mouth that cracked when she gave a small smile.

If the custody sergeant was surprised to find a well-dressed woman the wrong side of forty-five standing across from him, he didn't show it. Presumably he was past caring tonight.

'Name.'

Tia gave a hoot. 'Oh, this is going to be good.'

'Shut up,' the sarge shouted, then looked back at Liberty. 'Name.'

'Liberty.' She watched him scribble it down. 'Liberty Greenwood.' She watched the pen stop moving. 'Shall I spell that for you?'

Redman brought two coffees over to the corner table in the canteen where Rose was counting the number of perps they'd detained.

'How many?' he asked.

'Thirty so far.' Redman whistled. 'The cells are full here.'

Redman pulled a Twix from his pocket, tore open the wrapper with his teeth. 'Do we have a rough idea what percentage we'll be able to charge?'

'That was never the point of this exercise.'

'I know.' He offered a finger of the Twix to Rose. 'But some convictions would be the icing on the cake.'

She took the chocolate without answering. A few convictions would indeed help the stats and please the management but, frankly, she'd be happy if the bloke she'd nicked walked away and saved her the paperwork.

Redman chomped his finger of Twix. When his phone rang he had to swallow it quickly. 'Yeah.' Rose watched him listen, the colour draining from his cheeks. 'How the hell did that happen?' He listened some more, then hung up.

'What?' Rose asked.

'That was the custody sergeant,' Redman replied. 'One of the people down there is Liberty Greenwood.' Rose had heard the name, of course. 'When the chief super hears about this, he'll go bat shit.'

'Did they find anything on her?' Rose asked.

Redman threw down the rest of his Twix. It bounced off the table and landed on the floor. 'Of course they didn't find anything on her. She's not a street dealer.'

'Then we'll let her go when time's up.'

Redman slammed the table with his palm. 'Have you any idea of how much trouble she can cause us? She used to be a lawyer, for Christ's sake. We'll have the IPCC on our backs like this.' He snapped his fingers. 'And the chief will hang us out to dry.'

Rose watched panic seep from the roots of Redman's yellow hair down to his face and pool in his throat. 'Then we'll have to make sure something sticks on Ms Greenwood, won't we?' she said.

Redman snorted. 'Like what? She's been searched and there's nothing.'

'Oh, come on, Joel. Think about it.' Rose tapped the side of his head. 'We've got thirty local dealers locked up. Do you really think no one's going to give her up?'

'Trust me, no one will go against the Greenwoods.'

Rose leaned down and picked up the remains of Redman's Twix. 'Honour among thieves hasn't existed for a very long time.' She handed the stub of chocolate back to him. 'Half of these dealers are users themselves who'd give up their granny to avoid a night in the cells. The rest are a bunch of kids who will panic at the thought of doing any real jail time.' Redman looked like he might cry, and Rose was very nearly out of patience. 'If we manage to put Liberty Greenwood away for something, the chief won't hang you out to dry.'

'You reckon?'

'Joel, he'll be offering you a promotion.'

Liberty sat on the edge of the bunk in the cell, her legs stretched out in front of her. Outside the door the other prisoners and the police were talking, shouting and laughing. Someone in the neighbouring cell banged on their door. 'I want my brief,' he yelled. 'Get him here now.'

It was going to be a very long night. Liberty let her head hang.

The flap in the door clanged. A beady eye peered in, then the door opened, and Tia waltzed in.

'Ayyy,' she said, with a grin on her battered face.

When the door was securely closed, Liberty budged up for her. 'What's happening out there?'

'Man, they've nicked everyone on the Crosshills and the Peabody.'

Liberty shook her head. A coordinated strike. This was exactly why she'd been trying to drag the Greenwood business away from all that shit. Every day was a battle just to stay one step ahead of the police.

Tia lay back across the width of the bed, letting her head rest against the concrete wall. She wasn't remotely worried about being arrested. Liberty thought about the last couple of times she'd found herself on the wrong side of a caution, how her stomach had churned with fear.

'It'll be fine,' said Tia. 'They've got nothing on us.' She closed her eyes. 'Just have to wait for Raj to get here and insist they let us out.'

The lad next door started up again. 'I know my rights,' he screamed.

Tia banged her fist against the wall. 'Shut. Up.'

'Who d'you think you're chatting to?' he shouted back.

'Some ball bag who can't do his time quietly, innit?'

Liberty bent forward and let her fingers touch the floor. It was going to be the longest night of her life.

Hutch drove his car through the estate with Gianni in the front passenger seat and Sol in the back. Amy Winehouse was on the radio confirming her reluctance to go to rehab. Sol couldn't say he blamed her.

Gianni's mobile rang and he took the call.

'You gonna tell me what we're doing here, Hutch?' Sol asked.

Hutch smiled and pulled over by a wall covered with multi-coloured tags. To their right a square of scrubland was strewn with rubbish, an abandoned sofa plonked in the middle. Two wooden-tops were raking about in the empty pizza boxes and plastic bottles, rain beating down on them.

Hutch pulled out a hip flask and took a drink. Sol could smell the whisky and smiled when Hutch offered it to him. 'That's police work,' said Hutch, pointing at the cops running their fingers down the back of the sodden sofa, hoping there were no used needles buried there. 'Good old-fashioned ground work.' Sol drank, enjoying the burn of the alcohol in his throat. 'And we both know that it's bloody pointless.' Hutch took his hip flask back, raised it to the poor buggers getting drenched. 'If they're lucky, they'll get a few collars. Low-level dealers who'll be replaced in hours.'

Sol had heard it all before and he had some sympathy. But what was the alternative? Legalise drugs? Spice had been legal not so long ago, and look how that had turned out.

'What we want to do,' said Hutch, 'what we're going to do, is

bring in the big boys. The Ricky Vines of this world. Keep doing
that and we might get somewhere.'

Sol fancied a fag and shoved his hand into his jacket pocket,
turning his lighter over in his fingers. 'If it was that simple, they'd
all be doing it.'

Hutch turned around to face him. 'It *is* that simple. It's just that
they *can't* do it.'

'Because?'

Hutch glanced at Gianni, but he was still on the phone, one
finger in his ear, face screwed up in concentration. 'You've seen
how close we can get to these people.'

Sol waited. The video file had shown someone deep in Ricky
Vine's territory. Yet Hutch had admitted it wasn't an undercover
officer. That could only mean one of the crew wore a wire. Getting
someone to take that risk was a huge task, the leverage usually
involving a plea deal. 'What happened to your last informant?'

'Not what you're thinking,' said Hutch.

'What am I thinking?'

'That Vine found out.'

'And he didn't?' asked Sol.

Hutch shook his head. 'Other events unfolded. But we want to
send someone else in.'

Sol pulled out his fags and stuck one into his mouth. He opened
the door to step out, but the rain was lashing now. He pulled up his
hood, got out and lit up. The uniformed coppers were done and
went back to their car soaking wet. He bent to Hutch's window,
which was open just a crack. 'So, what do you need from me?'

'We need a handler,' Hutch replied.

Sol frowned. There was only one reason to use a handler not on
the force: deniability. He had a heap of questions, but his mobile
rang. He checked it, raindrops splattering his screen. He wiped
them away with his thumb to read caller ID and was shocked to
see Frankie's name. As far as Sol was aware, Frankie had never

called him before. Or Crystal. Or Jay. The Greenwoods treated Sol with the suspicion of any and all police. The only reason he had their numbers in his contacts was because Liberty had insisted 'in case of emergencies'.

'Yeah.'

'That you, Connolly?' Frankie asked.

'Uh-huh.'

'Look, Liberty told me to call you.'

A tingle of concern ran down the back of Sol's neck. 'About what?'

'Don't worry,' said Frankie. 'She hasn't mugged you off. Though that wouldn't be a bad idea.'

'What do you want, Frankie?'

Frankie sniffed. 'She asked me to tell you that she's been nicked.' Sol couldn't speak. 'Possession with intent to supply.'

'Has she been charged?' Sol spluttered.

'Dunno. As soon as I've got anything concrete, I'll bell you.'

Frankie hung up, leaving Sol staring at his blank phone, water dripping from the hood of his coat onto his now dead smoke.

Raj Singh shrugged off his waterproof with a mutter. 'This weather plays holy hell with my turban.' He touched the orange cloth. 'It'll smell like a dog's arse, later.'

Liberty was pretty sure she already smelt like a dog's arse. 'Thanks for coming, Raj.'

'Your wish is my command.' He plonked himself down on the opposite side of the desk in the police interview room. 'Though the missus isn't best pleased. She'd invited Kulvinder Mandeep over for tea. Don't ask me why, they can't stand each other.'

He reached down to the battered briefcase at his feet. The clasp was broken and the stitching coming apart. Inside were hundreds of papers, an empty Tupperware box and handfuls of chewed biros. Raj grabbed six and proceeded to try them on a piece of paper. The first three had run out.

Liberty usually kept one fountain pen in her handbag and she regularly checked the ink cartridge. 'Why don't you just chuck the dead ones, Raj?'

He finally found a red one that worked. 'Where's the fun in that?'

Liberty laughed. Everything about him spelled chaos, from the hem coming down on his trousers to the jewel missing in his right cufflink. But she wasn't daft. Raj's appearance belied a mind like a steel trap. She'd witnessed him outsmart a lorry load of police officers and prosecutors in his time. The experienced ones knew never to underestimate him.

'Go on, then.' His biro was poised above an A4 notepad. 'Tell me what the hell you were doing up the Crosshills with a known drug-dealer.'

'Just shooting the breeze,' Liberty replied.

'At night? In the rain? On a settee someone's gran chucked out in 1978?'

Liberty opened her palms. 'What can I tell you, Raj? I live a life of glamour.' He put down his pen. 'Listen, mate, we both know this is bullshit. No drugs, no money, nothing. The coppers who nicked me will tell you that all I was doing was sitting there.' She smiled at Raj. 'And since I last looked, that's not a crime.'

Raj slid the pad and pen back into his briefcase and heaved himself to his feet. When he got to the door he turned. 'Can I say something?'

'Course.'

'And I don't want you to reply. In fact, I'm telling you not to reply.' His hand hovered on the door handle. 'You had a bad start in life, I get that. But you worked your nuts off to put it all behind you. I mean really grafted, right?' Liberty nodded. 'So, I don't understand why you're throwing all that away.'

112

'I'm not. I'm . . .'

Raj put up a hand to stop her. 'I know you feel guilty and I know you think you've got to right some wrongs. But where does it end? Because if this carries on, you'll end up in jail and there's not going to be anything I can do to stop it.'

'You're a genius, Raj. We all know that.'

He rolled his eyes. 'I'm not chuffing Harry Potter. Keep living this life and it will catch up with you. It always does.'

Rose walked along the line of cells in the custody area, looking through the flaps at the prisoners inside. Some flipped her the finger, one showed her a bare backside, but a few were already on their bunks, clutching their stomachs as they started to cluck.

She checked the custody records for each one, trying to spot the most likely suspect.

At last she peered inside cell seven and discovered two women. One on the toilet and one laid flat out on the floor, hands covering her eyes. Neither looked at her. *Bingo.*

She nodded for the custody sergeant to unlock the door. He muttered under his breath but did as he was asked.

'Evening, ladies.' She checked the records. 'Who's who?'

The woman on the toilet bent forward with a groan as her insides slid away. 'Why?'

'I'm hoping we can get you out of here soon,' Rose replied.

'Carmen Garcia.' The woman pulled up her jeans without wiping herself clean. 'That's Kelly Scott.' Rose smiled at Kelly, who dragged herself to a sitting position. 'We're not dealers,' said Carmen.

Both Carmen and Kelly had been arrested on the Crosshills and had tried to swallow their drugs. The PC who pulled them from the women's mouths was probably checking his tetanus was up to date.

113

'You had twenty rocks between you,' said Rose.

'Personal use,' Carmen replied.

'Win the lottery, did you?' Rose looked Carmen up and down. 'It's not gonna fly. You're looking at a three stretch and you know it.'

Carmen sank back onto the rim of the toilet. The stench was horrific, but she didn't seem to notice. 'Thought you just said we could get out.'

'I need information,' said Rose.

'We're not going to grass,' said Kelly, as she climbed onto the bed and faced the wall.

Rose turned to Carmen, still perched on the foul-smelling bowl. This was just the start of the withdrawal. Sickness, diarrhoea, shaking. But soon enough she'd begin to feel like every bone in her body was crumbling and Carmen knew that was in the post. It was the fear that Rose was gambling on. Once Carmen was in the throes of it, she'd be a waste of space, but right now, when she had all that horror stretching in front of her, there was leverage.

'A bit of information and you'll get your bail,' said Rose.

'Have you got any idea what happens to someone who snitches?'

Rose shrugged. 'How will anyone know who said what?'

'It'll be a bit obvious when we walk,' said Carmen.

Rose paused and listened to the noise. People screaming and shouting. A steady stream of coppers and prisoners moving up and down the corridor. 'It's chaos out there. No one has any idea what's going on. Least of all anyone in a cell.' She laughed. 'I mean do you know who's in here and who's been let out?' Carmen shook her head. 'Exactly.'

Carmen chewed her lip and glanced at Kelly, who shivered resolutely, face to the wall. 'What is it you want to know?'

Chapter 9

9 September 1990
Matt insists on giving me a lift again, even though I've said like a thousand times that I'll get the bus. At least he doesn't talk to me on the way, just reaches behind him for a cassette and puts on the Cocteau Twins.

I told everybody I'm feeling ill, but I don't know if they believed me.

Matt grinds the gears as we head off and I curl my fingers around the wet and snotty sleeves of my sweatshirt. But when we get to the crossroads, he doesn't turn left, like he should, but keeps going.

'You've gone the wrong way,' I say.

He smiles, nods at a McDonald's up ahead. 'Do you mind if we stop in there? I'm starving.'

I shrug that he can do what he likes, but when he pulls into the car park and gets out, I don't follow him. I've no money. He slopes across the tarmac in his mucky rugby top and a couple of lasses sitting outside in the sunshine nudge each other as he passes. Not that he seems to notice.

At last he comes back with a paper bag of food and puts a bag of fries on my knee.

'I'm not hungry,' I say.

He doesn't answer but tosses a sachet of ketchup at me. I bite it open and try not to think about how much our Frankie likes red sauce. He'll eat it on anything, he will. Then I'm crying again, and I'll give Matt his due, he still doesn't say a word.

He opens up his burger and fishes out the slice of gherkin.

'I don't know why they even put them in,' I say. 'No bugger likes 'em.'

'The bins must be full of them at the end of the day,' he says.

I nod and squeeze ketchup over my chips, then eat every last one because I'm actually famished.

On the journey back to mine, we carry on listening to Victorialand. The singer's voice dances like magic, fluttering like fairy wings. I can't make out any of the lyrics, but it doesn't matter. I don't bother asking Matt to drop me off outside the Fast Chick Inn but show him the spot to park right outside our flat. I haven't the energy to lie or walk.

'Thanks,' I say.

'You know Kitty's an idiot,' he says.

'What?'

He turns the music down but not off. 'She thinks it's so cool that you live on your own.'

'I don't,' I say. 'I share with my mate.'

'I mean you don't live at home.' He picks at the dried mud on his knee. 'It doesn't occur to her that someone our age would not be with their mum and dad. Not unless there was something pretty bad going on.'

Living with Mam and Dad seems like a long time ago. 'They're dead.' It's easier than explaining why I wasn't with them even when they were alive. 'Look, you don't need to feel sorry for me. Me and Rob are doing okay.'

'So why have you spent the whole day crying?'

I laugh at that. 'Not the whole day.'

Then Matt smiles. 'You're a bit of a one-off, you, aren't you?'

'Yes, I am.'

I get out of the car and wave as I press the buzzer, and I'm feeling a whole lot better as I take the stairs up to the bedsit and knock for Rob to let me in. But when he opens the door, his face is serious. I know something's up because Rob is almost never serious. One time we got jumped by some lads on the way home from work. It was our own fault, really – we cut through an alleyway and the streetlamps were all busted – but Rob was still laughing and joking even when they went through our pockets.

116

'What's up?' I ask him.

He steps aside then, and the breath leaves my chest. I run across to the settee, well, it's only three or four feet but I run them anyway, and throw my arms around the person sat there.

'Fucking hell, Lib. You smell like a dead dog.'

I slap him, then hug him and kiss him and slap him again. At last I stand back and look deep into his eyes. 'What are you doing here, Jay?'

Present Day

Sol sprinted to the entrance at the police station and tried to push it open. The door didn't budge even when he gave it a good shove. What the hell?

A bloke inside watched him from the other side of the glass, then pointed to the side.

'What?' Sol demanded, breath coming out in a cloud.

The bloke pointed to the same spot and at last Sol noticed the sign – 'Automatic Door'. He groaned, took a step back and waited for it to slide slowly and quietly to the side. Sol had worked at this nick for more than five years but had never once used this way in.

'You won't be the first to do that,' said the bloke, Vans cap pushed so far back on his head that Sol wondered how it didn't fall off. 'It's like that programme on the telly. You know the one?'

Sol shook his head. Was there a show about people trying to get through doors? (It wouldn't surprise him – nothing would after he'd seen half an episode of the one where some people baked cakes. He'd been a bit pissed at the time and wondered if he'd missed something vital. But, no, apparently the cameras followed some people in a big tent as they iced some buns.) '*Crystal Maze*,' said the bloke. 'All them impossible tasks.'

Sol looked back at the door, then at the bloke, blinked a few times and went up to the desk. 'You've got Liberty Greenwood in custody,' he said.

The policewoman on reception gave a smile. 'You asking or telling me?'

'I need to speak to the officer in the case,' said Sol. 'Please.'

'Take a seat.' She pointed to the metal bench where the door bloke had taken a pew. 'Can I have your name?'

'Sol Connolly.'

The policewoman stopped at that. 'Didn't you . . .'

'Yeah.'

She pressed a button on the internal phone attached to the wall and turned her body so when she spoke into it Sol couldn't hear. So, this was what it felt like to be on the wrong side of the fence.

'You do not have to say anything, but it may harm your defence if you do not mention something which you later wish to rely on in court.' Angel gave the caution as she scooted her chair closer to the table. 'Anything you do say may be given in evidence. Do you understand, Miss Greenwood?'

Liberty licked her lips. She followed perfectly well. Not so long ago, like most ordinary punters, she'd believed that an innocent person would wish to explain themselves to the police. Now she knew that this was bollocks.

'Miss Greenwood understands the caution,' said Raj. 'But she will not be answering any questions today.'

Liberty eyed the two police officers. Angel, all common-sense boots and an accent she'd worked hard on. Those aitches had been hard to drop. You could take the girl out of Chelsea. On the other hand, Redman was a local lad. If he hadn't got into the job, he'd have become a plumber like his mates. And he'd have been happy too. Maybe happier than he was playing happy families with the likes of DI Angel.

'Does your client not want to set the record straight?' Angel asked.

118

'What record?' said Raj. 'You've no real evidence that a crime's been committed.'

'Your client was arrested with a known drug-dealer in an area where drug-dealing takes place.'

Raj folded his arms. 'Let's be honest here. You've done a massive sweep tonight, picked up as many dealers as you can.' He gave a magnanimous smile, which Liberty knew meant he was going to trash their case. 'Where did you get your intel? Here, there and everywhere?' Angel didn't give any ground, but Redman's cheeks flushed. 'You're bound to pick up some innocents along the way.'

'If your client is innocent why doesn't she explain what she was doing with Tia Rainsford?'

Raj gave a chuckle. 'Come on now, lass. Maybe Miss Greenwood stopped to chat about the weather or maybe to ask about the big fat bruises Tia's got all over her face. Could be anything. Here in Yorkshire we're friendly like that.' So Raj, too, had noticed Angel wasn't from round here. 'Isn't that right, Officer Redman?'

Redman looked into his hands, bright scarlet spots glowing on each cheek.

Angel's mobile vibrated on the table and she checked it, smiled, passed it to Redman. 'We've just completed a search of the area where your client was arrested.' Redman smiled too. 'And a large quantity of class As have been retrieved.'

Raj shrugged. 'Nowt to do with my client.'

'Yes, well, we have a witness who says otherwise.'

Rose watched Liberty Greenwood being led back to her cell.

'You're sure about this?' Redman asked. 'Because the chief super will not be happy if this won't stick.'

Rose sighed. 'We've enough to charge her, which buys us time to shore up any cracks. We're allowed to keep on digging, Joel.'

She was relieved when the custody sergeant called her over, bored with Redman's nervousness.

'Someone wants to talk to you,' said the sarge. 'About Greenwood.'

'Oh, yeah?'

'Sol Connolly,' said the sarge. 'Used to be DI Sol Connolly.'

'What does he want?' Redman asked.

'I expect he wants to know why we've nicked his missus.'

Rose watched Connolly through the automatic door. He was pacing the wet pavement, trying to smoke a cigarette in the rain. 'That's him?' she asked Redman.

What had she expected? Greenwood was slick. Even covered with mud and having spent a few hours in a cell, the woman was cool and unruffled, her hair still glossy, her skin still clear. Connolly, on the other hand, was the definition of a scruff, all knackered boots and dirty fringe covering his eyes.

She took a step towards the door, so it opened, a blast of cold air thundering inside. 'Mr Connolly?' He flicked away his dog-end and strode inside. 'I'm DI Angel.'

'You've arrested Liberty Greenwood,' he said.

'I'm just about to charge her.'

Water dripped from the ratty ends of his hair onto the collar of his Puffa. 'With what?'

'Conspiracy to supply class-A drugs,' said Rose.

'Bail?'

'I'll leave that up to the magistrates tomorrow.'

Connolly turned to Redman. 'The chief okay with this?' When Redman didn't answer, Connolly laughed. 'Doesn't know, eh?' He ran a hand under his fringe to wipe his wet forehead. 'See you tomorrow.' Then he marched out of the station, giving a salute.

'I hope you know what you're doing,' said Redman.

Rose ignored him and used her pass to leave Reception.

Liberty leaned against the wall of her cell with Raj's words ring-ing in her ears. *This life will catch up with you in the end.* How many times had she said that to her brothers and sister? How many times had she warned them that their business was a road to jail or worse? Yet she'd still allowed herself to get sucked in. Oh, she'd told a good tale, that she was trying to legitimise the family, that these things took time. And, in the meantime, things had carried on as normal. Drugs, pornography, prostitution and everything that went with it. And now she was paying the price.

Tia nudged Liberty's tray with her foot. 'You eating that?'

Liberty wrinkled her nose at the beige chicken nuggets and round container of orange mush. 'What even is that?'

'Carrots?' Tia shrugged.

'Why would anyone mash up carrots?'

'Do I look like Jamie Oliver?'

Liberty pushed the tray at Tia with her own shoe. Whatever it was, she wasn't putting it into her mouth. 'You don't seem worried.'

'About what?'

'The fact we're banged up.'

Tia slid to the floor and shovelled in the nuggets, two at a time. 'It won't be for long.'

'How can you be sure?'

Tia licked her greasy fingers. 'One, they can't prove those drugs were ours and, two, there's no way your family are going to let this happen.' She grinned. 'Lucky for me we got nicked together.'

Liberty watched Tia polish off the rest of the food. The kid was right. Raj would work his magic and, if he couldn't manage it, Crystal would be in the background activating the dark arts.

'I'll eat my pants if we don't get bail in the morning,' said Tia.

Liberty nodded at the possibly-carrot mash. 'Well, they'd probably taste better than that.'

Hutch took a long gulp of Jim Beam and passed the bottle to Sol. It was almost half empty.

'You know what?' Sol asked.

'That we should be in a pub?' Hutch said.

Sol took a swig. After Hutch had caught up with him on his way from the station, he didn't want to be where there were any people. So, they'd bought a bottle in the nearest off-licence, headed to the park on the estate and sat on the swings in the rain.

'Everything's fucked.' Sol's tongue tripped on the *f*. 'Totally fucked.'

Hutch held the chains at ear level and gave a little push with his feet. The movement didn't go down too well, and he burped. 'She'll get bail.'

'That's not the point.' Sol took another drink. 'She's still . . . you know.'

'A perfect ten?'

Sol pushed the mouth of the bottle into his cheek, held it under the bone. 'I had to give up my job because of her.'

Hutch got off his swing and staggered towards the slide. He bent to investigate some sort of memorial that had been set up, steadying himself on the rusty steps.

'And now I haven't got anything to do all day,' Sol shouted, across the playground. 'She's busy playing Michael frigging Corleone and I'm . . .' He dug the glass rim into his flesh. 'I'm cleaning the fridge.'

Hutch picked something up from the memorial and swayed back to Sol. It was a little teddy bear, brown fur all soggy. 'Come work for me. Be my handler.'

'I've just told you that my girlfriend is a fucking gangster, Hutch.'

'Well, I'm not looking for someone too squeaky clean, am I?' Hutch swapped the bottle for the bear. It had a little ribbon around its neck, so tight it was more of a noose. 'I need someone who can see the bigger picture.'

Sol wandered over to the slide, put the bear back in his place with the dead flowers and sodden football scarves. 'Come on, mate, who's the informant?'

'Her name's Madison,' said Hutch. A woman was unusual but that didn't bother Sol. 'And I'm going to be honest now.'

'First time for everything.'

Hutch held up the bottle to toast that. 'She's fifteen.'

Sol laughed at the joke, saw Hutch's face and realised it wasn't. 'Oh, shit.'

Chapter 10

8 September 1990

I pour boiling water into the Pot Noodle and stir in the little sachet of curry sauce. Then I watch our Jay wolf it down, opening his mouth around gobfuls to let out the steam.

'You could just let it cool down,' I tell him.

'Bossy cow.'

His hair's grown back since the last time I saw him, and he'd got a skin head. It's a bit spiky on top now and jet black like his eyebrows. He looks a lot like Dad.

Rob smears margarine over a slice of bread and hands it to Jay, who grabs it and dips it into the plastic pot. It's like watching a dog bolt Pedigree Chum.

'How did you find me?' I ask. I haven't sent my address to Jay because they read all the letters coming in and I was worried that someone would put two and two together and come and get me. I mean, there probably isn't anyone who gives a shit where I am, but you never know with social workers.

'I went round to see that lass you used to knock about with.' Jay's mouth is full of bread crust and noodles. 'The one with the hair.'

'Tiny?'

Jay nods and I turn to Rob. He wrote her a few letters when he first got to Manchester, but she never wrote back.

'Is she all right?' he asks.

124

'Due any minute by the size of her,' Jay answers, and spoons down the last dregs of his dinner. 'But she said she thought you were here, so I jumped the train.' I take the empty pot and hand him a tea towel to wipe his hands and face. He burps and accepts a cig from Rob. 'I know I can't stop here, Lib. I just really needed to see you.'

I hug him and smell his curry breath. 'If we had more room it'd be okay. But I'm already here on the QT.'

'It's fine, Lib,' he says. 'I'll get myself sorted. Oh, and while I'm here I brought you this.' He fishes into his jacket and pulls out a CD. Vanilla Ice. 'Happy birthday.'

Rob grabs it and sticks it in his music system. Those first terrible beats belt out and I laugh. This has got to be the worst song released this year. Rob hisses out the lyrics and pulls me to my feet. Pissing our sides laughing, we dance around, Rob cupping his balls through his boxers.

'You two are fucking mental,' shouts Jay, which just makes us laugh even more.

When the track ends, we collapse onto the settee in hysterics.

'Jay, mate, you're going to have to stay for a bit,' says Rob. 'If only to get a proper education in music.'

'You sure?' I ask.

'How's he ever going to get a bird buying that sort of shite?'

'To be fair, I didn't buy it,' says Jay.

Present Day

Sol's hangover was at DEFCON 1, his hands shaking around a takeout coffee. He looked in good company with the smokers outside the magistrates' court.

'At least it's stopped raining,' said the woman at his side, the split in her pencil skirt displaying an impressively tattooed thigh. Some sort of native with a bow and arrow. Three rows of writing in what looked like Arabic. And a rose that seemed to be dripping blood. 'Can't stand the damp, me,' she said. 'Lumbago.'

Sol looked into the sky. Right now, some cool raindrops would be welcome on his burning face. At last he saw who he was waiting for, plastic slip-ons squeaking like a kids' toy. 'Raj.'

The solicitor's grin displayed a new gold filling. 'Christ on a bike, Sol, you look like a bag of knackers.'

'I feel worse.'

'The other half gets indisposed and you're straight out on the lash, eh?'

Sol laughed, then wished he hadn't. The movement of his head sent a pain from one eye to the other across the bridge of his nose. 'Shall we talk to Bucky?'

'I'm betting she's already rolled out the red carpet.'

Indeed, Tessa Buckland was ready and waiting for them, bare feet up on the table in the CPS room. She'd changed the colour of her hair since the last time Sol had seen her. From pillarbox red to a sort of grey. Not old-man grey, of which Sol had more than he liked to admit, but a sort of silvery blue. Not that he'd ever dye his. (Mad hair colours like Bucky's were a sort of fashion statement, he got that, but dyeing your hair its own colour, what was that about? Going from brown to another brown? Who would actually spend time and money doing that?)

'Here comes the cavalry,' she boomed at them.

'Bucky.' Raj smacked his briefcase on her desk. 'This is like Groundhog Day.'

'I'm a prosecutor and you're a defence lawyer,' she said. 'Our paths are bound to cross, Mr Singh.'

Raj dug around in his pocket, pulled out a biro and slid it under his turban to scratch his head. 'I mean the police trying to fit up my client.'

Bucky roared with laughter and turned to Sol. 'Aren't you going to stick up for your old muckers, then?' She flicked his belly. 'Wasn't so long ago you were trying to put her away.'

'Oh, he's putting her away, all right,' said Raj, sifting through Bucky's files as if he owned the place.

Everyone in the room hooted at that. Sol knew he should at least try to join in. He had the banter coming, no question. Copper takes up with one of the local faces? It was the gift that kept on giving.

'Being serious, though, Bucky,' said Raj, 'this isn't something that's going to stick.'

She snapped her fingers at a file in Raj's hands and he tossed it to her. She shook it open and ran her eyes down the first page. 'Arrested with a known dealer in a location known for dealing.'

'Circumstantial.'

'Drugs found at the scene.'

Raj wagged the biro at her. 'After the fact. I'll be looking at that chain of evidence very closely.'

'Witness statement.' Bucky's thumbnail traced the notes. 'From a Miss Carmen Garcia.' Sol couldn't believe it. He'd nicked Carmen a hundred times when he'd worked in Vice. 'Says she bought several rocks of crack cocaine from someone matching your client's description.'

'You cannot believe that,' said Sol.

Bucky shoved the file at him with a wink. 'Read it yourself, Sol. I can't just chuffing ignore it, can I?'

'For fuck's sake.' Sol chucked the file back at her and the papers scattered across the floor. 'This isn't a joke.'

Bucky's smile washed away. She took her feet off the desk and stood inches from Sol. He could smell her perfume, the strong one she always wore, and it made his stomach churn.

'Listen to me, pal.' Her voice was low. 'Don't come in here still half cut and acting like the big I am. The only reason I'm even talking to you is because we go way back.'

Raj leaned down to collect up the papers, popped them back on the desk and dragged Sol out of the room.

Liberty allowed herself to be led from the police van into the secure area at the back of the magistrates' court. It had stopped raining, but the wind whipped around her face. At least it was clean fresh air, a relief after spending a night in the cells. Tia chatted to the other prisoners, most of whom worked on the Crosshills.

Another meat wagon pulled in and more prisoners were hauled onto the concrete.

'Hill's people,' said Tia.

A bloke with a neatly trimmed beard stretched his back and gave a tut when he caught sight of Tia.

'You fucking tutting at me?' Tia asked, with a laugh.

The bloke chuckled. 'I'll do more than that, you skanky little bitch.'

Despite the language, it was good-natured. They were all in the same boat.

'Any idea what's going on?' he asked.

'Not a Scooby,' said Tia.

A guard brought them all to the entrance and uncuffed them one by one. Liberty rubbed her wrists and buttoned her coat. The mud had set hard, forming a stiff brown carapace down her front. She tried to brush it away but only managed to cause a storm of brown flakes.

A couple of Hill's youngers giggled, and Tia's smile dropped.

'You shit yourself, love?' one of them called out.

Liberty put a hand on Tia's arm, but the kid was already squaring up to them. 'Think you're funny?' When the younger barked another laugh, Tia turned to the bloke with the beard, all bonhomie gone. 'Keep your people in line.'

He screwed up his face. 'Are you giving out orders?'

The Greenwood youngers went silent, and that should have

been enough of a warning, but maybe the bloke didn't want to back down in front of his troops, or maybe he was too knackered to spot what was coming.

Tia sneaked a look over her shoulder at the youngers at her back and Liberty caught the smile. She could stop this. Tia was fired up, but she would leave it if her boss told her to. Instead Liberty just blinked at Tia. It wasn't that she wanted to see anyone hurt, more that she needed everyone to know who was in charge. Then Tia balled her fist and punched the bloke in the throat. His mouth opened and he let out a choke. Then one of the Greenwood youngers, a pretty girl with a stud in her nose that sparkled in the cold morning light, kicked out at the bloke's legs and he went down on the concrete, like he'd been shot. A trainer belonging to someone else stamped down on his nose and it exploded across his face.

When the guards realised things were kicking off, an alarm sounded, and batons were drawn, Liberty grabbed Tia and tucked her away. The girl with the nose stud got a face full of pepper spray and was heaved off.

'She'll be all right,' said Tia, sucking her hand. 'No previous and she's only fifteen.'

Rose checked the FME's report as she raced up the stairs from the cell area to the CPS room. Virtually a full can of pepper spray had been used, but the kid wouldn't suffer lasting damage. She thrust the report at Redman who was at her side. 'We can add GBH to the girl's charge sheet,' she said. 'When we get a statement from the victim.'

'We won't get one,' Redman replied.

'Then we'll offer a plea of ABH or common assault, so the kid doesn't file a complaint.' Rose took the last step. 'Everyone's a winner.'

Redman grabbed her elbow. 'Which part of "We won't get a statement from the victim" do you not understand? If he says he slipped, we can't charge the kid with anything.'

Rose shrugged him off. The victim had a gash on the back of the head and a broken nose where he'd been stamped on: of course he'd talk. Especially if Rose offered to drop the drugs charges looming over him.

'And what are we doing about Liberty Greenwood?' Redman was gabbling now. 'Because there's going to be a call from the chief any minute.'

She knew he was bone tired – they all were. It had been a long night and the adrenalin of the op had worn off hours ago, but his jitteriness was testing. They had a perfectly good case against Greenwood. Not rock solid, but more than enough to keep going until they found more.

Outside the CPS room the solicitor, Singh, was deep in conversation with the boyfriend, Connolly. Neither of them noticed her until Rose was right behind them and gave a polite cough.

'DI Angel,' said the lawyer. 'Nice day for it.'

'I hear there's been a bit of a fracas involving your client,' said Rose. When the solicitor gave a puzzled frown, Rose returned a smile. 'It all kicked off in the yard.'

'Is Lib okay?' Connolly asked.

Rose smiled again. He'd been a copper, a good one by all accounts, but he was obviously loved up with Greenwood. Turning up at the station and now here at court, he didn't care who knew about his relationship with her.

'Oh, she's fine,' said Rose. 'Got her people to do the dirty work.' Connolly narrowed his eyes. 'Two have been rushed off to the hospital. Awful business. One of them is only fifteen.'

'I'll go down and see what's happening,' said Raj, and charged off.

Connolly didn't take his eyes off Rose until two men walked

towards him, their dark hair and eyes a facsimile of Liberty Greenwood's. 'Frankie.' He nodded at the younger one. 'Jay.' They didn't shake hands and there was no warmth in the greeting. Connolly might have found favour with the big sister, but the siblings didn't seem enamoured.

'I'm sure we'll see each other soon,' said Rose, and wandered into the CPS room.

Liberty clocked Sol, Jay and Frankie in the public gallery and nodded. Jay shook his head with a grin, Frankie blew her a kiss, but Sol's face was like thunder. She sighed. It was undoubtedly unpleasant seeing your girlfriend in this situation, especially if you used to be a copper but she was the one in the dock.

Bucky gave her a strange look and Liberty couldn't blame her for it. Although Liberty had always liked the other woman, they were squarely on different sides today.

'Nice hair,' Liberty said to her.

Bucky laughed at that and pointed to Liberty's mud-stained coat. 'Nice threads.'

'I'm setting a trend,' said Liberty.

The guard brought in Tia and she slid into the dock next to Liberty with a yawn. Frankie scowled at her.

'Oh, I thought this would be my fault,' Tia called out at him.

Liberty shushed Tia.

As the magistrate entered, she glanced at the defendants, brow furrowed.

'Who represents the defendants?' she asked.

Raj jumped up. 'Madam, I do. And I need to say from the off—'

The magistrate put up a well-manicured finger, the nail short, round and glossy red. 'We're overrun with cases this morning, so can we save the grandstanding?' She turned to Bucky. 'You want to transfer the case to the Crown Court?'

'Yes, madam.'

'Done.' In different circumstances Liberty would have admired the efficiency. 'Bail?'

'I'd say both my clients are excellent candidates for bail, madam,' said Raj.

The magistrate smiled. 'To misquote Mandy Rice-Davies, you would say that, wouldn't you, Mr Singh? What are your views, Miss Buckland?'

Bucky gave a shimmy. 'The first defendant has several convictions for drugs-related offences and no viable other means of support. I'd say Miss Rainsford will more than likely offend again.'

'That's a bit of a stretch,' said Raj.

'What will she live on? Fresh air?' Bucky opened her arms. 'She doesn't have a job, she's not in receipt of benefits and her mother doesn't appear to be in the picture.'

'What about Miss Greenwood?' the magistrate asked.

'She's a lawyer,' Raj confirmed.

'Who hasn't practised any law in over twelve months,' said Bucky. 'The Crown understands that Miss Greenwood now runs the family business.'

'She helps out from time to time,' said Raj. 'That's not a crime.'

'But much of the family business is.' Bucky pulled herself up to full height. 'Drugs, gambling, prostitution.'

'If there was any evidence of that, you'd charge them all.'

'We *have* charged your client,' said Bucky. 'Look, we all know that the Crosshills estate is awash with drugs. Every single day we all come to this court and see the victims of it. Lives ruined. And it's common knowledge which family is at the top of the food chain.'

Raj laughed. 'You can't base a case on common knowledge.'

'We're not,' Bucky replied. 'We've got drugs and we've got a statement.'

'From a witness you know will never give evidence.'

Bucky turned to Raj, eyes flashing. 'And why's that, eh? Why do all these witnesses evaporate?'

Liberty looked over at the public gallery. Sol was on his way out. He knew as well as she did that, despite the courtroom fireworks, she was on her way to jail.

'I thought they'd send you to a secure unit at your age,' Liberty told Tia.

'They would if there were any places,' Tia replied, as she jumped out of the meat wagon. 'Anyway, you'll be glad of the company.' She grinned into Liberty's face, her own a multi-coloured bowl of cuts and bruises, ranging from midnight blue to Bird's-custard yellow. Liberty followed her to a door marked First Night Centre. 'This is like that place between Heaven and Hell.'

'Purgatory?'

'That's the one.'

A guard opened the entrance and the new arrivals surged in, a sea of bad teeth and hormones. Tia pushed her way through, so she was first at the desk. A trustie in standard prison uniform of royal blue sweatshirt and joggers looked her up and down. 'All right, jail bait?'

A few women whistled and laughed. Tia gave the trustie the finger and pointed to a shelf behind the desk. 'Got something for my face?'

'Just some sloppy kisses, sweetheart.' The trustie leaned over, tongue out, and the other women roared with laughter. 'How about I start up top and work my way down?'

Tia gave a finger on both hands and the trustie smacked some items onto the desk. Soap, shampoo, an e-cig. Tia grabbed them and gestured for Liberty to step up. 'If you've got any brains at all, you won't start on this one,' said Tia. The trustie folded her arms, unimpressed, so Tia grabbed the list of new inmates and jabbed a dirty thumb at Liberty's name. 'Read it and weep, paedo.'

The trustie did read but didn't weep. 'That you?' she asked Liberty.

Liberty checked the list, saw her name and nodded. The trustie quickly collected a heap of groceries, including three e-cigs.

'Ta,' Tia called, and dragged Liberty down the corridor before skidding to a halt at another door. 'Medical room. Tell them you're depressed, and we might get some pills.'

The door swung open and a doctor in a white coat appeared. 'Name?'

'Liberty Greenwood.'

'Step inside.' The doctor peered at the haul of goodies in Liberty's arms. 'And don't ask me for any uppers, downers or calmers. This is prison, not the Priory.'

Hutch was waiting for Sol at the house. Considering how much booze he'd put away the previous night, he looked fresh. Sol didn't need to check a mirror to know that he still looked like shit. He unlocked the door in silence, left it open so that Hutch could follow him inside and headed straight to the kitchen where he pulled out a Tupperware box that acted as a first-aid kit. Among the bandages and tubes of Savlon there was a box of codeine. Sol pushed out two pills from the blister pack, popped them into his mouth then drank them down with water straight from the tap.

'Bad day?' Hutch asked.

'My girlfriend just got remanded to prison.'

Hutch nodded slowly. 'That constitutes a pretty bad day.'

'I'd offer you a coffee,' said Sol, 'but I can't be arsed.' He slid into a kitchen chair. 'Explain to me why you can't take down Vine the usual way.'

Hutch dragged out the other chair, scraping it across the tiles.

The noise ran through Sol's thick head like a rusty saw. 'They tried. Spent a lot of money and man hours.'

Sol nodded. Nothing scared off the top brass like wasted resources. Then again, that was why he'd thought Liberty would be safe. Any tiny appetite the chief had to go after the Greenwoods had died with Amira. She'd managed to convince the chief super to put eyes on Liberty, but when that had gone tits up, Amira had found herself out in the cold. She'd probably have been shunted to Traffic if she hadn't run into a burning building. But something had evidently changed upstairs and the Greenwoods were back on the table.

'I moved into the private work to reinvent myself, to be honest.' Hutch tapped his right eye. 'But I soon saw a way to have another pop at Vine.'

'Not strictly above board, though?'

'Look, Sol, they give me a budget to collect intel. If I start telling them how I do that, it's not going to play.' Hutch laughed. 'But when I have a case on Vine . . .'

'They'll take the credit,' said Sol.

'Frankly, my dear, I don't give a damn. I just want to put Vine and Clarke where they belong,' said Hutch. 'And I'm asking you to help me.'

'Vine and Clarke don't mean shit to me.'

'True,' said Hutch. 'But I'm assuming you miss the game. And with the missus otherwise engaged, it's not like you're busy.'

After Hutch left, Sol took out a bottle of Sauvignon Blanc from the fridge. It was one of Liberty's favourites. There weren't any clean glasses, so he poured the wine into a mug and lit a fag. He should probably eat, but cooking was way beyond him, so he found a packet of peanuts and emptied them from the packet into his mouth.

Then he let himself flop onto the sofa in front of the telly.

He'd never been one for spending much time staring at the box. All the shows people talked about at work seemed so long. Who had time to watch four seasons to find out who had committed the murder? Sol could tell them who it would be from the off.

He flicked it on and began to scroll through some of the box sets he'd heard about. Things considered binge-worthy. And why the hell was that considered a *good* thing? It wasn't that Sol was a stranger to bingeing, but it was something he was always trying (mostly without success) to avoid. When he was married to Ange, they'd made a pact every new year to pack in smoking and cut down on drinking. They rarely made it past a day.

The first show was something about serial killers in the seventies. Sol definitely didn't fancy that. But then he saw one that Liberty had been threatening to start. *Orange Is the New Black*. Well, Liberty was getting the real deal tonight. He lifted his mug to toast her, wherever she was, and pressed play.

Chapter 11

8 September 1990

We take our Jay to work with us. Well, what else can we do? If we leave him back at the flat, he's bound to get up to no good. And, anyway, I want to be near him. I can't really explain it because obviously I haven't seen him for months, but now he's here I just need to keep touching him. On the bus, I slipped my hand into his and he didn't pull away, so I think he feels the same. He just watched the world go by out of the window and gave my fingers a squeeze.

'This is my brother,' I tell Tony. 'He won't get in the way.'

Tony laughs as if it hadn't occurred to him that he would. 'He can help you look after Pete, if he likes.'

Pete's a big-name DJ come up from London. I've met him before and he's a bit shy. His girlfriend asks for a few things – drinks, fags, a bacon roll – but nothing fancy. I doubt it'll take both me and our Jay to keep them happy.

I introduce him to Steph, who gives him a wink and a free bottle of water, then to Red, who says we look alike.

'I'm the pretty one, though, right?' says Jay, fending off my slaps.

'Oh, aye.' Red gives Jay a cig. 'Lib's proper ugly.'

'I know. Lucky she's got some brains to see her through life.'

A bit later, we're helping clear up a spilled bottle of pop by the decks when Pete's girlfriend bounces over. Her hair is short and bleached white blonde. It suits her. 'Sorry to bother you, Lib,' she says.

I scrunch up the wet paper towels. 'Don't be daft.'

'Just wondering if you could get us a few bits and bobs?'

'Course.'

She smiles and disappears into the crowd.

I get this a fair bit. There's the official rider, then there's the stuff no one wants to write down. The first time I was worried, especially after Connor got sent to prison for dealing. But then I realised that I'm safe, as long as it all happens inside the club. For some reason the police never come in here. It's a bit like the rider: there's the official police line on drugs, then there's what they actually do. Like I've heard of people getting searched outside but never being charged with owt. The drugs just get handed over and that's the end of it.

I catch the eye of one of the Cheetham lot I've scored from before. He's wearing a pair of baggy dungarees over a Bob Marley T-shirt, shoulder-length hair gelled off his face. I think he's called Sean.

'All right, Lib?' He kisses my cheek. 'New boyfriend?' It takes me a second to realise he means our Jay. 'Good on you, mate.' He shakes Jay's hand. 'We were beginning to wonder if she were a nun.'

'Actually, he's my brother,' I say. 'And since when were you lot keeping tabs on my love life?'

'What love life?' asks Sean, and our Jay cracks up at that.

'And how many girls have you got queuing up?' I say.

Jay holds up his hands. 'Give us a chance, I only got released yesterday.'

'How long were you away, mate?' Sean asks.

'Only three this time,' Jay replies.

He's showing off, making out like he's the big hard man who's done lump after lump, no bother. He learned inside that any sign of weakness will result in a battering.

Sean chucks an arm around his shoulders. 'Must be time to let your hair down.'

'Love to but I'm completely skint.'

'I'm sure we can work something out,' says Sean. 'Lib's bloody royalty around here.'

Jay steps away from Sean. Like me, he learned early on that no one does anything for nothing in this life. But things work a bit differently here. No one bothers the Cheetham lot, even though everyone knows what they're up to. So the Cheetham lot say their thank-yous in their own way. I'm guessing they give the bouncers a cut. I've seen money changing hands at the end of the shift. I don't get involved in any of that, but as part of the family, Rob and I don't pay for drugs.

'It's fine,' I tell Jay.

'I don't like owing,' he says.

'Chill out, mate.' Sean hands him a pill. 'You're not inside now.'

Present Day

As soon as the morning lights went on, Liberty and all the other inmates were frog-marched from the first-night centre across the exercise yard. Carrying their stuff like packhorses, breath huffing into the frosty morning, they tried to keep up with the prison officers. It didn't help that Liberty had twice as much as everyone else.

'Can you give me a hand?' Liberty asked Tia, as she dropped a bottle of shampoo for the second time.

'It's better for everyone to see how much you've got,' said Tia. 'Then they know the score.'

'Fine,' said Liberty, and pressed her chin into the top of her pile to stop a couple of bars of chocolate crashing to the ground.

Once on the wing, the noise was deafening. There wasn't a woman in the place who spoke in a normal voice. Instead, every single inmate either shouted or screamed or whistled. When they finally reached a cell, Liberty thought her ears might actually be bleeding and dropped her gear onto the bottom bunk in relief.

Tia opened the cupboard next to the toilet and checked inside. She shook a tampons box – empty – then sniffed a bottle of something green, like it might have been a pint of milk gone off.

'That is minging,' she said, but put it back anyway.

A screw stuck his head in. He was handsome and couldn't have been more than twenty-five.

'Oi-oi,' said Tia.

'Canteen's open, ladies,' he said.

'Thank God,' said Tia. 'We're desperate for a full English.'

Breakfast turned out to be toast, toast and toast. All white and pre-smeared with margarine. Liberty was forcing down half a slice when a woman passed by their table and slid a small plastic pot of jam at them. Someone else deposited Marmite.

Tia went to pick it up, but Liberty grabbed her hand. 'We don't want to owe anyone anything.'

'It's fine,' Tia replied. 'These are your people.'

'What are you talking about?'

Tia rolled off the top on the Marmite and stuck her finger into the brown gloop. 'They work for you lot. Or some of their family does. Or they're from the estate or whatever.' She sucked off the Marmite. 'They're not daft, just want to make sure they're in your good books.'

Liberty watched as another woman, one side of her head shaved to reveal a tattoo of three stars, dipped her hips as if giving a small curtsy and dropped four sachets of sugar onto the table.

Tia pointed a brown fingertip at a group of women at the far end of the canteen who glanced over occasionally from a game of cards. 'They're Paul Hill's people. We'll need to watch them.'

'We've no beef with him.'

'Maybe. Maybe not.' Tia shook one of the packets of sugar and ripped it open. 'But there's always a bit of friction, you know?' She poured the sugar over her toast. 'Let's just keep our eyes and ears open.'

By the time, they'd finished eating, Liberty had accumulated a pile of pots and sachets. Coffee, powdered milk, ketchup.

And back in the cell other items had been left on the bunk. Tia whooped at the sight of a pair of woolly socks rolled into a ball.

'Cold feet?' Liberty asked.

Tia shut the door and unravelled them, shoved her fingers inside one and pulled out a mobile phone. 'Just so you know, coming to jail with you properly works for me.'

Tessa Buckman had one foot on her desk and was painting her toenails darkest purple. The whole CPS room smelt of the polish. Her mobile vibrated next to her ankle.

'I don't even need to look at it to know who's calling,' she told Rose.

'Chief super?' Redman asked.

Buckman finished the nail on her little toe and smiled at her handiwork. 'Hell, yes.'

'I'll bring him up to speed later,' said Rose.

'And what will you tell him?' Buckman asked.

'That you were happy to proceed against Greenwood.'

'Happy's not the word I'd use,' said Buckman, and swung her feet down. 'But there's no way I was going to let Sol Connolly push me around. And you said you had a witness statement.'

'I said we'd get one.' Rose crossed her arms. 'In the meantime, there's the other evidence.'

Buckman screwed the top back on the bottle of polish and chucked it into her handbag. 'You nicked her in a dodgy place with a dodgy person. Not going to stand up, is it?'

'Drugs were found at the scene.'

'After she'd left,' said Buckman, and reached across for a sheet of paper. 'Your chain of evidence is going to be shite, and if you do manage to get a judge to swallow it, I'm betting Rainsford will cough to it before she lets the boss go down.' She fanned her feet with the paper to dry the varnish. 'We all know you need that statement.'

'I'll get it,' said Rose, and walked out.

She drove across town to the address Carmen had given when they'd bailed her, while Redman drank from a bottle of 7Up in silence. Suddenly she noticed that his hair wasn't yellow but brown. Ordinary-hair-colour brown. He must have dyed it the previous night.

'What?' he snapped.

Rose just shook her head that she had absolutely nothing to say.

Carmen's place was a downstairs flat close to the park where Rose had been attacked. The door was open and a woman in her fifties was outside watering a bay tree in a tub. A toddler wobbled at her calves in a pair of Pokémon pyjamas. The woman tore off a leaf, rubbed it between finger and thumb and held it for the boy to smell.

'Is Carmen home?' asked Rose, and flashed her warrant card.

'Still in bed,' said the woman.

'Can you get her for us, please?'

The woman picked up the child. 'You might as well come in.'

They followed her into the sitting room of the flat, which was dominated by a grey velvet sofa and a television. Rose's stepfather had always made plain his views on large telly screens. A picture with the word 'love' sprayed graffiti-style across green and white stripes and various photographs in frames hung on the wall. Carmen appeared in a few with a teenage boy, spiral curls covering most of his face.

The woman popped the toddler on the sofa, scooped a bowl of grapes from the floor and handed it to him, then scurried away, presumably to raise Carmen. The little guy rolled a grape around the bowl then bent his head and lifted it with the pink tip of his tongue. It immediately fell off, which made him laugh.

'Can I get you a cup of tea?' The woman appeared back in the room. 'It's going to be a while until she can speak.'

'No, thanks,' said Redman.

'Just had one,' said Rose.

The woman pursed her lips, reached into the toddler's bowl for a grape and pushed it into his mouth. 'What's she done this time?'

'We just need a statement from her,' Rose replied.

The woman rolled another grape into the toddler's mouth, though it was obvious he hadn't eaten the first. Both his cheeks puffed out, like Marlon Brando's in *The Godfather*.

'Is he Carmen's?' Rose asked, nodding at the little boy.

'Aye.' She ruffled his hair. 'I had to fight the social tooth and nail to keep him. They said I hadn't exactly done a good job on my other two.' She glanced at the photograph of Carmen and the teen with the curls. 'But I did my bloody best.'

Rose ran her finger around the edge of the photo frame. 'Where's the boy?'

'Strangeways.' The toddler looked up at the woman, cheeks like a hamster's, and she smiled at him. 'He only went in for breaching his bloody probation, then he gets caught up in something.'

'What sort of thing?' Rose asked.

The woman shook her head as if she didn't want to say, then shrugged as if none of it mattered. 'He shanked a drug-dealer. Big name in these parts. That's why they had to move him to Manchester,' she said. 'Not that he's safe there. Has to stay in seg most of the time.' She looked at Rose sadly. 'Doing life in solitary. Can you imagine?'

'Who was the dealer?' Rose asked.

'Jackson Delaney,' she said. Redman let out a puff of air and the woman sniffed. 'Exactly. But if you think my boy did that on his own, you're mad.'

Rose turned to Redman for information.

'Word on the street was that it was ordered by Hill,' he said. 'Or the Greenwoods.'

'Do you know what?' Rose told the woman. 'I will have that tea if you're still offering. Doesn't look like Carmen's in a rush to talk to us.'

The woman snorted. 'Takes her an hour before she can move.'

Liberty lay on the lumpy mattress and stared at the underside of the top bunk. It was covered with the names of previous inmates. Bex, Colleen, Cherri. Plus lines of street names scratched into the metal. Princess Lo, Poison Ivy, Krasher.

The mobile vibrated and she grabbed it. A text from a number she didn't recognise. *I'll call in 5 F xx*

While she was waiting, Liberty considered calling Sol. He'd want to know she was all right. Or maybe he wouldn't care. She sighed. He told her he loved her, and she sometimes said it back. But if she really loved him shouldn't she have just left him alone? He'd had a job he was good at, a home, a wife who adored him. In time there might have been kids.

On the dot, the phone buzzed. 'Frankie?'

'All right, jailbird,' he said. Liberty felt relief wash over her at the sound of her brother's voice. 'How's tricks?'

She looked over at Tia on the bog, joggers around her ankles, reading the list of ingredients on an individual box of Frosties. 'It's like a holiday.' Frankie laughed. 'I'm thinking of trying the spa later.'

'You banged up with Fuckstick?'

Liberty watched Tia open the Frosties and pour the flakes directly into her mouth from the box. 'Indeed I am.'

'At least she knows what's what,' said Frankie.

'Are you calling me soft?'

'Wouldn't dare,' he said. 'Listen, I've spoken to Raj and he doesn't seem too worried.'

'He's not the one in here, is he?' she replied.

'We'll get you out soon enough. Just keep your head down,' he said.

'What's happening with you?' Liberty asked.

Frankie paused for a second. 'The police grabbed a lorry load of our lot. They're only just getting out. And we've lost a ton of food. Same with Paul Hill.'

Liberty's heart sank. 'What's happening with the crew from Moss Side?'

'They've pretty much jumped into our spots,' said Frankie. 'Hill wants to hit back.'

'Did he find out anything about who they are?'

Tia finished both her ablutions and her second breakfast, lobbed the empty box at the bin and missed, then pulled up her trousers, but not before Liberty got a good look at her lady garden. Eyes burning, she rolled onto her side to face the wall.

'He's asked to meet later,' said Frankie.

'Try to get him to keep calm,' said Liberty.

'I'll try, Lib, but he's got a point,' Frankie replied. 'We can't have these muppets strolling into our patch and taking what's not theirs. It's not even about the money.'

Liberty understood. If word got around that the Greenwoods didn't hit back and hard, they'd be considered a spent force. Easy pickings for anyone else who fancied their chances. 'What did Crystal find out?' she asked.

'A couple of names,' he said. 'She told me she'll come to see you when we've spoken to Hill.'

There was the sound of laughter in the background, then music cranking up. He must be in the Cherry. Liberty never thought she'd live to see the day when she missed being in the club with its sticky floors and whinging dancers, but she did. If she was honest with herself, it felt like home.

'Gotta go, Lib,' said Frankie. 'I'll see you soon.'

'Hope so.'

'And tell that stupid little sket that if anything happens to you I'll personally cut her legs off.'

Liberty remained on her bed, trying to think, but the noise level had reached football-stadium status. In the cell next door, a television blared. One of those shows where folk washed their dirty laundry in public. Several inmates screamed and demanded DNA tests. She knew there was nothing she could do in her current predicament, but that didn't stop her worrying. From what Frankie had said, things were about to kick off. Even if she hadn't been in jail there probably wasn't much she could have done.

Then there was Sol. How would he react to this situation? Since the moment they'd met, he'd been forced to cross boundary after boundary. Of course she'd never asked him to do that, but the lines were always there, drawn with a dirty finger in the sand. If he wanted to be with her, he needed to move to the other side.

Time after time he'd done things for her that he shouldn't. When she'd asked him why, he'd said simply that he didn't believe she was a bad person. Did he still believe that? Or would he take this opportunity to free himself from all the problems? She couldn't blame him if he did that. Hell, she was the queen of running away, had gold medals for it.

There was a beep over the Tannoy system and whoops went up across the wing.

'Let's get out of here,' said Tia.

Liberty's eyes opened wide. 'What?'

'Exercise.' Tia slid her feet into her trainers. 'We get half an hour in the yard.' She picked up one of Liberty's shoes and threw it at her. 'Or would you rather stay here and stew?'

Liberty snatched her other shoe. Right now, she'd give a kidney for a breath of fresh air.

Hutch picked up Sol and drove across town. His hair was damp, and a whiff of chlorine clung to him. Sol tried to recall the last time he'd been for a swim. It must have been on his honeymoon. Two weeks in Croatia, all blue skies and clear seas, Tash in a different bikini each day. Truth be told, he'd been a bit bored, continually wondering how crap people's lives must be that this was the highlight.

'Tell me about the kid,' he said.

The car in front turned without signalling. 'Is it a problem with your finger?' Hutch yelled and pressed the heel of his hand on the horn. 'Madison Moser.' He dragged his eyes from the offending car to the road ahead. 'Goes by Mads.'

'And she's fifteen?'

Hutch nodded. 'Don't go thinking she's some Girl Guide, Sol. She's got form for everything from possession with intent to robbery. She got nicked not long ago for battering some younger. Hammers were involved.' He pulled the car over outside a laundrette. A woman stood at the door, a plastic tub in her arms crammed with clothes, the strap of a pink bra snaking over the rim. 'She would have gone down for that, but she had it away on her toes.'

'And that's what you'll use as leverage?' Sol asked.

'That and a couple of other things I've got up my sleeve.' The woman caught Sol looking at her bra and kissed her teeth as if he were a flasher, which made Hutch roar with laughter. 'Seems like your luck with the fairer sex has run its course, mate.'

Sol closed his eyes. Wasn't that the truth?

They waited until a white van stopped a few feet ahead, the wheels on the right-hand side mounting the kerb with a squeal of rubber.

'Gianni cannot drive for shit,' said Hutch, and got out.

Gianni jumped out of the driver's door. 'I'm getting the hang of this thing at last.'

Hutch waited for him to open the back, then hopped inside. Sol followed suit.

The kid was slumped in a seat, elbows on her knees, chin in her hands. When Hutch grinned at her she didn't grin back. 'Who's that?' She jerked her head at Sol. 'Another fucking pig?'

'Nice to see you too,' said Hutch, and took the seat next to her.

Gianni shut the door behind him and flicked on the light. It was a tight squeeze with three grown men and the girl, and the air already smelt of stale smoke.

'This is Sol,' said Hutch.

'Hi,' said Sol, but the kid didn't answer.

As his eyes grew accustomed to the gloom, he noticed that Madison's wrists were covered with red weals. He glared at Hutch. This whole thing was dodgy enough without keeping the kid chained up.

'Mads got herself into a bit of a situation,' said Hutch. 'Isn't that right, Mads?' She stared at him with enough venom to knock him out. 'Got herself grabbed by one of the locals.' He reached to touch her face, but the kid backed away, displaying raw wounds across her throat. 'Might have killed you, if we hadn't got you out.'

Sol reached into his pocket for his fags and offered one to Madison. When she didn't react, he took one for himself, lit up and tossed the packet into her lap. She stared at it for a second, then helped herself to one. Sol handed her the lighter.

'I'm not a grass,' said Madison.

'He'll never find out,' Hutch replied.

Madison laughed, smoke streaming from her nostrils. 'Ricky knows everything. He's got untold coppers in his back pocket.'

'We're the only people who will ever know about this,' said Hutch. 'No one else.'

Madison gazed at the three men in turn. 'Any one of you could tell him.'

'Why would we do that?' Hutch asked. Madison shrugged. They all knew the answer was money. 'Look, Mads, we can't make you do this for us, but you know we'll make the other problems go away if you do.' Madison considered these problems and flicked her ash. 'The affray charge gets dropped. Tia gets nowhere near you.'

'Tia?' Sol asked. 'Tia Rainsford?'

'You know that bitch?' Madison shouted, and held up her injured wrists. 'She's the one that done this to me.'

Sol nodded and tried to cover his shock that she had caused Madison's injuries. Tia worked for Frankie, but Liberty kept an eye on her. Surely Liberty couldn't know what Tia had done to this kid.

'She's in prison,' said Hutch. Madison's eyes popped open. 'And we can make sure she stays there.' He smiled. 'All we need is for you to get back in touch with Ricky and feed us some information.'

Chapter 12

10 September 1990

I haven't seen our Jay since last night, and when he rolls up, he's got a new top on. 'Tell me you've not been on the rob,' I say.

He pulls a pack of Benson's from his pocket and sparks up. 'I haven't.'

I'm trying to do the washing-up, but there's no hot water and the grease won't come off the pots. I throw down the cloth and it lands on the draining board with a wet thump.

'Since when did you get all squeaky clean?' Jay asks, fag hanging off his bottom lip.

I dry my hands on the front of my hoodie with a sigh. It's not that I'm perfect, but I know I'm not going to be caught, don't I? What happens in the club stays in the club. It's like a kingdom of its own. 'I just don't want you going back inside,' I tell him.

He flops onto the settee and blows smoke at the ceiling. 'I can't survive on fresh air, Lib.'

'So, you have been on the rob?'

'No,' he says. 'I just did a few deliveries for somebody.'

That floors me. I mean, our Jay doesn't know anyone in these parts. Then it strikes me that there is one person he knows. 'Tell me you don't mean Sean.' He doesn't answer. 'Chuffing hell, Jay. You know he's a drug-dealer?'

Jay laughs. 'Well, I met him when you were buying drugs off him so, yeah, I know that's his game.'

'And what do you think you're likely to be delivering for him?' I can't believe this. There was me worried he'd get done for shop-lifting when actually he's moving pills around. If he gets nicked, it'll mean years, not months. He won't be the hard man then, will he?

'Look, I'm not taking it up full time,' he says. 'But I needed a bit of cash and he offered as a favour to you.' He laughs. 'He fancies the living arse off you.'

'Well, he can do me a favour by not getting my brother sent down.'

Jay rolls onto his side and flicks his ash into a saucer. I've got to admit that the black T-shirt does him a lot of favours, the handsome bugger. There's a knock at the door and I assume Rob has forgotten his key.

'Do not say a word about this to him,' I say.

Jay mimes zipping and locking his lips. I roll my eyes. I should be so mad at him, but he can always get round me.

When I open the door, I don't find Rob there, hands deep in his pockets trying to find his key.

'Hi,' says Matt.

'How did you know which flat it was?'

'Nice to see you, too,' he says.

He looks over my shoulder into the flat. I stretch my arm out across the door frame, but I don't know why I bother cos Jay is already on his feet and bounding over.

'Who's this, then?' asks Jay. 'Boyfriend?'

'No,' I say. Matt holds out his hand and our Jay just looks at it. 'You'd better come in.'

Matt, hand still out, blushes. 'It's fine. I shouldn't have come unannounced.'

'Well, we do prefer it if folk let us know,' says Jay. 'In writing.' I smack him one. 'Ow. Mate, be glad you're not the boyfriend because she gets violent and I wouldn't want to see you get your head kicked in.'

Matt laughs at that. 'Look, I was passing, and I just wondered if you fancied coming over to ours for a few beers. But if you're busy . . .'

'We're not,' says Jay.

I flick him. 'He didn't mean you.'

'Obviously you're both welcome,' says Matt. 'I wouldn't invite one flatmate without the other.'

'Invite me where?' Rob appears on the landing behind Matt.

'Party at this bloke's,' says Jay.

Rob rubs his hands together. 'Nice one.'

Present Day

The exercise yard was full, although there wasn't a fat lot of exercising to be seen. The rusty netball post at the far end was ignored. To be fair, Liberty couldn't see a ball even if anyone had an urge to play wing attack. Instead, the prisoners mooched about, leaned against the wall or sat on the concrete. Quite a few women just carried on with whatever they'd been doing inside: one was hunched over a letter, pencil stub in hand, another plaiting her cellmate's hair.

Tia chatted to various inmates and played a game of noughts and crosses someone had drawn in the dirt.

Liberty spotted the group who had been playing cards over breakfast strolling the perimeter, sucking on their e-cigs. They kept glancing at Liberty then away again.

'I'm going to speak to them,' she told Tia.

'I wouldn't.'

'There's no problem between me and Paul Hill,' said Liberty. 'So there's no need for any bad feeling in here.'

Tia marked a cross in the muck that made three in a diagonal and drew a line through them. 'Let them come to you.'

'What?'

'You're the head of the Greenwoods.' Tia stood, wiping her dirty finger down her thigh. 'They're just some low-level girls from the Peabody. I bet they barely know Paul Hill.' She stared at the women in question. 'They should know their place.' She caught the eye of one and waved. The other didn't wave back.

'Don't ramp things up,' Liberty snapped.

Tia's shoulders stiffened and Liberty anticipated a long-winded tirade about respect and rank, but then she noticed Tia was watching a prison guard marching towards them. 'Liberty Greenwood?' he said.

'We haven't done nothing,' said Tia.

The guard ignored her. 'Greenwood?' Liberty nodded, heart pounding. 'Visitor.'

The guard said nothing as he showed Liberty down a long corridor that led to a door marked 'Visitors' Centre'. The bunch of keys he produced was huge and it took several attempts to find the right one. At last he managed to open the door, and they entered, greeted by absolute silence.

'Where is everyone?' Liberty asked.

'Apparently, it's just you, princess.'

He wafted a hand at a table and Liberty took a seat. She looked around her at all the empty tables and chairs. How had Crystal managed this? Securing a visit so quickly was nothing short of miraculous, but to get them to open up the centre especially for her was incredible. How many palms had she greased for that?

As they waited, the guard tapped the tip of a key against the wall. The sound seemed to travel directly into Liberty's brain-stem. Hopefully Crystal would bring good news.

The door opened and Liberty looked up. The face staring back at her wore a smile: it wasn't Crystal's.

'Hello, Liberty.' It was the detective who had interviewed her. She had short sensible hair, neither blonde nor brown. What Mam would have called 'mousy'. 'I'm Rose Angel.' She held out her hand, nails clipped and clean. Liberty shook it, then Angel sat down. 'You were expecting someone else.'

'I didn't know who it was going to be.'

Angel laughed. 'But you were hoping for someone more fun than a copper.'

Liberty eyed the other woman. Of course she was gutted not to have her sister on the opposite side of the table, telling her she'd sorted bail and found out how to get rid of the gang from Moss Side, but she wasn't going to give anything away. Growing up in care had provided years of poker-face practice.

'You used to be a solicitor,' said Angel.

'Still am.'

'Don't you get stripped of all that if you have a criminal record?' Angel asked.

'I don't have a criminal record,' said Liberty, and Angel waggled her hand from side to side as if the issue was debatable. 'If you thought you'd get a conviction, you wouldn't be here now.'

'Why do you say that?'

Liberty coughed to gain the guard's attention. 'Can I leave, please?'

'Come on,' said Angel. 'Surely you're curious as to why I'm here.'

The guard looked up from his key tapping, as if surprised to find Liberty still there. 'You don't want the visit?'

'Carmen Garcia ring any bells?' Angel asked. Liberty stood and nodded at the guard. 'She gave a statement that you sold her some drugs. Your lawyer said she wouldn't put it in writing, but she did. I don't suppose he knows the full story.' She grabbed Liberty's hand. Liberty tried to pull away, but Angel gripped tightly. 'He won't know the name Lucas Garcia, will he?' Liberty froze. 'You know him, though.'

Liberty glared at Angel, but she just smiled and jerked her head at Liberty's chair. Liberty sank back into it.

'Make your mind up,' the guard muttered.

'Lucas is Carmen's brother,' Angel said. 'Imagine that for a coincidence. And imagine how angry she is that her brother killed someone for you, and that you left him to rot.' Angel leaned over and dropped her voice. 'Imagine the world of bad things that are descending on your head right now.'

Liberty's own voice came out barely above a whisper. 'What do you want?'

'Now, that's more like it,' Angel replied.

Sol chose a chicken shop on the other side of town where he was pretty certain they wouldn't be seen. It was amazing how small the area was that most criminals stuck to. Often the kingpins ruled little more than a few blocks of flats.

'What do you want?' Hutch asked Mads.

'Fifteen nuggets, chips and a strawberry milkshake,' she said, without checking the menu.

'Sauce?'

'Barbecue,' she said. 'Two sachets.'

Hutch took his place in the queue, which was surprisingly long for mid-morning. Sol took a seat on a plastic banquette and slid a mobile phone across the table to Mads. 'Is it unlocked?' she asked.

'Yup,' he said.

Without hesitation she programmed in a pass key. He took it back and set himself up as a contact. 'That's me. You call me or text me at least twice a day.'

'To say what?' Mads asked.

'That you're still alive.'

Mads checked the number, then flipped the phone over so the screen was against the table top. She looked at the queue and sighed.

'If I don't hear from you in twenty-four hours, I'll come and get you,' he said.

'How?'

Sol picked up the phone, went into settings and showed her the find-my-phone display. He didn't point out that if the phone was broken, destroyed or even just turned off he would have no idea where Mads was.

'What's in all this for me?' she asked.

Hutch had already explained that if she didn't do as they asked, she'd face the outstanding charges and maybe Tia Rainsford into the bargain – but, as Sol's mum always said, you catch more flies with honey than vinegar.

'You're fifteen, right?' he said. 'As soon as you're sixteen, we'll put in a word with social services to get you your own flat.'

Mads groaned. 'There are never any places. Everyone knows that.'

'There aren't places for normal punters,' he said, 'but there are always some for anyone considered especially vulnerable.' He smiled. 'We'll make the case.'

Hutch arrived with the food and three sachets of barbecue sauce, which Mads grabbed as she jumped up.

'Tell them you got nicked or something,' said Hutch.

'I think I'm probably a better liar than you,' said Mads.

Hutch laughed and they watched her leave, grabbing a straw for her milkshake on the way out. Poor kid. She had absolutely no idea how good at this Hutch was.

'You sure about this?' Sol asked. 'If Vine works out what she's up to . . .'

'He won't,' said Hutch. 'He's like some bloke who was in the C band at school, not a criminal mastermind.'

'Well, if he's that thick, how come you haven't caught him yet?'

Back in the cell, Liberty sent a text to Frankie asking him to call her urgently while Tia fiddled with the buttons on a portable television that had appeared.

'Can you step outside a minute?' she asked Tia.

The girl pouted as she managed to find ITV. 'What? You don't trust me now?'

'It's not about trust,' said Liberty. 'But some stuff is family business.'

Tia huffed but made for the door. 'Keep the telly on. If the screen flickers, the screws have got phone scanners out on the landing.' She opened the cupboard and pointed to the empty tampon box. 'Stick it in there.'

The mobile vibrated on the mattress and Tia made herself scarce.

'Frankie?' Liberty asked.

'He's on the streets trying to figure out who's still around,' said Jay. 'Is that a telly I can hear?'

'Yeah.'

'Bloody hell, next you'll be telling me you've got Netflix and your own shower.' Jay laughed at his own joke. 'Far cry from when I last got sent down.'

Liberty checked the television screen. The picture was grainy, but she couldn't see any flickering. 'We've got a problem, Jay.'

'Tell me about it,' he replied. 'These jokers from Manchester have jumped into every free spot. They're literally riding around on the estate picking up our punters. I know you're not happy about making a statement but here we are.'

'Thing is, Jay, we've another issue.' The picture folded in on itself, once twice, then again. 'Shit, I've got to go.'

'Lib?'

'The Delaney thing.' Liberty rushed to the cupboard and grabbed the box. 'The police know all about it.'

'What the . . .'

Liberty hung up, pulled down her joggers and jumped onto the toilet just as the door burst open. The handsome young guard held a phone scanner, like a prize on sports day.

'Cell search,' he said.

'Fine,' said Liberty, and held up the tampon box. 'Don't mind me. Women's business.'

Strangeways – or HMP Manchester, as it was now called after its post-riot rebranding – was on lockdown.

The guard who met Rose and Redman didn't have the full details. 'It all kicked off on K wing. A dodgy batch of spice they think.'

The landings were empty, but the sound of angry voices seeped from under each cell door.

'How does it get in?' Redman asked.

The guard threw out his arms and circled them. 'It's like bloody water. We plug up one hole and it finds another. You know they can impregnate paper with it now?' Rose nodded. She'd heard about letters and cards full of the stuff being found. 'I wouldn't care if it just made them zombies. I mean, they can sit in their own piss all night for all I care. But some of 'em start hallucinating and the next thing they're frigging psychotic.' He glanced at a door that someone was hammering on from the other side. 'We've all been attacked at one time or another. A mate of mine got the end of his nose bit right off.' He tapped his own, which was covered with freckles. 'Still, at least he got compo. He'll be able to buy a black cab now.'

'That's a win right there,' Rose murmured.

Eventually they came out at a small office where every surface housed a half-drunk cup of coffee. The guard collected up two in each hand and shoved them to the corner of a desk. 'We'll bring him here – if that's all right?'

Rose went to the chair but found an open tin of Quality Street on it. Only the orange creams were left.

'Help yourself,' said the guard, and popped off to get the prisoner.

'And you thought being a copper was rubbish,' Rose said to Redman, as she chucked the Quality Street alongside the cups.

Ten minutes and two orange creams later, the guard appeared with Lucas Garcia in tow. Carmen's brother had lost his spiral curls but was still recognisable as the sullen skinny kid in the photo.

'Sit down, Lucas,' said Rose.

The lad plonked himself down and stared at them suspiciously, dark circles under each eye.

'We met your mum earlier,' said Rose.

He looked startled. 'Is she all right?'

'She's worried about you,' said Rose. Lucas shrugged and his eyelids became heavy. He'd probably been hearing that since he was ten. 'She doesn't think it's fair that you did what you did and haven't been looked after for it.' Lucas picked at a stain on his trousers. 'Stuck over here in a Cat-A prison.' Rose reached for the Quality Street and offered it to him., Lucas took a handful and stuffed them into his pocket. 'Your mum thinks that the Greenwoods haven't done what's right.'

'I don't know who you mean.'

'Yes, you do,' said Rose, and took a chocolate for herself even though she certainly didn't want another. 'How old were you when you did that favour for them? Eighteen? Nineteen?' Lucas nodded. 'You'd have been out before your twentieth birthday. But now how long have you got to do?'

'At least ten.'

'Ten years.' Rose turned to Redman who whistled. 'That's a lot of hard yards. If you make it,' she added. 'Can't be sure Delaney's people won't get to you, eh?' Rose unwrapped the orange cream and bit into it. The cakey sugar covered her tongue and she instantly regretted it. 'Can't say I'd be overjoyed if I were in your shoes.'

'I'm not going to grass,' he said.

'Just a little help,' said Rose. 'You scratch our back and we'll scratch yours.' She ran her tongue across the roof of her mouth to get rid of the orange paste. She'd been sure that Lucas would be sufficiently aggravated by his situation to turn on the Greenwoods. 'We can make life inside a whole lot easier,' she said.

Lucas shook his head. 'Not going to happen.' He stood now,

reached across for another handful of chocolates and gave a half-smile. 'Sorry you wasted your time.'

Rose looked through the office window for the guard, already dreading the return journey across the Pennines with Redman and his told-you-so face.

'What about your nephew?' Redman asked. Both Rose and Lucas were shocked to hear him speak. 'What sort of life do you want for him?' Lucas licked dry lips. 'I'm assuming you don't want him going into care. Can you imagine what that would do to your mum?'

Lucas, who was several inches taller than Redman, squared up to him. 'Leave him out of this.'

'Not up to me, mate.' Redman put up his hands in mock surrender. 'Carmen's back living at your mum's and she got herself nicked again. Fifteen rocks.' Lucas's eyes flashed. 'I don't think the social worker's going to be too impressed, do you?' Rose felt her mouth fall open. She wouldn't have thought Redman had it in him. 'But if we don't charge Carmen, then who's going to tell the social worker?'

'You people, you're all the fucking same.' Lucas sat back down. 'You think the Greenwoods are bad people, but you're just the fucking same.'

Three beeps sounded from the Tannoy system across the prison and every inmate scrabbled for whatever they needed before bang-up and lights out.

Tia thrust her hand under her mattress and pulled out the stub of a candle and a lighter. As soon as the guard on landing duty had done their check, she lit the wick. 'We'll ask around for a torch tomorrow,' she said.

Liberty wondered how someone could smuggle one in, thought about the shape and decided not to ask.

The night brought with it a drop in noise levels but no silence. Women still shouted to one another. A whistle pierced the air and Tia took the candle to the window. Soon an envelope attached to what looked like a long white rope appeared from above. Tia grabbed it and whistled back.

The rope was made from pieces of sheet knotted together. It must have taken an age to craft. But Liberty had quickly realised that time in jail was glacial. Spending three hours carefully ripping a sheet into strips, then tying those strips together wasn't a problem. No one here was busy.

Tia opened the envelope and produced a pre-rolled blunt and three razor blades. She sparked up the joint and reached for a toothbrush. 'Can I have this?' she asked. 'You've got three.'

Liberty nodded and watched as Tia melted the back of the head of the brush and pressed the razor blades into the waxy plastic. Then she blew on it until the plastic set. 'Got to be prepared in here,' she said, and handed Liberty the spliff.

It had been years since Liberty had smoked weed, but if ever there was a time to start again, this was it. She took a long draw and held the smoke in her lungs, smiling as her head spun.

'I know you said it was family business.' Tia climbed onto the top bunk. 'But you can tell me stuff, you know?'

Liberty passed back what was left of the blunt. 'I grew up on the estate.'

'I know that.'

'Then I left.'

Tia leaned over the side of her bed, ponytail dangling in the candlelight. 'Why?'

Liberty frowned. If Tia asked Jay that question, he'd say his sister got scared. If she asked Crystal, she'd say Liberty was a selfish bitch who only thought about herself. And what would Frankie say? He'd been a baby back then and wouldn't have understood. But what did he think about it now? 'Complicated,' she said.

'But you're glad you came back?' Tia asked.

Liberty considered that one. Of course she was glad to have her siblings back in her life. Even Crystal. But she'd done so many things since her return. Things she would have never dreamed of doing. She'd lied. She'd cheated. She'd hurt people. And there was Delaney. She hadn't touched a hair on his head, but she'd given the nod.

'Complicated,' she said.

Chapter 13

10 September 1990

When we hop the gate at Kitty and Matt's house, our Jay bursts out laughing. 'You're joking.'

'Don't make a show of me,' I warn him.

'No, Jay.' Rob puts on a ridiculous accent that he thinks sounds posh. 'One mustn't make a scene or big sister will get terribly upset.'

I cuff him round the back of his head. Then I cuff Jay for good measure. 'Don't test me.'

They're both still cracking up when we get to the door and find Kitty outside with the girl in the shoulder pads who cried when it all kicked off in the club. They're both holding a glass full of what looks like wine and smoking roll-ups.

When Kitty sees me, she comes running up and hugs me, clearly already pissed. 'You made it. Matt wasn't sure if you would.' She smiles at Rob, then at Jay. 'And who's this?'

'My brother, Jay,' I tell her, and he holds up a four-pack of Boddingtons he bought on the way.

'Are you as fun as your sister?' she asks him.

'You think Lib's fun?' Jay grabs the roll-up from Kitty and takes a drag. 'You'd get more laughs out of Peter Sutcliffe.' She pulls him through the hallway to the kitchen. Now I know for a fact that our Jay has never been anywhere like this in his whole life, but he's never going to let that slip and swaggers along like the cock of the north.

163

Someone's set up a sound system outside, so Rob immediately goes off to have a nosy at the record collection while I help myself to a handful of cocktail sausages and some crisps. There are lots of people here all milling around, drinking and chatting. Rob manages to convince some bloke to let him have a go on the decks and soon enough he's got ten lasses dancing to 'I've Lost Control' by Sleezy D. I bob my head in time.

A lad appears at my shoulder. 'Don't you find this music a bit repetitive?'

'I think that's the point,' I say.

'Beep, beep, fucking beep.' He's got hair cut short at his ears and long at the back and the smell of some sort of incense comes off his Motörhead T-shirt. 'Music for the brain dead.'

'Brains are overrated,' I tell him, and dance away.

Matt wanders over and hands me a can of cider. 'You could at least pretend to like my friends.'

'Why?'

'Because they're nice.' He looks over at the bloke with the hair, who's moaning to someone else about the music. 'Actually, he's a dick, but the rest are nice.' A couple of lads rush across the lawn, bare-chested, waving their rugby tops. 'Okay, most of them are dicks.'

I take a swig of the cider. 'You're nice, though,' I tell him. 'I mean, you're a bit of a dick, but still nice.'

'Thanks,' he says. 'I think.'

Then he starts dancing and that makes me smile. He's pretty crap, neck going back and forth, like a chicken's, but he's enjoying himself. When Rob drops the next track, I cheer. 'Chime' by Orbital. Not long ago it would have made me feel a bit sad, because of Connor, but tonight I realise I'm just happy to hear it.

Rob must have caught the look on my face because he leaves the records, dances over to me and picks me up. I put my arms around his neck and let him swing me around, like we're a pair of kids in the playground.

Then I see Jay in the kitchen doorway, holding himself up, face white. Rob has seen him too because he puts me down and we hurry over.

'What's up?' I ask.

Jay puts his free hand on his thigh and bends forward like he might be sick. 'It's that lass,' he says. 'The one that lives here.'

'Kitty?' I look round for her. 'Where is she?'

'In her room,' says Jay. 'I don't think she's breathing.'

We race up the stairs and find Kitty on her double bed. She's not wearing a top, just a white bra with a little bow on each strap. Her skin is wet and cold when I give her a shake. There are twin streams of blood trickling from her nostrils.

'What's she had?' Rob asks. Jay shivers. 'What's she taken, mate?'

'Just a bit of brown.' Jay catches my look of horror. 'She asked me if I had any gear. I didn't offer.'

'And what the fuck are you doing with smack?'

'Sean gave me a few bits and bobs to sell,' said Jay. 'She told me she'd done it before.'

I point wildly around the room. 'Does that seem very likely, Jay?' He looks around sheepishly. 'Go home,' I say, but when he doesn't move, I shout, 'I'm serious.'

Rob grabs his shoulder. 'She's right, mate.'

'I didn't do owt,' says Jay.

I push him to the door. 'Unless you want to go back to jail for a very long time, get the fuck out of here.'

He looks at Kitty, lifeless on the bed, then legs it. I wait for thirty seconds until I'm sure they've gone, then run downstairs to the phone and dial 999.

Present Day

That morning's toast came with a few teaspoons of beans that Liberty avoided.

'You are so picky,' Tia told her, as she scooped her own helping into her mouth and reached for Liberty's. 'You know if there was an apocalypse, like with zombies and shit, you'd have to eat whatever you could scavenge.'

'I'll worry about that when the time comes,' Liberty replied.

When a guard called her over and informed her that she had another visit, Liberty's heart sank. Another run-in with DI Angel was not high on her to-do list.

'Who is it?' she asked.

'Do I look like your social secretary?' the guard shot back.

Fine. Liberty would go along, and if she found Angel sitting there, she'd turn around and walk back to her cell.

Unlike the previous day, the visitors' centre was full. Every table taken. A few husbands and boyfriends holding a prisoner's hand, but mostly mothers and sisters who had brought in the kids. A trolley run by trusties was doing a brisk trade in Fruit Shoots and Quavers.

In the corner, cocky as you like, it wasn't Angel but Crystal. She eyed up Liberty as she approached. 'Well, don't you look glamorous?'

Liberty took in her sister's drawn face. 'You don't look so hot yourself.' Though her sister didn't react, Liberty immediately regretted the dig. 'Still better than me, though.'

A kid raced past with a packet of Maltesers and a grin from ear to ear. Liberty watched Crystal for any sign of emotion but there was none. She wanted to ask her about the pregnancy, but if there was a worse time, she couldn't think of one.

'The police woman came to see you?' Crystal said.

'Yeah. She knows about . . .' Liberty hesitated to spell it out.

'Delaney?' Crystal laughed at Liberty's discomfort. 'Relax, they can't listen in.'

Liberty looked up at the cameras on the far wall. What were the chances they could pick up sound? 'She says the Garcia kid is talking.' The trustie wheeled the trolley between the tables, nodded at Crystal when she reached her and placed a Yorkie between them, then continued on her way. 'She didn't have a statement or anything, but if she arrests me for it, I've no chance of getting bail.'

'Fed up already, sis?'

Liberty opened the chocolate bar and pushed it at Crystal. 'Murder trials can take a year to get to court.' Crystal pushed the chocolate back to Liberty. 'If you think I'm worried about being in here that long, then you're spot on.'

'As I see it, we can play it two ways,' said Crystal. 'The first option is the obvious one.'

Liberty snapped off a chunk of the Yorkie. Crystal meant get rid of Garcia. Easily done. The kid was in prison where violent attacks happened all the time. 'What's the second?'

'Do what Angel wants.'

Liberty had not expected that and laughed. 'Be a grass?'

'You give her some information and the Delaney thing goes away,' said Crystal.

'I cannot believe you of all people are suggesting I help the police.'

Crystal leaned forward. 'On our terms. We only pass things along that will help us. Let her get rid of the crew from Manchester and Hill while we're at it.' She smiled. 'No point having a dog and doing all the barking yourself.'

'Someone will work it out.'

'Not if we're quick,' said Crystal. 'We get things done, then that's an end to it.'

'And if Angel doesn't want to end it?' asked Liberty.

'By that time, we'll have enough dirt on her to shut that shit down.'

Back in the cell Tia was checking her lip in a compact mirror, pressing gently on the cuts that had still not healed. Liberty remained certain that they'd needed a stitch. Trust Crystal to gloss over that. It was like there was something missing inside her. Growing up, Liberty had met a lot of damaged kids. The care homes were full of them, all big balls of temper and desperation. They'd learned to dampen down their emotions until something kicked off and then they spilled over, like molten lava. But she'd never met anyone quite like Crystal and that worried her. No, it scared her.

'See, when we get out,' said Tia, 'I'm going to track down that Mads and break every bone in her body.'

'What would you do to get out of here?' Liberty asked.

Tia laughed. 'Pretty much anything.'

'But are there things you wouldn't do? Lines you'd never cross?'

Tia shrugged and licked her split lip. 'You've got to work it out as it comes up. Only a fool makes rules before the game even starts.'

Sol checked his phone for the umpteenth time.

'For God's sake.' Hutch took it from him. 'She's fine.'

'I told her she had to stay in touch,' said Sol. 'If she can't even follow the basics . . .'

Hutch waved his mug at Scottish Tony for a refill. 'It's a different carry-on when they're not job. You must have used people on the street. You know what it's like.'

'I've never used a kid before.'

Scottish Tony arrived at the table with a fresh cuppa. It wasn't steaming. Hutch took a sip and winced. 'Any chance you could actually put the kettle on, Tone?'

'Boiler's broken.'

Hutch shook his head in despair, as Sol's phone vibrated. He snatched it back. It was a text from Mads asking to meet in a shopping centre.

'What did I tell you?' said Hutch.

Sol jumped up and threw a fiver on the table for his breakfast.

He waited outside the door of Claire's Accessories, a poster of a baby wearing a bow the size of its bald head staring back at him.

Just inside the door, a girl sat on a stool, waiting to have her ears pierced. The assistant cleaned her lobes with an antiseptic wipe and produced the earring gun. She glanced at Sol and frowned. He couldn't blame her. What business did a scruffy man in his forties have loitering outside this place?

At last Mads arrived, a checked shirt tied around her waist.

'You're late,' said Sol.

'I don't work for you.'

'It's not like that,' said Sol. 'I need to know you're safe.'

Mads snorted. 'If you gave a shit about me being safe you wouldn't send me in to do this, would you?'

He ran a hand under his fringe, scratching his hairline. Hutch was adamant that Mads could look after herself, but he wasn't convinced. The girl on the stool squealed as the gun popped a stud into her ear. Mads kissed her teeth as if she'd never seen anything so pathetic.

'What's happening?' Sol asked.

'The feds cleared up the estates,' said Mads. 'Picked up a load of locals.'

'And you lot have stepped in?'

'What do you think?'

'I think you need extra supplies if business just doubled,' said Sol.

Mads nodded. 'A packet arrived before I got back, but we'll soon be cleaned out.'

'Has anyone mentioned when a new one's coming?'

Mads twisted the loose cuff of her shirt around her hand. 'One of the boys says Caleb will be across tomorrow, but I don't know if that's true.'

'Caleb's bringing the drugs in person?'

'Supposedly,' said Mads. 'Things are getting hectic, so he wants to bring it himself and talk to everyone.'

There was little chance that Vine or Clarke would turn up carrying a ten-stretch worth of gear. That was the whole point of setting up these county lines. But then again, these were exceptional circumstances. A chance to expand his empire had fallen into Vine's lap and a man like him would find that hard to resist. But it would need organising, and would Ricky Vine trust that to anyone except his number two?

'See if you can find out a time and a place,' said Sol. 'And call me, okay?'

'Yes, Dad.'

The chief super was a simmering pot of fury. Rose had dealt with all types of bosses before. The shouters, the swearers, the ones who threw files across the room. The simmerers were always the worst.

'This operation was about picking up street dealers,' he said.

'That's correct,' Rose replied.

'Then explain to me how Liberty Greenwood was arrested.'

Rose didn't need to look at Redman to know his face would be a shade of puce. 'Sir, she was with a person well known to us.' She noticed that there was no offer of coffee today as the chief tapped his desk with his thumbnail. 'And we do have a statement from a witness confirming she bought drugs from someone matching Greenwood's description.'

'Do you know the history between this station and that woman?'

'Officer Redman has appraised me, sir.'

The chief pressed his lips together so tightly they disappeared. 'Then why is she in prison?'

'The prosecutor felt she was a bail risk,' said Rose. 'And the magistrate agreed.'

'Well, let me make this crystal-clear for you. Your case had better be watertight.'

'I don't think any case can be that, sir.'

Redman waggled his foot and Rose could feel the stress radiating from him, but they'd discussed how to play this beforehand.

170

'Then drop the charges,' the chief hissed.

'Isn't that a matter for the CPS now?'

'If you tell them your witness is unreliable, they will be only too happy to discontinue,' he said. 'Miss Buckman's department has no desire to pursue a case she will not win.'

'I'll speak to her,' said Rose. 'But in the meantime, we should really start picking up our new dealers before they bed in.'

'What?'

'Sir, the whole point of the operation was so we could smoke out the county lines and send them back home as quickly as possible.'

The chief sighed. 'This whole thing is a mess. I've used a ton of manpower and for what? A few low-level drugs convictions if we're lucky.'

'That wasn't the point, sir.'

'Well, DI Angel, the point is this.' He narrowed his eyes. 'Sort out this Greenwood problem, *then* come back to me about the county lines.'

Back in Redman's car, he looked like he might throw up with both hands on the wheel and his head down. After he'd played the social services card with Lucas Garcia, he'd gone right up in Rose's estimation, but the state of him now told her that he was not a natural in this game.

'Chill out,' she said. He threw her a look of disgust. 'I'm serious. The chief has ordered us to drop the case against Greenwood, which is good news.' She held out the car keys to him. 'There won't be any questions when she walks out of prison tomorrow.' She tapped his hand to urge him to start the engine. 'And Greenwood will think we're honouring our side of the deal.'

'But what if she won't make the deal?' Redman's hands shook as he tried to push the key into the ignition. 'What if she tells you to do one?'

Rose laughed. 'She won't.' Redman wasn't convinced. 'I've got her number. She might be part of the Greenwood family, but underneath she's soft. There's no way on God's green earth she could do a stretch of proper jail time.' The engine started and she grabbed the seatbelt. 'It's a win–win, Joel. We'll send the county-lines crew packing and have the Greenwoods nice and close. Then maybe the people round here can start sleeping at night.'

When the guard told Liberty she had another visit, Tia burst out laughing. 'You must be the most popular person in here.'

But when Liberty saw Angel and Redman it didn't seem funny. That said, the fact that they were there again so soon after Angel's first visit told Liberty they were eager to seal the deal. One of the first things she'd learned in corporate negotiations was that you needed patience and balls of steel. Leave the offer on the table and walk away.

'Return customers,' said Liberty. 'Must be the food.'

'And the general ambience,' Angel replied.

Liberty pointed to Redman's hair. 'Nice colour job. Do it yourself?'

He blushed deeply, even more so when Angel chuckled. They were on their own again in the visitors' centre, but the place hadn't had a proper clean since the last session and there were crisps scattered across the floor. Liberty crushed one with her shoe.

'Have you thought about what we discussed?' Angel asked.

'Of course.'

'And?'

'It's a big decision. I need time to consider it.'

She was pretty sure that time was what they didn't have. Whatever they wanted from her they needed quickly, and she could use that as leverage.

'What's there to think about?' Angel asked. 'Either you do

what we want or face a charge of murder. That'll put you in prison for a very long time.'

Liberty crossed her arms. 'I don't know if you've noticed, but I'm already in prison.'

'We can get you out,' said Redman.

'Oh, he speaks,' said Liberty, and turned to Angel. 'Is that allowed?'

'We can make both cases go away,' said Redman.

Liberty had lied about his hair. The brown was too dark and didn't suit him. Plus, he'd somehow managed to stain the top of his ear. 'When?'

'You can walk out of here tomorrow,' said Redman.

'What about Tia?'

'Who?'

'Tia Rainsford,' said Liberty. 'My co-defendant.'

Redman checked with Angel, who nodded. 'She can walk too.'

Liberty paused. Of course she wanted to get out of jail. And of course she wanted that for Tia too. She might be a royal pain in the arse, but she was just a kid, and this was no place for her. But providing the police with information? Even if she accepted Crystal's take on it, was that a price too far?

At last she nodded. 'Fine.' Angel grinned and held out her hand. Liberty spat on her own and shook, enjoying the horror on the detective's face.

Chapter 14

10 September 1990

The ambulance sways from side to side and I have to hold on to a handle. A medic straps an oxygen mask to Kitty's mouth, but as we career around a corner, the tank rolls off and a tube breaks free. The medic swears and reattaches it.

'Have either of you got any idea what she's taken?' he shouts above the siren. Matt shakes his head. 'Did she mention anything at all?' the medic asks me. 'It could save her life.'

'Sorry,' I say.

'What about your brother?' asks Matt. 'Might he know anything?'

'Why would he?'

'I saw him with Kitty before.'

I shake my head. 'Him and Rob left the party ages ago.'

'Why?'

'Because a load of posh kids getting pissed out of their minds isn't really their scene,' I say. 'Anyway, do you really think people like us have the money to be buying drugs?'

Matt looks into his lap and I feel a bit shit, but I've got to put him off the scent. If anyone finds out what our Jay did, he'll get sent down for a very long time. Matt's shoulders heave and I know he's crying. He was lovely to me when I was upset but I don't know what to do for him.

When we arrive at the hospital, the ambulance doors get thrown open and more medics pull the stretcher outside. Then they're off, racing Kitty into the hospital. Me and Matt run after them, dodging through all the folk, but we can't keep up.

'I think I'm gonna puke,' says Matt.

I see a bin by the side of a water-cooler, grab it and hold it for him while he chucks his guts up over a load of paper cups. When he's finished, I give him a bit of toilet roll I've got in my pocket. 'Sorry, it's used,' I tell him.

He wipes his mouth with it and drops it on top of the pukey cups. I pop the bin back where I found it, which is really minging but I can't think of owt else to do with it.

'Kitty'll be all right,' I say. 'They know what to do in these places.'

'You think?'

'Yeah. There was this lad at the club and his eyes rolled completely back into his head,' I say. 'I thought he was dead for sure, but he was back the next night, right as rain.'

Of course we hadn't rung for an ambulance. The Cheetham lot had carried him out and put him in a minicab, paid the driver double fare to get him to A and E. But I don't tell Matt any of that.

He decides he needs to call his mam and dad from the payphone. Apparently, they're away because it's their anniversary. I don't suppose they're going to be too happy when they find out there's been a massive party in their lovely house and their daughter has overdosed on skag.

But when Rochelle turns up with some bloke that I assume is Matt's dad, there's no shouting. She just hugs Matt and asks him if he knows what's going off. It turns out they've given Kitty a big injection of adrenalin. Weird that they have to give you a drug to get rid of a different one.

A nurse lets us have a quick visit. I give a little gasp when I see Kitty. She looks like she's actually died, but with her eyes open. For a second, I worry that she'll tell on Jay, but she doesn't look like she can even talk.

When we're ushered out of the ward, we end up in a line on a metal bench. Rochelle's between her husband and Matt, all holding hands like a chain-link fence. I'm on the end, sort of with them but not. 'I should probably go,' I say. 'Now we know she's okay.'

Rochelle looks up at me. 'Of course. Your parents will be terribly *worried about you.' I look at Matt, but he doesn't put his mam right about my situation. She turns to Matt's dad. 'Do you have any money for Lib to get a cab?'*

'Of course,' he says, digging in his pockets.

I look at the crinkled twenty quid he's just given to me. 'This is too much.'

'Don't worry,' says Rochelle. 'I just need to know you're going to get home safely.'

Matt jumps up and gives me a hug. 'Thanks, Lib.'

Guilt sweeps over me. I should be saying sorry to this family on bended knee, but instead I leave them in the hospital. When I get outside, I'm looking for a taxi when I spot the N33. I jump on it and pay my bus fare, crunching the twenty-pound note into my pocket.

Present Day

As soon as the morning lights went on, a screw opened up the cell. 'Get your stuff.'

'Why?' Tia jumped off her bunk. 'You're not splitting us up?'

The guard yawned. This was the end of a long night shift. 'Just get your bloody stuff,' she said, and wandered off.

Liberty watched Tia grab a hundred sachets of sugar and drop half of them. 'If they're shipping us out somewhere else, we can't risk taking the phone,' said Tia. 'I know some girls put 'em up, but I'm not about that life.'

'Give it all to next door,' said Liberty.

Tia was aghast. 'We can manage to bring some of it with us. They might send us miles away and there won't be half as many of your people in there. Maybe none.' She shoved a bottle of shampoo down her knickers. 'I mean, I know your family will see us right, but it could take a while to filter through.'

'Give it to next door.'

Tia growled as the shampoo bottle escaped through the elastic and slid down the leg of her joggers. 'It's a complete nightmare on basic rations.' She reached up the leg of her trousers and pulled out the bottle. 'Wait and see.'

The kid bitched all the way down the corridor to Reception and didn't shut her mouth until the screw produced a see-through plastic sack of the belongings she had come in with.

'What's going on?' Tia demanded.

Liberty leaned close to Tia's ear and whispered, 'We're going home.'

Liberty unlocked the Black Cherry and pushed back the velvet curtain. Jay and Mel were at the bar counting cash into piles.

'You'll be declaring that to the tax man?' Liberty said.

When they looked up, Mel clucked like a hen and Jay ran over and hugged her. The door of the office opened, and Frankie appeared, arms full of leather whips. He whooped when he saw his sister and groaned when he saw Tia.

'Behave,' said Liberty. 'This one looked after me inside.'

'Oh, she knows which side her bread's buttered,' said Frankie.

'I didn't ask for nothing,' said Tia.

'No, but I bet you took anything on offer.'

'Enough,' said Mel. She grabbed the whips from Frankie and plonked them in Tia's arms. 'You, put these in Frankie's boot. Then you can help wipe the tables.'

'What did your last slave die of?' Tia asked.

'Giving me lip.'

Tia gave a tut but took off with the whips as Liberty kissed Frankie.

'Well, isn't this a touching scene?'

They all looked around to find Crystal by the curtain. Liberty went over and put her arms around her sister. Crystal stiffened but didn't push her away. 'You took my advice, then?' she asked.

'Of course I did.' Liberty smiled. 'And you think we'll be able to play the policewoman?'

Crystal pulled out a packet of Juicy Fruit, snapped a stick of gum in two and pushed one half into Liberty's mouth. 'Trust me.'

'I do.'

Crystal gave something that was almost a smile and turned to her brothers. 'Right, then, what are we going to do about our new friends from Manchester?'

'Do we need to do this now?' Liberty asked. 'I haven't even had a shower.' She didn't mention that she hadn't seen or spoken to Sol yet.

'This can't wait, Lib,' said Jay, and pulled out four chairs at the table nearest to the bar.

The Greenwoods each took a seat. Mel put a glass full of ice in front of each of them with a smile.

'What are you so happy about?' Frankie snapped.

'This is how it should be,' said Mel. 'You lot function better when you work together.' She plonked bottles of orange juice, Diet Coke and Jack Daniel's in the middle of the table. 'Now figure this out.'

Liberty pushed all thoughts of Sol from her mind and they got down to business.

Sol had spent the night drinking and thinking. There had come a point when the drinking had hindered the thinking and all he'd had in his brain was a swirling mass of names: Angie, Natasha, Amira, Madison. And Liberty. Always Liberty.

The sound of his mobile woke him with a start, and he fell off the sofa. With his head in an ashtray on the floor, he knew he hadn't made it to bed.

By the time he found his phone down the back of a cushion

it had stopped ringing. But he recognised the number in Missed Calls as Madison's and hit reply.

'What's the point nagging me to keep in touch if you don't answer?' she said.

'Sorry.' He burped into his fist. 'Is everything okay?'

'You asked me for a time and a place,' she said.

'Go on.'

'Two o'clock,' she said.

'Where?'

'Someone called Mad Brian's place.'

Sol brushed ash from his chin. 'Where's that?'

'You're the fucking five-oh.'

Then she hung up and Sol ran to the bathroom to chuck his guts down the pan.

Jay poured them all a measure of bourbon, then raised his glass. 'Welcome home, sis.'

They all clinked glasses and drank, except Frankie, who pushed his glass at Liberty with a wink and opened a Diet Coke. It was far too early for a JD, but Liberty had been in prison. All bets were off.

'Go on, then,' she said. 'How bad is it out there?'

Frankie rattled the ice in his drink. 'They've pretty much taken over.'

'So they think,' said Jay.

Liberty reached over and laced her fingers through his. 'Have you spoken to Paul?'

'He's raging.' Jay laughed. 'Thinks we should tool up the lads and go break some heads.'

'Do we have enough people for that?' Liberty asked. 'It seemed like a lot of them got picked up.'

The door opened and Tia waltzed back inside. Mel threw a

179

cloth at her and waved at the tables at the far end of the club. Tia sighed but got on with wiping.

'About half got bail,' said Jay. 'Not enough for all-out war.'

'Then we need to be strategic,' said Liberty. 'Paul can go scrap it out if he wants, but we need to hit them where it matters.'

'Do we know their stash houses?' Jay asked.

The silence told Liberty that they didn't.

'There's Mad Brian's place.'

They all looked at Tia, who was scrubbing a stain on a table by the stage.

'Go on,' said Liberty.

'Mads told me they were cuckooing his flat,' she said. 'Poor bloke's not the full ticket. Probably has no clue what's going off.'

Liberty looked around her siblings. 'Seems like we've got a target.'

Sol rolled down his window to let the smoke from his fag escape. He'd been watching the block of flats for an hour and needed a pee, but sod's law said the moment he went to find a toilet, something would happen.

A lad came out of the block, all box-fresh Nikes and tracks in his buzz-cut.

'Know him?' Sol asked.

Mads had her hood up and eyes closed in the passenger seat. He nudged her arm with his elbow until she opened her eyes. 'That's Stacks,' she said.

'What's he do?'

Mads shrugged. 'Same as us all. Package the food and serve it up.'

Sol nodded. From questioning Mads, it seemed that Vine didn't run a pyramid, like a lot of crews. He had a whole gang of

180

youngers, who did the work for little in return. Then a few guys, who kept the pipeline flowing in the area. Then Clarke, who moved the product and people up-country.

Mads yawned and closed her eyes again. 'Not being funny, but if this is what you do all day, it's stupid.'

The ash from Sol's fag dropped onto his jeans and he sighed. He opened the door and got out to take a leak. He'd drunk three litres of water to try to clear his head and that had been a mistake. There was a tree on the corner, the base of the trunk thick with bin bags and rubbish. It would have to do.

Sol was mid-flow over the nappies and syringes, when Mads got out of the car.

'Gotta go,' she said.

He gave himself a shake and trotted after her, grabbing her arm.

'You haven't even washed your hands.' She shrugged him off. 'Which is rank by the way.'

'Where are you going?'

Mads waved her phone at him. 'I need to work. If I don't, they'll know something's up.'

'But as far as you can tell Clarke is still coming here today?'

'As far as I can tell, yes.' She glared at him. 'But you know how it is. I'm nothing and nobody so I don't get told shit.'

He let her go and went back to the car, took another swig of water, batted on the radio only to hear some song he hated by Drake. Then his phone beeped. 'Yeah.'

'We've just seen your girl wandering past us,' said Hutch.

'Well, yeah,' Sol replied. 'She can't go on the missing list for too long without raising suspicion.'

'You got anything?' asked Hutch.

Sol glanced over at Mad Brian's block. 'Absolutely nothing.'

Frankie drove across town with Liberty in the front seat. Tia, in the back, kept messing with all the buttons, turning the heated seats on and off, opening and closing the windows.

'If you don't stop that I won't be held responsible for my actions,' said Frankie.

'You've got anger issues,' said Tia, and lay across the seat, wiggling her backside so that her joggers made little mouse squeaks against the leather.

'I know, I know,' said Liberty, to her brother. 'You're going to kill her.'

They pulled up outside Mad Brian's block.

'This it?' Frankie asked.

'Yup,' Tia replied.

'Which flat?' Liberty asked.

'I already told you I don't know,' Tia said, as if she was dealing with idiots. 'I've been there like once.'

Frankie snapped his head around. 'Which floor?'

'Second, I think,' she said. 'I wasn't paying attention, was I?'

Liberty put her hand over Frankie's. She understood his frustration, but it wasn't down to Tia. She'd already given them a heads-up about the stash house. The fact she couldn't pinpoint it wasn't a cause for rebuke. 'All we have to do is wait,' she told him. 'Sooner or later someone will lead us to the right flat.'

'When did you get so zen?' Frankie asked.

'You try spending time in jail,' Liberty replied. 'There is absolutely nothing to do all day except chat to your cellmate.'

Frankie looked over his shoulder at Tia, who had her feet on the window. 'In your shoes I would have strangled her and done the time. No question.'

Soon enough two lads cycled past, hoods up over their baseball caps, steering with one hand, a McDonald's drink in the other. As they chained up their bikes, one lifted the straw from his cup with his teeth and blew drink through it at his mate with a high-pitched laugh.

'You recognise them?' Liberty asked Tia.

'Yeah,' she replied, and went to open the door.

'Don't be stupid,' said Frankie. 'If you know them, they'll know you.'

'Well, everyone around here knows *you*,' she snapped back.

'It'll be me, then,' said Liberty, and stepped out of the car. 'Play nicely while I'm gone.'

She took her time, walking to the entrance of the block, checking her phone and pretending to tie up her boots so that she was behind the boys. One of them pressed the intercom.

'It's Cayden.' The boy spoke into the metal grille. 'Open up.'

The door buzzed open and Liberty raced forward, her hand on the frame before it closed behind them. She slipped inside and followed them up the stairs. Cayden sucked up the last of his drink, the gurgling sound bouncing off the walls and ceiling.

Tia had been right about which floor the flat was on as the boys peeled off at the sign marked '2' and went along the walkway to a flat with filthy nets at the window. Cayden banged on the door and the grey lace was pushed aside.

'Let us in, Brian,' Cayden shouted, and when the door opened, he pushed his way inside.

Liberty bounced down the stairs and went back to the car.

'Is it the right place?' Frankie asked.

'Definitely.'

He gunned the engine. 'Let's go talk to Jay and Crystal and decide what to do.'

Sol couldn't believe his eyes. At first, he thought his mind was playing tricks on him but, no, there she was entering Mad Brian's block, then reappearing two minutes later.

A jumble of questions hurt his brain. When had Liberty got out of prison? Why hadn't she called him? And what the hell was she doing here?

Chapter 15

11 September 1990

When I wake up the next day, Rob's already in the kitchen filling the sink with a kettle. Our Jay's still spark out on the floor, my coat over him.

'All right?' I ask Rob.

He's about to wash his hair so he's got a bottle of Johnson's and a Tupperware box on the side. He bends over the sink and scoops a boxful of water over his head. With his hair dripping, he grabs the bottle and squeezes a good slug onto his hair. 'I think I'm going to stay at Donna's for a couple of days,' he says.

'Is she okay with that?'

Donna lives with a bunch of other lasses who go to the poly and their landlord is awkward about them having their boyfriends over.

'She'll put up with me for a bit,' he says, kneading the bubbles into his scalp. 'Thing is, Lib . . .'

He's got soap running down his forehead, aiming straight for his eyes, so I stop the flow with my finger. 'You need our Jay gone when you get back.'

'It's not that I don't like him,' he says, 'but if Kitty tells anybody who gave her the gear, there'll be ructions.'

'They can't prove owt,' I say.

'I know, but they can cause a lot of bother for us all.'

He leans back over the sink to rinse, but I take the box and do it for him, making sure the soap's all out, especially around his ears. 'One last shot of cold?'

'You're a cruel woman,' he says.

'I've told you, it stops it getting greasy as quick.'

'Go on, then.'

I fill the box with water from the cold tap and pour it over. Rob gives a scream, which makes me laugh and our Jay fart as it wakes him up. That makes us both laugh.

'I'm worried about you as much as myself.' Rob gives his hair a rub with a tea towel that's not even clean. 'At some point they'll have to let you see your Crystal and Frankie again, but not if they think your Jay's mixed up in drugs and you're letting him live with you.'

When Rob's got off, I make two cups of tea and kick our Jay awake. 'Ow,' he shouts.

I put his brew on the floor. 'We need to have words.'

An hour later, we're in a Chinese restaurant on the high street where they're advertising a half-price lunchtime special. It's dead so they let us share sweet-and-sour chicken balls with two portions of egg-fried rice.

Our Jay's stuffing his face. 'When I'm rich, I'm going to eat this stuff every day.'

'And how will you pay for it?' I ask. 'Drug-dealing?'

'It's not like I've got too many choices right now, Lib.' A waitress brings over a basket of prawn crackers. 'Sorry, we didn't order them,' he says, and she gives him a wink even though she's twice his age. At least. I can see that this will be it from now on with lasses falling over themselves to drop their knickers. As if he's not in enough trouble.

'We could call social services,' I say. 'You're still in care.'

'So are you.'

'But you're younger than me,' I say.

He shoves the last chicken ball into his mouth and gets up from his chair. 'If you think I'm going back to live in some unit, you've lost the plot.' He marches out, runs back for the basket of prawn crackers and takes them with him.

Later that night, with Rob at his girlfriend's and our Jay still off sulking somewhere, I'm in the flat on my own, working on my Mansfield Park *essay when there's a gentle knock on the door. So gentle that I know for a fact it can't be my brother.*

When I open up, I find Matt standing there and my heart leaps into my mouth. 'Is it Kitty?' I ask him. 'Has something happened?'

'Apart from her overdosing on heroin, things are pretty quiet,' he says. 'Any chance I could come in?' He holds up a bottle of Lambrini. 'I've brought provisions.'

I let him in, move my books and that off the settee and fetch two mugs from the kitchen. I give him the one that isn't chipped, and he fills them both up.

'Is she home?' I ask.

Matt nods. 'And refusing to say a word about what happened. Honestly, I feel like strangling her.'

Me, I feel like kissing her. Which is bad, obviously. But the thought of our Jay going down again makes me panic. Every time it changes him just that bit more.

Matt grabs my hand and I pull it away. 'I'm not going to shag you, if that's what you think,' I say.

'Lib?' He looks shocked. 'No. I didn't mean . . . I just wanted . . .'

'What?' I eye him over my mug of fizzy wine. Because he wants something from me. No one gives lifts and bottles of booze without some sort of wish list. Except Rob. But he's special. 'You're here for a reason.'

He gulps some wine. 'I wanted to apologise. Last night in the ambulance it must have sounded like I was accusing your brother but, honestly, I was just in bits.' Face bright pink, he jumps up, spilling what's left of his drink into his lap so it looks like he's wet himself. 'Sorry, I shouldn't have come over.'

Then he's gone, slamming the door behind him, and I'm left on my own again, so I go back to my essay on Austen's portrayal of social mobility. From what I can tell, all the lasses in Mansfield Park *had to rely on getting married. Bugger that. I'm the clever one. I'm going to university to study law and then I'm going to get the sort of job that lets me make my own decisions.*

Present Day

When Liberty entered the back office of the Black Cherry, she found Crystal heaving down the mirror that always hung in front of the safe.

'Let me help,' Liberty said.

'I'm fine.'

Liberty grabbed hold of the other side and tried to take the mirror from her sister, but Crystal wouldn't let go. 'It's too heavy for you,' said Liberty.

'What are you talking about?' Crystal asked. 'I move this thing all the time.'

'But not in your condition.'

Crystal let go of the mirror and Liberty stumbled backwards with it, whacking her thigh on the side of the desk. She yelped as pain coursed through the muscle, and leaned the mirror against the wall. Rubbing the back of her leg, she tried to smile at her sister. 'Harry told me,' she said. Crystal was rooted to the spot, looking the nearest thing to scared that Liberty had ever seen her. 'He's worried about you.'

'Have you told Jay and Frankie?'

'No.'

Crystal stared at her. 'Well, don't.' Then she turned and tapped the code into the safe keypad. It beeped and the door opened. She bent to check inside, then fed the hungry mouth with bricks of cash.

'Are you going to keep it?' Liberty asked. She saw her sister's spine straighten, but there was no answer. 'I know it's hard.' Crystal closed the safe door and relocked it. 'We didn't have a normal family growing up, but look at Jay – he's doing a good job as a dad.' Crystal remained facing the safe and Liberty watched her shoulders rise and fall as she breathed. 'Just don't end up like me.'

The door opened and Frankie came in, laden with a Chinese takeaway from the Jade Garden. He lined up the foil boxes

187

and peeled off the cardboard lids. Prawn toast, spring rolls, crispy seaweed. Then Jay sauntered in and added the obligatory sweet-and-sour chicken balls. He pulled three plastic forks from his back pocket, handed one each to Liberty and Frankie and kept one for himself.

'I'm assuming you've already eaten, Crystal,' he said.

'Yeah,' she replied. 'But I might have a prawn cracker.' They watched open-mouthed as she took one and nibbled the edge. 'What?'

Jay stabbed a chicken ball with his fork. 'So, you found the stash house then?'

'Yeah.' Liberty took a spring roll. 'And there are youngers coming and going, so it's being used.'

Frankie picked up the box of seaweed, poked around in it and scooped some into his mouth. 'We should go over there and kick the door off.' The moss-green shreds crackled as he chewed them. 'Batter whoever's in there and take the drugs.'

'Or,' Liberty held up her spring roll like a greasy finger, 'I could tell Angel. She wants information so I'll give it to her. Let the police kick the door off.'

'That'll take too long,' said Crystal, still working on the cracker. 'By the time she gets the say-so from top brass, days will have passed. We need to get this done. Moss Side's a serious problem, and it'll send a message to everyone else round here that we're still in the game.'

'They won't take it lying down,' said Liberty.

'Course not,' said Jay. 'Our people will have to be ready for the backlash.'

'The few we've got left,' said Liberty.

Frankie picked at a piece of seaweed that was stuck between his teeth. 'I say we team up with Hill for this.'

'Agreed,' said Jay.

'Agreed,' said Crystal.

They all looked at Liberty and waited. The last thing she wanted was a war on the streets. Violence only ever brought more violence. But she couldn't for the life of her see a viable alternative. At last she nodded. 'Agreed.'

Sol threw two rucksacks onto the bed and yanked open the bedside drawer. He never balled his socks in pairs but just slung them in. It didn't matter. He only ever wore the same plain black ones, so they all matched each other. He grabbed a handful and dropped them into the nearest bag.

He checked his phone. Another three missed calls from Hutch. Nothing from Liberty. With a snarl, he pulled the drawer from its runners and held it upside down over the rucksack.

He finally answered Hutch to stop the man ringing.

'What the actual fuck, Sol?'

The built-in wardrobe spread across the whole of the far wall, but Sol's clothes filled only five or six hangers. Jeans, T-shirts, jumpers. One suit for court. 'Something personal came up,' he said.

'And you couldn't let me know?' Hutch was furious. 'We've been hanging around like a pair of twats waiting for you to tell us when Clarke arrived.'

'It's an emergency.'

'And what about Mads?'

'She's somewhere on the estate serving up,' said Sol.

'She might go back to the flat,' said Hutch.

Sol grabbed both pairs of jeans and rolled them up. 'Not going to happen. Mads knows they're going to suss anything out of the ordinary.' There was a black pair somewhere. Maybe in the wash basket. 'Showing up accidentally on purpose at the exact moment Clarke surfaces would look too dodgy.'

Hutch sighed. 'I just wished you'd told us you'd got off.'

189

He hung up before Sol could apologise, which he wasn't going to do.

Ten minutes later, Sol's worldly possessions were packed and he was riffling through the dirty laundry for his black jeans.

'Lost something?'

He looked up and found Liberty in the doorway. 'When did you get out?'

She shrugged, walked to the bed and peered into the rucksack. 'You're leaving?'

He sniffed the jeans and decided he could manage without them. Then he took the bag from Liberty and pulled hard on the toggle at the top. 'I was hoping we could both leave.' She sank onto the bed and unlaced her boots. 'A lot of bad things have happened that we can't change, but we can make a fresh start.'

'You know I can't.'

'Can't or won't?'

She pulled off the left boot and tossed it aside, then did the same with the right. 'My family need me.'

'And what about me?'

'It's not the same,' she said.

She rubbed her feet as if the joint of every toe ached and, for a second, he was tempted to kneel in front of her and take over. But then he remembered all the times Angie and Natasha had accused him of putting the job before them. Well, now he knew exactly how it felt always to come second in line.

'I have to go,' he said. She nodded, but when she looked up at him, there were tears in her eyes. 'Don't you ever just want a normal life, Lib?'

She gave a sad laugh. 'A long time ago someone told me that normal is overrated.'

'And what did you say to that?'

'I said I wouldn't know.'

He put one of his bags over his shoulder. 'It's not that I don't love you, but I can't live like this.'

'Where will you go?'

He picked up the other bag. 'I'll work it out.'

Rose and Redman were at their desks doing the paperwork on the street-dealing operation. Redman kept licking the end of his pencil and the tip of his tongue was grey.

Rose tried to type up a report, but everything was coming out in capitals. She deleted the line and restarted with the same result. Redman leaned across and tapped the Caps key on her laptop. A tiny light went out and the letters began to behave themselves in lower case. 'You tell the chief that Greenwood was out?' he asked.

'Sent him an email,' Rose replied.

'Did he reply?' Rose gave him a look and Redman chuckled. 'You really know how to make friends and influence people, eh?'

He went into the pocket of his jacket, which was hung on the back of his chair, and brought out a Twix, tore it open and offered Rose a stick. The chocolate was beginning to melt but she took it happily. 'Can I ask you something?' she said. He nodded and bit into his share of the bar. 'Why do you keep dyeing your hair?' He blushed. 'What's wrong with the real colour?'

'It's grey.'

'What?'

'I went to this RTA involving a lorry and there was a family that went into the back of it.' He tugged at a lock of his hair. 'The driver was decapitated. My hair went grey overnight.'

'Sorry,' said Rose.

He went back to his pencil and paper.

Rose watched his face intently. 'That's not true, is it?'

He crossed his heart with a smile, and she grabbed his pencil and stabbed the back of his hand with it.

'Can I ask a question?' asked Redman, and Rose tipped her head at him. 'What do you expect to get from Greenwood?'

'Information,' she said. 'Someone that high up must know everything that's going on, right?'

Redman finished his finger of Twix and wiped his mouth. 'But she's only going to tell us what she wants us to know.'

'Well, duh.'

'So, how are we going to get the full story?'

Rose typed the final word on her report and pressed save. 'Come on, Joel, we don't ever get the full story, do we?' She shut the lid on the laptop. 'Do we even want it?' She pulled herself to her feet. 'Right, we've cleared the streets of the local dealers, sorted out Greenwood, and now we need to deal with the county lines. We've waited too long as it is.'

'The chief told us to hang back.'

Rose pulled on her jacket. 'So, if we see people committing crimes we're meant to ignore that now?'

'Do you ever follow the rules?'

'Not if I can help it.'

Bunny Hill's cream leather sofa was so squashy Liberty thought she might disappear into it, like quicksand. Somehow her knees were at the same height as her chin as her backside sank deeper and deeper into the leather.

'You're looking good,' Liberty told her.

'People keep saying that and you know what I tell them?' Bunny asked. Liberty shook her head. 'A gold facial massager. I think they come from Korea. Or was it Corsica? But the important thing is they're made of gold.'

'Right.'

'I'm not going to say they're cheap,' said Bunny, 'but they cost less than a face-lift.'

Paul entered the living room, impeccably dressed as always, but he looked older and thinner, the lines around his eyes deep.

'I keep telling Paul to use it,' said Bunny.

'Can you leave us alone, Bun?' said Paul.

Bunny pouted but did as she was told, struggling out of the gravitational pull of the leather and heading to the door. 'If anyone needs anything, you know where I am.'

Paul waited until she'd gone. 'Sorry about that.'

'Don't be daft, I love Bunny,' Liberty lied. She noted that Paul perched on the arm of the sofa rather than take his chances. 'Can we talk about this crew from Moss Side?'

'I told Frankie what I think.'

'And we agree with you,' said Liberty. 'We just need to coordinate this properly.'

Paul went over to a drinks cabinet and lifted a bottle of single malt. Liberty shook her head and he poured himself a good slug. 'I don't know, Liberty. Back in the day we just did what we did. Now it's like living in the fucking Matrix.'

Liberty pushed herself out of the sofa, ignoring the suction noise that sounded not unlike a fart, and joined him at the cabinet. There was a dish of lemon slices on top, presumably left there by Bunny. Liberty took one and chewed the rind, enjoying the sharpness on her tongue.

'We'll hit the main stash house while your people take out as many of their youngers on the street as you can,' she said. 'No need for any serious violence. Just get the gear and send them away with a flea in their ear.'

Paul swirled his glass. 'Scare them back to where they came from?'

'Exactly that.'

'You been to Manchester recently?' he asked. Liberty sniffed her fingers, now citrus-coated, and shook her head. 'Absolute shithole. Can't move for the spice heads in Piccadilly Gardens.' He drained his glass. 'So, when are we doing this?'

Liberty checked her watch. 'How long do you need to get your people ready?'

'We're always ready, love.'

Frankie pulled the car over outside Mad Brian's block. 'Stay here,' he told Liberty.

'You and me are both staying here,' she said. She waved at Tia and some lad called Kane in the back. 'They can handle this.'

Kane pulled out a cosh and a flick knife. Tia was slapping the end of a baseball bat into her palm. Two more youngers were already waiting at the entrance under a streetlight.

'This is my estate,' said Frankie, and opened his door.

Liberty patted his knee. 'Do you think you can manage not to kill anyone or get yourself killed?'

'They're a bunch of kids,' he said, with a laugh. 'We'll do more barking than biting.'

'Speak for yourself,' said Tia, and got out, bat over her shoulder.

'Can you watch out for her?' said Liberty. 'Please.'

'You're a soft touch, you. It drives me mental.' Frankie opened his door. 'But it's also one of the things I fucking love about you.'

'And what are the others?'

Frankie tapped his nose and slammed the door.

Liberty sent a text to Paul Hill. *The party's started.* And waited. After a few minutes she got out of the car. By now they should be in the flat and have things under control. When another minute passed, she had visions of Tia torturing people. Then another minute went by. What could be happening? Another minute, and she locked the car and headed to the entrance, which Tia had wedged open with a house brick. At the bottom of the stairs, she knew something was wrong. She'd made it very clear that this was to be a lightning job. In and out. If she found out that Tia or Frankie was having a field day in there she'd go ballistic.

Suddenly a shot rang out. Then a scream. Jesus. Had one of the youngers brought a gun?

She took the stairs two at a time and was at the entrance to the first floor when a bloke hurtled past her from above. He carried on down. What the hell was going on?

When she got to the second floor, Liberty turned into the walkway and was almost knocked off her feet by a group of kids rushing past. Outside Mad Brian's flat was Kane, hands on either side of his head. More screams from inside the flat.

Liberty ran to the door and saw Tia, her body twisting like a corkscrew. It took Liberty a second to realise that she was the one screaming. Then she saw the blood. Rivers of it. Tia's trainers paddling in it. Then the body, lifeless, on the carpet. A hole in the chest.

The Travel Inn was precisely what Sol had expected: two single beds with duvets that didn't reach the foot, a kettle that had to be filled in the bog and one sachet of decaffeinated coffee. There was no minibar, and in the room next door a couple were shagging to porn-film standards.

When his mobile rang, he had no intention of entering into another round of bollockings from Hutch, but when he saw it was Mads's number he picked up.

'Sol?' She sounded frantic.

'Yeah, what's up?'

'There's been a shooting,' she said.

'Are you okay?'

'No.' Mads was crying. 'I went back to the flat to see if Caleb was there. I thought maybe he might say something useful that I could tell you.'

Sol's heart sank. Mads should never have done that. 'What happened?'

'Everything was fine.' She gulped down the phone line. 'He brought a load of gear with him, told us the new pricing and all that, then the door got kicked off by a local crew. That one called Tia was with them.'

'Jesus Christ,' said Sol.

'I thought they'd just rob us but then Caleb pulls out a gun,' said Mads, choking down sobs.

'Who got shot?'

'One of the Greenwoods,' she said.

Sol felt the breath stop in his lungs, as if freeze-dried in an instant. His heart beat so loudly he could hear it above the couple having sex.

'Which one?' said Sol.

'A bloke,' Mads replied. 'He runs the estate.'

Sol hung up and ran from the room.

Liberty was on her knees, hands over the gunshot wound in Frankie's chest, mouth to his, blowing in oxygen.

Tia was screaming into her mobile phone to the emergency services and, somewhere above, Liberty could hear helicopter blades. Her hands slid from her brother, slick with blood, but she immediately put them back onto him to stop the life falling out. 'Don't you die on me!' she shouted at him. 'Don't you dare die on me, Frankie Greenwood!'

Chapter 16

14 September 1990

I haven't seen our Jay since Tuesday, when I find him waiting for me outside college, laid flat out on a bench in the sunshine. All the lasses eye him up as they pass.

'Oi.' I'm dead mad at him and he deserves a bollocking, but when he leaps up to give me a massive hug, I can't help but hug him back.

'What's this, then?' He's got a new checked jacket on and some high tops I've never seen before. 'Been shopping?'

He pulls out a fag and I notice his lighter's new as well. A proper Zippo one that stinks of gas when he sparks up. 'Let's not row, Lib.' He puts an arm around my shoulders. 'I don't know about you, but I'm starving.'

The weather's so nice, we decide to go to a fish shop and eat outside on a patch of grass. Our Jay insists we get one of each, which is daft because we'll never get through all the chips, but he's not having it.

'You staying at Sean's?' I ask him.

He blows on a chip. 'I know you think he's a wrong 'un . . .'

'It's not that,' I say, and I mean it. I don't judge folk on what they have to do to get by in life. Not my business. Back when I was at Orchard Lodge and my room-mate Vicky went on the game, Fat Rob and that lot were horrified. But it's easy to think you'll never do owt like that when your family will always put a roof over your head, isn't it? 'I'm just worried you'll get caught.'

His tray's empty and he's waiting to see what I leave. I pass it over and he gets going on the shrapnel of batter and chips I can't face.

'It's just in clubs.' He sucks his greasy fingers. 'The bouncers always get weighed in.'

'It's not the bouncers I'm bothered about, you div.'

Later on, at work, I try not to notice what our Jay's doing, though he's hardly hiding it. And when I see Sean, I give him the cold shoulder. I mean, I know none of this is really his fault but still. He looks like he might be about to come over to talk to me when I hear yells from Tony's office. When I go inside, his bin's on fire and he's trying to put it out by whacking it with a V-neck jumper. There's a bottle of Irn-Bru on the side, so I yank off the lid and pour it over the flames, which go out in a hiss of orange fizz.

We try to open the window, but it's stuck fast so I grab the bin and head outside with it. Red watches me as I shake the black bits of paper and sandwich crusts into a skip. 'Everything under control, I see.' He lights up a spliff and offers it to me. There aren't any rules as far as I know about smoking at work. There aren't any rules as far as I know about doing anything at work, so I have a puff and give it back.

'Your brother will be all right, Lib,' he says. I look inside the empty bin, sides a bit burned. 'If he's got his head screwed on like you, he'll cop on quick.'

I nod and go back into the club, just hoping that our Jay has got his head screwed on.

Present Day

The hospital car park was full, so Sol abandoned his car by the machine.

A man on crutches scowled at him. 'You can't leave that there.'

'Police,' Sol shouted.

'No, you're not,' said the man. 'Where's your badge then?'

Sol ignored him.

Inside the hospital, Sol didn't need to ask where Frankie would be. It had to be ICU. He knew exactly where it was and high-tailed it over.

In the corridor, heads bowed, were the whole clan. Liberty, Jay, Crystal, Harry, Mel. Pacing up and down was Tia Rainsford.

Liberty looked up at him, most of her face grey-white, but with scarlet smears of blood around her mouth and chin. There was so much blood on her hands it was as if she was wearing red gloves.

'It's bad?' Sol asked.

Liberty didn't even nod, so Sol put his arm around her waist and led her away. 'I'll clean you up.'

In the ladies' toilets, Sol brought Liberty to the sinks. 'You're okay,' he said, and yanked a handful of paper towels from the dispenser. When he'd wet them under the tap, he gently wiped her face.

'He's going to die,' she said.

'Nah,' Sol replied. 'We thought that last time and look what happened.'

The wet paper wodge was soon soaked with blood and Liberty's face was no nearer to being clean, so Sol jammed the plug in the hole and filled up the sink. As gently as he could, he pushed her head down and when it was inches from the bowl, he cupped his hands in the water and washed her face. He released the plug to let the bloody water run away and dried Liberty's face. Then he ran the tap and put each of her hands under it in turn, rubbing the skin until it was clean.

There was dried blood on her clothes, of course, but there was nothing Sol could do about that.

'I agreed to this,' she said. 'It's on me.'

Sol put a hand at either side of her head and looked into her eyes. 'When are you going to learn that none of this was ever on you, Liberty Greenwood?'

199

Liberty held his gaze, then bent into the sink and threw up.

For that time of night, the alley was quiet. A few junkies milled around, muttering to one another, but no one was dealing.

'I thought nature abhorred a vacuum,' said Redman.

'Shut up,' Rose replied.

When there was no sign of business, Rose directed Redman to drive over to Salty's garage where she hammered on the door. 'Need to talk to you, Salty,' she shouted.

As the garage door opened, the smell of vomit assaulted them.

'Jesus,' Rose shouted.

Salty shivered in reply. At the back of the garage the source of the stench became apparent as a girl hurled into a grey plastic bucket.

'Drought,' said Salty, his nose running unchecked. 'Can't get any gear for love nor money since you rounded everyone up.'

'What about county lines?' Rose asked. 'They've been handing out their number all over town.'

Salty dragged a flyer from his pocket and threw it at her. 'No one's answering the phone.' His shoulders heaved and he doubled over, depositing a puddle of vomit and snot inches from Rose's shoes. 'Probably to do with that shooting at Mad Brian's.'

Redman and Rose gave each other a look. What the hell?

The word 'quiet' could not have been used to describe the scene at Mad Brian's. Half a dozen squad cars were pulled up, flashing blue lights reflecting off the slick black tarmac. Overhead a helicopter whirred. Coppers in uniform and plain clothes came in and out of the building and a SOCO team jumped from their van, already suited up.

Rose flashed her badge at a wooden-top, and he lifted the caution tape to let them through. Up on the second floor a

200

PLAYING DIRTY

DI stood at the door to Mad Brian's flat, dragging hard on an e-cig.

'What happened?' Rose asked him.

'The victim came to collect something, I'm assuming drugs or money.' The DI blew vapour out of the corner of his mouth. It smelt of burned apples. 'But what he got was a bullet to the chest.' A beam of light from the helicopter blinded them all for a second. 'Eye in the sky's been combing the area for a car we think the shooter might have got away in, but nothing yet.'

'Do we have an ID of the victim?' Rose asked.

'Oh, yeah,' said the DI. 'And this is not going to bring peace to our streets.' He vaped another lungful. 'Frankie Greenwood.'

'You're joking,' said Redman.

The DI pulled some shoe covers from his pocket. 'I sincerely wish I was.'

As they watched the DI pad into the flat in a rustle of paper protection, Redman groaned. 'This is very bad.'

Rose leaned against the wall, the concrete scratching the nape of her neck. She'd told the chief they needed to move fast. If they'd got cracking while most of the Greenwood people were still locked up, this wouldn't have happened. 'Let's speak to Liberty,' she said.

'Do you really think she'll want to talk to you right now?' Redman asked.

'Of course not,' Rose replied. 'But I'm not handing out choices.'

The lift doors opened, and Angel and Redman stepped into ICU. Anger, hot and dirty, bubbled in Liberty. Her brother had just been shot and they'd got the cheek to turn up at the hospital.

'How is he?' Angel asked.

'Well, the doctors are trying to pull a bullet out of his chest, so what do you think?'

'I'm sorry.'

Liberty turned away and the ends of her hair, still wet where Sol had washed off the blood, stuck to her cheek. DI Angel had coordinated the operation to nick the local dealers, leaving the streets clear for the Moss Side crew to waltz in with their fresh supply of drugs and guns.

'Our deal is off,' she said.

The lift doors opened behind them and a nurse appeared, all hairspray and fabric softener. Angel waited until she'd entered the ward. 'Our deal stands. Or you face charges.'

Liberty let out a laugh that sounded hollow. 'Bucky's discontinued the drugs charges.'

'I mean for the murder of Jackson Delaney.'

Liberty prised the strands of hair from her face. She wanted to tell this idiot to go fuck herself, but that was something Frankie would do.

'Do you really want to fight a court case at a time like this?' Angel leaned in to Liberty. 'Spend time on remand when you should be with your brother?' Liberty wanted to punch her. The feel of her knuckles connecting with Angel's mouth would be delicious. 'All we need is a bit of information.'

'Like what?'

'Who was in the flat?'

Liberty swallowed a barrage of abuse. 'If I knew that, do you think I'd be stood here now?'

'I seriously suggest you leave this to us,' said Redman.

The stain on his ear from his DIY hair job had almost gone, the skin red where he'd been scrubbing.

'That's a great idea,' said Liberty. 'Because you're clearly on the tail of whoever did this.' She slapped her forehead. 'Oh, wait, you've come to me precisely because you lot have no clue.' She pushed past them, entered the lift and stabbed the button. 'I need to make a call.'

'Don't do anything stupid,' said Angel, as the doors closed. 'Your family need you.'

Outside, Liberty took a drink of cool air and pulled out her mobile. She knew she would have to give Angel something. There was no way that bitch was sending her back to prison, even for a week. Not when she had no idea if Frankie was going to live or die. Trouble was, she didn't actually know anything yet.

She called Paul Hill a couple of times, but he didn't pick up.

The pressure of hands on her shoulders made her jump. 'Okay?' Sol asked.

The fact that he'd followed her out to check on her made Liberty want to cry. 'I need to find out who did this.'

'That's not your job.'

'Well, it's sure as hell not yours.'

She shouldn't have said that. Sol had left the police because of her, not because he wanted to. He'd been a good copper. She was just lashing out because she could.

'I just meant that this isn't top priority right now.' Sol put his face close to hers. 'That's got to be Frankie, right?' A tear slid down her cheek and she batted it away. 'Let's go back inside,' he said.

'I will,' said Liberty, 'but you don't need to be here.'

'Where else would I be?'

'You just left me, Sol,' she said.

'I was angry.' He wiped away another tear. 'It doesn't matter now.'

Liberty nodded. 'Yeah, it does. Things are going to get ugly and I'm not pretending any more.'

★★★

Sol caught up with Mads in the chicken shop. She was terrified, picking apart her nuggets but not eating them. Sol sipped a black coffee, which wasn't bad, considering.

'Is he dead?' Mads asked.

Sol shook his head. 'You see it?'

'I was in the bedroom when I heard them come in the flat.' She pushed the box of shredded chicken away. 'There was shouting and that.' She picked up her drink, pumped the straw a couple of times, then abandoned it alongside the nuggets. 'I went to see what was happening.'

'And what was happening?' The door opened and Mads whipped her head around to check who was arriving. Some bloke and his toddler in matching football tops with their names printed on the back. The dad was Daniel and the son Kraig. Kraig-with-a-K. Kraig-let-me-spell-that-for-you. Why would you do that to your own kid? Sol patted Mads's hand. 'What happened?'

She turned back to Sol. 'I don't even know. One minute that Greenwood bloke is laying down the law. Then Caleb pulls out his piece. So, I'm thinking that's that.' She pressed her thumb against the bridge of her nose. 'He's proper hard, Greenwood, but a gun's a gun, right? Then Tia shows up.'

'From where?'

Mads shrugged. 'Maybe she'd been in the kitchen all along. But she barges in with this baseball bat and she's swinging it like fucking Negan.' She raised her arm as if holding the bat. 'And she almost takes Caleb's head off, man. Then bang.'

'Caleb shot Frankie?'

'Yeah. I mean I don't know if he meant to or if the gun went off 'cos Tia smacked him, but Greenwood flies across the room, like he's Spider-Man or something.'

'Where's Caleb now?' Sol asked.

'I dunno,' Mads replied. Sol tilted his head. 'I don't! As soon as we all saw Greenwood on the floor, we knew it was bad. There's no way he's getting up from that, you know?' She closed her eyes, as if she couldn't stop watching the scene play out. 'Caleb just legs it, so we all do the same.'

'I need to find Caleb,' said Sol.

'I just told you—'

'You can get to him.'

Mads looked at him, eyes pleading. She was just a scared kid who'd witnessed a shooting, probably traumatised. He should hand her in to social services and convince Hutch to leave her be. But he had to find Caleb Clarke before Liberty did. If she found him first, she'd kill him and that would be the end of the woman he'd met and fallen in love with.

'Tell me where Caleb is, and we can work something out.'

Back in the ICU, Jay made Tia go over the sequence of events for the fourth time, but Liberty zoned out, her head pressed to the glass of another person's room. The nurse from earlier tended the patient's lifeless body with a gentleness that made Liberty's chest ache.

When she came out of the room, the steady rhythm of the ventilator leaked out. The suck and sigh of air that the patient could no longer breathe for himself. 'Is he going to live?' Liberty asked the nurse.

She put a hand on Liberty's arm. 'I'm praying he will.'

'Where are his family?' Liberty asked.

The nurse gave a sad smile. 'Not everyone is as lucky as your brother in that department.'

Chapter 17

16 September 1990
*I'm taking a video back to Blockbuster when I see Matt's car parked at the
end of the road. He gets out and smiles at me a bit sheepish, like. 'Any
good?' He nods at the copy of* The Blob *in my hand.*

'A bit daft,' I say.

*He's wearing an 'Axe the Poll Tax' T-shirt and denim shorts, squinting
into the sunshine. 'I'm sorry about the other night.'*

'Are you just going to apologise every time I see you?'

'Probably,' he says. 'I'm posh so it's what we do.' *I smile at that.*
'Look, my mum's got it into her head that this is going to be the last day
of good weather and she's insisting we have a barbecue.' *He looks up into
the cloudless sky.* 'Do you want to come over?'

'I've got to return this.' *I wave the video at him.* 'Or I'll get fined.'

'I'm sure the burgers can wait the extra ten minutes,' *he says.*

*I don't know what to do. In some ways I was hoping never to see any of
the Spencers ever again. I'd rather forget about what happened with Kitty
and our Jay.* 'I expect your mam might want a nice family gathering,' *I say.*

'Oh, Christ.' *Matt laughs.* 'What with Kitty virtually a hermit in her
room, and Tobe acting like Rainman because he doesn't know what's going
on, I think Mum would be very happy to welcome some guests.'

'I can't stay long,' *I say.* 'I've an essay to hand in tomorrow.'

'A couple of hours,' *he replies.* 'Fill your boots on potato salad and then
I'll bring you home.'

PLAYING DIRTY

When I arrive, Rochelle does seem happy to see me, giving me a peck on the cheek and insisting Matt fetch me a beer. 'I know you're not strictly old enough, but the French do it, don't they? Watered-down wine with their dinner.' I just smile cos I've no idea how old you have to be to drink in France.

Matt's dad waves at me from the barbecue. It's like a big metal cooker and he's sweating cobbs prodding at bits of meat with a long fork.

When Matt appears with a bottle of beer for me, he's got Tobias in tow. Tobias stands very close to me, staring at my face. I take a step back, but he just follows me.

'Tobe.' Matt puts his hand under his brother's chin and forces him to look at him. 'Not cool, mate. Understand?'

'She's pretty,' says Tobias. It's the first time I've ever heard him speak and the fact that he's as posh as Matt and Kitty surprises me a bit.

'She is.' Matt smiles. 'But we don't say it out loud.'

Tobias frowns. 'Why not?'

'To be honest, I don't know the answer to that one.'

I snort and they both look at me.

'Funny,' says Tobias.

I nod. 'Yeah. Very funny.'

There's a wooden table piled high with food. Stacks of different types of salad and bread. Matt's dad ferries across a tray of sausages, the skins as black as the burned bin at work. Rochelle pops one on a plate alongside some lettuce and a spoonful of coleslaw. 'Could you take this up to Kitty?' she asks me.

'Mum,' says Matt, 'it's not for Lib to do that.'

'I know.' She seems almost about to cry. 'It's just that she's barely eaten in days and I thought she might try for her closest friend.'

It's a bit strange that she called me that. I mean, I only met Kitty a couple of weeks ago, but I take the plate. 'I'll see what I can do.'

Kitty's bedroom curtains are drawn and the telly's on, although she's got the sound muted. She's at her desk drawing what looks like a dragon. I put the food down next to her. 'Your mam sent this.' She looks at the sausage as if it's a piece of burned dog shit. 'You need to eat something.'

207

'How's Jay?'

There's a lump in my throat at his name. 'He's gone to stay with a mate.'

'I hope you didn't send him away on my account,' she says. 'I'm never going to tell anyone.'

She turns from her sketch and smiles at me. I suppose I was being ridiculous to hope she'd forgotten what happened just because I wanted to. The good thing is she seems to want to keep it to herself. I'm about to thank her when Matt walks into the room. 'Never going to tell what, Kitty?'

Present Day

Frankie had been in theatre for four hours when Liberty called Jay, Mel and Crystal down to the hospital car park. It was dark now and the wind lifted their hair and clothes. A woman swore at the ticket machine as it vomited back the change she had fed it, the coins clanking in the metal hole, like a pay-out in Las Vegas.

'Here's what I think we should do,' said Liberty. 'Jay and Mel go back to the Cherry. We need everyone to know that it's business as usual.'

'It's not, though, is it?' said Jay.

Liberty smoothed his shirt, running her palm from his chest to his belly button. 'Yes, it is. The world versus the Greenwoods, just like it's always been.'

'She's right,' said Mel. 'They've grabbed the drugs. Next up could be the clubs.'

Jay bristled at that. The Black Cherry was his pride and joy. Over his dead body would anyone take it from him. He kissed Liberty's cheek, gave Crystal's arm a friendly punch. 'Keep me in the loop.'

When Jay and Mel had gone, Liberty turned to Crystal. 'You stay with Frankie.'

'No.'

'Yes. He needs someone here and it's going to be you.'

'Harry can do it,' said Crystal.

Behind them the woman kicked the ticket machine with a desperate sob, then marched past. Her mascara ran like black rivers down her face and her hair blew wildly.

'Harry's not pregnant,' said Liberty.

'I haven't agreed to keep it yet,' Crystal replied.

'I know that. And if you decide to get rid, I'll drive you to the clinic myself. But that would be your decision and I'm not having it taken away from you. Understand?'

Crystal nodded. 'So, where are you going?'

'I'm going to find out exactly who was in that flat.' Liberty pulled out her phone. 'And I'm going to find out why Paul Hill isn't taking my calls.'

There were still police outside Mad Brian's block. Two of them stopped anyone who entered to ask a few questions.

Tia sniffed. 'As if they'll get anything from anyone round here.'

'Will we?' Liberty asked.

'Brought a few bits and bobs that might help matters along,' said Tia, and pulled out the waistband of her joggers. Underneath she was wearing two pairs of pants and, wedged between them, numerous baggies of powder and pills, plus at least five hundred quid in used tenners.

'Where did you get those?'

'From your Crystal.' Liberty laughed. 'And if they don't work there's always this.' Tia lifted her jacket and showed Liberty the handle of a gun.

They entered the Spar across the street and filled a wire basket with crisps and sweets. Liberty smiled when Tia dropped in a Kinder Egg. At the till the assistant, a chunky lad with hair in cornrows, scanned them all.

'Eight sixty-three, love,' he said, and Liberty handed him two tens. He handed one back. 'Too much there.'

'No, it's fine,' Liberty replied. 'Just wondering, though, if you saw what went on over at the flats.'

The lad looked at the dirty ten-pound note, dithered for a second, then closed his hand. 'Some bloke got shot.'

'Christ,' said Tia. 'That was on the news. She's not giving you an Ayrton for that.'

'Did you see anyone come out?' Liberty asked. 'Right after?'

'A lot of kids,' said the lad.

'What about a bloke?' Tia chirped in. 'Slicked-back hair, beard.'

'Maybe,' said the lad.

'Oi, she ain't handing out tenners for "maybe",' said Tia.

'Yeah, there was a bloke,' he said. 'Got into a big car.'

'What sort?'

The lad opened his hand to give back the money. 'I don't know.'

Tia went to take the note, but Liberty smacked her hand away. 'Keep it. You've been really helpful.'

After the Spar, Tia marched over to an alley. Halfway along there was a makeshift shelter: a tarpaulin stretched across some wooden pallets. 'Knock-knock.'

'Fuck off,' came a voice from inside.

'It's Tia. I have food if anyone's hungry.'

A flap flew open and a teenage boy smiled at them, nose running in the light of a candle. He frowned at the sight of Liberty. 'What does she want?'

'Your body,' said Tia.

The boy sighed so that his grubby dreads shivered. 'I don't do women.'

'Pretty sure you do whoever pays you enough for a dig,' said Tia.

The boy looked Liberty up and down and bit his lip, then shuffled to one side. 'Fine. But I don't do oral.' Inside the shelter,

Liberty could see the boy's worldly belongings. A stained mattress, a bin bag of clothes, a biscuit tin of needles and pipes. 'And she keeps her fingers out of my arse.'

'Do you think you can manage that?' Tia asked Liberty.

'It'll be hard to resist,' she replied.

Tia crouched in front of the flap. 'Look, she doesn't want to shag you.'

'Thank fuck.' He gave Liberty a weak smile. 'No offence.'

'None taken.'

'Go on, then.' He reached into a second biscuit tin full of dog-ends and sifted through them with his finger. 'What do you need?'

'After the shooting in Mad Brian's, did you see some bloke come tearing out?' Tia asked.

The boy popped a dog-end, with a few millimetres of tobacco left, into his mouth and reached for the candle. He held back his dreads and lit up. 'Black hair and beard?'

'Yeah.'

'He was in a right old mess, staggering all over the shop,' said the boy. 'Holding the back of his head, he was. When he drove off, I thought he'd crash before he got to the end of the road.'

'What car was it?' Tia asked.

The boy blew a mouthful of smoke at Tia, who gave an exaggerated cough. Then she stuck her hand down her pants and pulled out a baggie of brown. The boy's eyes registered want. 'Black Porsche Cayenne,' he said, eyes on the prize.

'Reg plate?'

'Dunno. New, though.'

Liberty nodded that that was enough, and Tia tossed the bag over his head. The boy scrambled to shut the flap.

Rose was certain Greenwood would get in touch. The threat of being arrested was too sharp. But it wouldn't be tonight. She yawned. It was time to call it a day, but what was there at home? A microwave fisherman's pie and a sitcom written by some grumpy men who thought there was nothing funnier than men being grumpy.

Another dance through the statements, and then she'd treat herself to some fish and chips. As she scrolled through the files, she came across the ones that had first given her the idea that county lines might be at play. Aaron Mason, Elijah Hunter, Naz Aktar and what was the girl's name? She read the top details and remembered there was only 'Madison'. The girl had refused to give her surname or address. How, then, had there been a connection with Moss Side social services?

Rose pulled up the custody record. Nothing there to explain it, but something shocked her. The arresting officer was one Joel Redman. Why had he never mentioned that?

Quickly, Rose pulled up the records for the other kids. She scanned the information about Elijah Hunter.

'Motherfucker.' Joel had been one of the officers who'd attended the hospital. She hardly dared open the file for Aktar. At first there was nothing, but then up he popped: Joel Redman had taken the statements of some witnesses on the estate. 'Motherfucker.'

Rose slammed down the mouse. Redman had been involved in three of the cases. How had she missed that? More importantly, why hadn't he mentioned his involvement? And why had he not made the connection to county lines? Sure, he wasn't the deadliest weapon in the arsenal, but he must have realised what was going on. Or, at the very least, suspected it.

Rose thought back to her time with Redman. He'd been difficult towards her from the get-go. Then he'd thawed when Rose had pressed him to look into Mason's murder.

The drive across to Redman's flat almost killed Rose and she banged the steering wheel at her own stupidity. Joel Redman, the idiot who showed off his ankles like they were a fashion statement, had played her. She'd been so busy playing Salty, Carmen and the big prize, Greenwood, she hadn't noticed that *she* was being played.

When she reached the flat, she turned off the engine and forced herself to calm down. Redman would have to admit he knew about county lines, but he'd react badly if she went in too strongly, of that she was certain. No one took an accusation of corruption lying down.

She reached into the glove compartment and rummaged around the items inside until she found the miniature bottle of Johnnie Walker she'd pocketed on a business-class flight to Prague. She uncapped it and poured it into her mouth. As the alcohol swept away some of her bad mood, she smiled and stepped out of her car, but before she could walk over to Redman's flat, another vehicle pulled up outside.

Rose jumped back into hers and watched. The driver was a big man, all neck rolls and crew cut. The passenger was older, with white hair and a lived-in face. Rose recognised him but couldn't place him. They hadn't met, she was clear on that, but she'd seen the face. As he made his way over to Redman's door, shrugging on a leather jacket, Rose racked her brains but still couldn't work out who he was.

Back at the station, she pulled up as many files as she could on the drug-dealers in the area. Anyone and everyone arrested on the estates. At last she found a picture of the man staring out at her. Not an arrest record, but a profile in the file of those who ran the area. There were the Greenwoods, gorgeous peas in a pod, and there was the next man along. Paul Hill.

Liberty and Tia sat on the sofa on the scrubland eating the haul from the Spar. Tia had a family bag of Maltesers open in her lap. She threw one into the air and snatched it with her teeth.

Liberty laughed. 'Jay does that all the time.'

'What's he like?'

'Who – Jay?' Liberty asked. 'He's the funny one.'

'What about Crystal?'

Liberty took a Malteser. 'She's the pretty one. I'm the clever one and Frankie . . .' Liberty's voice caught '. . . Frankie's the baby.'

Tia frowned. 'You know I don't really hate him.'

'Yeah, you do.'

'Okay, I do,' said Tia. 'But only because he's a twat to me. It's not like I'm happy this happened to him.' Liberty gave Tia a sideways glance that said she wasn't convinced. 'I'm not. For one thing, he's your brother and you've been good to me.'

'Me? What have I done?'

'You tried to help Dax,' said Tia.

Liberty had met Dax in London while he was moving drugs for a local gang. She'd brought him with her to Yorkshire, given him somewhere to live. She'd hoped to give him a second chance in life, but it had been impossible to keep him out of trouble.

'And you've tried to keep an eye out for me since he passed,' Tia added.

Liberty pointed to Tia's injured face. 'Haven't done a great job, though.'

'Things don't always go the way we planned. That's no one's fault. It's the intention that matters.'

Liberty didn't believe that. Cemeteries were littered with good intentions. The only things that mattered were results. 'Do you miss him?' Liberty asked.

'I get sad when I think about him,' Tia replied, 'so I don't think about him.'

'I'm freezing.' Liberty got up. 'Let's go.'

Tia shook her head and pointed to someone shuffling towards them. 'Here they come.' She pulled her waistband to check the bags of drugs.

'How will this help us?' Liberty asked.

'Seriously?' Tia let the elastic snap back. 'How many Porsche Cayennes do you think there are round here?' Liberty glanced about. The only vehicles were white vans and battered two-door jobs. 'Exactly. And one of our friendly zombies is bound to have spotted it.'

At least twenty motorbikes were parked up outside Scottish Tony's. And not cheap Honda crap. These were the real deal. Sol counted at least fifteen Harleys.

Inside, the bike owners filled the tables, all leather jackets and long beards. Sol found Hutch next to the counter. 'I didn't realise there were so many members in ZZ Top,' said Hutch. Sol tried to smile but failed. 'Look, I'm sorry about Frankie. I know he's family,' he added.

Sol tried to attract Tony's attention, but he was shovelling chips into a hundred hairy mouths. 'Frankie's not family.'

Hutch pushed across a plate with a half-eaten pie sitting in the middle. 'What does Mads know?'

'Caleb was the shooter.' Sol picked up the pie in his fingers and took a bite. Chicken and mushroom. Not bad. 'He suffered a blow to the head, so the chances are he's still in the ends.'

A working girl from Carter Street stuck her head into the café and the bikers shouted and whistled as one. She laughed and gave them a good-natured finger. Someone played a track on their phone and a few bikers banged on a table. The girl rubbed her fingers and thumb together in the universal sign for money. Four tenners were banged down and she took the huge pink ham of the forearm of one and climbed onto a chair, then the table. He spoke to her in German. She giggled that she didn't understand. He handed her a twenty and she understood that.

'Is Mads looking for Clarke?' Hutch shouted, above the noise.

215

'I've told her to get in touch as soon as she knows where he is,' Sol replied.

'The kid must be in a state,' said Hutch.

Sol finished the pie. 'She's fine.'

The café erupted as the girl whipped off her top to reveal a shabby greying bra to the sound of Nena's 'Ninety-nine Red Balloons'.

Just as Tia had predicted, several buyers confirmed sightings of a black Porsche Cayenne in the area and that it was now parked up on the estate.

'I tried the doors,' one addict, with a yellow beehive straight from 1963, told Liberty. 'Because I'm thinking a car like that must have something inside worth nicking.'

They found it easily enough outside a derelict house, the downstairs windows smashed, the door covered with gang tags. Tia reached around to the back of her waistband and pulled out her gun, but Liberty pushed it down into the girl's lap. 'Easy cowboy. We're not going in there like Al Capone.'

'Who?'

Liberty rolled her eyes. 'We need to work out who's inside there first. For one thing we know Clarke's armed.' Liberty held out her hand. 'Have you got a knife?'

Tia fished among the drugs and money, pulled out a flick knife and slapped it into Liberty's open palm. Liberty looked down at it and smiled. She slipped from the car, one eye on the house, and crept to the Porsche. Then she stabbed the back right-hand tyre with the blade. It went in more easily than she'd expected, and she heard the pleasing hiss of air. Silently, she moved around all four tyres. Caleb Clarke wouldn't be leaving in a hurry.

'You've done that before,' said Tia, when she got back.

'Shut up.'

216

'Where's your brand loyalty?' Tia asked.

'What are you talking about?'

'You've a Porsche.'

'Mine's a nine eleven. A classic,' said Liberty. 'That piece of shit is a four-by-four invented for people with money but no taste.'

Tia chortled and reclined her seat. 'No one could ever accuse you of having no taste.'

'You know I grew up on this estate,' said Liberty. 'We didn't have a pot to piss in.'

'If you love that car so much, why did we come in Frankie's?'

Liberty stroked the steering wheel of her little brother's Merc. 'Boot space.'

Before Tia could reply, someone came out of the house. A girl they both recognised.

'Oh, man.' Tia sat bolt upright. 'You should have let me kill that low-life when I had the chance.'

It was Mads. 'Can you follow her without chopping her head off?' Liberty asked. 'I mean it. I want to know where she goes.'

Tia rolled her head from side to side and got out of the car. She leaned back in and made two fingers into the shape of a gun, put it to her temple, mimed blowing her brains out.

'Don't let her see you,' said Liberty, as Tia slammed the passenger door.

Chapter 18

21 September 1990

Mr Simms hands the Mansfield Park *essays back to everyone except me. 'Can I see you after class?' he asks.*

Shit. I was so stressed out when I finished it last Sunday that I must have done a crap job of it. I should have asked Mr Simms for a bit of extra time, but I didn't want to make a bad first impression. That hasn't exactly worked out, has it?

When everyone's left, I stand at his desk, but he's already pointing for me to pull up a chair. This is going to be a right talking-to. I can feel it.

'Any news on Kitty?' he asks.

I don't know how much he's been told but I'm assuming Rochelle hasn't filled him in on the truth. 'I think she's still poorly.'

'No doubt her essay, when it finally arrives, will be worth the wait, eh?'

I decide it'll be best to dive straight in. 'Sorry about mine. I'll redo it.'

Mr Simms scratches his head. 'Redo it?'

'Yeah. I can do better.'

He opens a brown cardboard file on his desk and pulls it out. There are red scribbles all over it. I lean over to take it, but Mr Simms keeps his hand on top of it. 'What do you think was wrong with it?'

Well, I can't say for certain if he won't let me have a look at it, can I? 'The bits about who the daughters married. I think I went off on one a bit.'

'I'll say.'

'Sorry.'

He laughs and finally gives me my essay. 'I'm going to be honest, Lib, I don't think I've ever given that grade at the very start of the course.' I check it. 'The first essay is about helping students with the jump to A-level standard. But this essay . . .' he taps the letter A that he's circled '. . . is frankly brilliant.' I know I've always been good at school work, especially English. I enjoy finding all the patterns and connections. 'Are you having any thoughts about university?'

'I want to go if I can.'

'I meant have you had any thoughts about where you might apply?' he asks.

'I need to go somewhere that will look good when I apply for a job,' I tell him.

'Right then,' he says. 'How does Oxford sound?'

I'm still smiling to myself when I get to work and tell Rob about it.

'You're a chuffing genius, Lib,' he says. 'Haven't I always told you that?' He kisses my head. 'I'll miss you, mind.'

'It's not for another two years,' I say. 'A lot can go wrong in that time.'

The warm-up singer finishes and Rob's set's about to start so he cracks his knuckles and selects his first track. He hasn't even laid it down yet, and people are flocking to the dance floor. 'When you're rich, can we at least buy a bed?'

He goes for a big Chicago house number. 'Move Your Body'. And the roof goes off.

Half an hour later, with sweat raining down from the ceiling, I feel a hand grab my arm. When I turn, I find Matt looking right into my face, as close as he tells Tobias off for. He drags me through the throng of dancers to the door.

'Oi, mate,' Red shouts. 'What the fuck do you think you're doing?'

'It's all right, Red,' I say, and lead Matt to the skip.

He smells of beer and his T-shirt has got a stain down the front. 'You lied.'

'About what?'

219

'About Kitty and the drugs.' He leans against the skip, panting. 'Your brother gave her the smack.'

'Is that what she says?'

Matt shakes his head, sticky hair in ringlets. 'She didn't need to say anything. You might think I'm stupid, but I'm not.'

Present Day

Tinkly laughter filtered from the chief's office, setting Rose's teeth on edge. She'd been waiting fifteen minutes already.

At last, the visitor left the room, a smile still cemented to her mouth. Rose knocked and entered with a scowl attached to her face that she couldn't shift.

'I'm leaving,' said the chief, who was on his feet, packing away papers in a leather briefcase.

'It's urgent, sir,' said Rose.

'Put it in an email.'

'I think I should tell you this in person, sir.' She didn't wait for him to argue further. 'It's come to my attention that Officer Redman is working for Paul Hill.' The chief didn't react. 'I went to see Redman earlier and Hill arrived at his flat.'

There were three elastic loops attached to the lining of the case and the chief slid a fountain pen into each one so that their silver lids lined up. 'Perhaps they know one another.'

'Paul Hill is involved in organised crime, sir,' said Rose. 'A police officer should not be taking visits.'

The chief pushed the metal clasp together and smiled at the pleasing clunk it made. Then he picked it up. 'Why are you doing all this, Angel?'

'Sir?'

'I agreed to take you at this station because you had obviously been through the mill.' The chief put out his hand to open the door. 'And I am a great believer in second chances. But since your arrival you have brought nothing but problems.' Rose was gob-smacked. She'd worked hard ever since she'd arrived in Yorkshire. 'The team complained about your attitude, but I asked them to cut you some slack.'

Rose jutted out her chin. 'The team were antagonistic towards me from the off, especially Redman, and I now understand—'

'Joel Redman was the only person willing to work with you, DI Angel.'

'He wanted to keep tabs on my investigations, sir, so he could protect his position with Hill.'

The chief glared at her. 'Joel has been working these streets for years. He grew up on the Peabody estate.' He walked through the door, back rigid. 'You have caused chaos locally and good police will have to deal with it.' He stalked down the corridor, calling over his shoulder, 'Pack your belongings. You're suspended until further notice.'

'That's not fair. I'm just trying to do my job.'

'Call your union representative,' said the chief, and disappeared down the stairs.

Liberty kept one eye on the derelict house while she tried Hill's mobile once more. Still no reply. He must know by now that Frankie had been shot so why wasn't he taking her calls? Something about that was setting off all her spider senses.

The passenger door opened, and Tia jumped inside with a rush of cold air, then stared at her hands, folded in her lap.

'Spit it out,' said Liberty.

'You're not going to be happy,' Tia replied.

'Someone's trying to grab my family's business and they've just shot my brother,' said Liberty. 'Happy's not on the agenda today.' Tia gave Liberty a quick glance. 'Don't mess me about, Tia. Where did Mads go?'

'She met up with Sol.'

Liberty's eyes opened wide. 'Sol?'

'The bloke you live with.'

'Yes, I know who Sol is, but why would Mads meet him?' Liberty asked. 'Are you sure it was him?'

Tia bobbed her head that she was indeed sure. But what the hell did that mean? How on earth did Sol even know Mads? Liberty's brain hurt with it all so she bent forward and let her cheek rest on the steering wheel.

'What do you want to do?' Tia asked.

Liberty laughed. She wanted to rewind a couple of years. No, twenty-five years. She wanted to live her life again and make different choices that would lead to a different version of tonight. A scene where all her siblings were around a table listening to Jay's shit jokes, Frankie creasing up at her side.

Liberty straightened. 'I want to go inside that house and explain to everyone involved that they've picked the wrong place to try to set up shop.'

Tia reached behind her seat and grabbed the baseball bat. 'I'm ready.' The end was already stained with blood.

'How many do we think are in there?' asked Liberty.

'There's no way of knowing that,' said Tia.

Liberty pulled out her phone. 'Well, there's someone we can ask.'

'I don't think you should trust him,' said Tia. 'We've got no idea what's going on with him and Mads. For all we know, he's in with this lot from Moss Side.'

Liberty considered. She didn't trust many people. Paul Hill, she wouldn't trust as far as she could throw him. But Sol? Was it possible he was working against her? She tapped the call button.

'Lib?'

'I know you're with Mads and I need you to ask her something.' There was a pause in which she could hear Sol's ragged breathing.

'How many people are in the house with Clarke? Can you ask her that, please?'

Liberty heard muffled voices. Then Sol came back on the line. 'There's Caleb Clarke and one younger. But they're both armed.'

'Thanks.'

'Lib, listen to me.' Sol's voice dropped to almost a whisper. 'Do not go in there. He's already shot Frankie and he won't think twice about shooting you.'

'He won't get the chance.'

'Plus, there's a whole—'

Liberty hung up. She inhaled a deep breath and took the bat from Tia. 'There's Clarke and one more. Both packing.'

Tia pulled out her gun. 'Clarke's already half dead.'

'Don't assume anything.'

They got out of the car and checked up and down the street. Fortunately, the wind was howling so no one was around. Headlights approached so they waited for the car to pass, then moved silently to the gate. Liberty pointed that they should sneak around the back and Tia gave the okay signal.

'I wouldn't do that if I were you.'

Liberty froze at the sound of Angel's voice.

Rose's eyes slid down the length of the bat to the stain at the thick end. She peered at the fragments of skin embedded in the wood.

'A word?' she asked Greenwood. 'In private.'

Greenwood fished out car keys from her jacket pocket. It was a thick Puffa with a fur-lined hood, lots of silver buttons. Rose's stepfather would have called it 'classy' and Rose could see that it was. The sort of coat she imagined Italian women would wear in December as they sashayed across the cobbled streets of Rome. She never bought clothes like that. Not that she didn't like them, but when she went shopping, which she avoided unless necessary, she always homed in on the functional. Waterproof coats for autumn. Thick boots for winter. She had five jumpers lined up in her wardrobe for work, all ordered from the same brochure.

Greenwood tossed the keys to Rainsford and gestured that the younger should get into the car. Rainsford tucked something into the back of her trousers, presumably a weapon, and did as she was told. Greenwood moved into the shadows, where she could keep an eye on the house she'd been about to enter, without being seen herself.

'Redman and Paul Hill are tucked up in bed together,' said Rose.

'Their sex lives are no concern of mine.'

Rose gave a tight laugh. 'I want to take them both down.'

Greenwood put up her hood against the cold and it framed her face perfectly, the grey fur a gorgeous halo. Rose flipped up her own hood, but it was nylon and kept blowing back until she pulled the toggle tight under her chin.

'Whatever's going on in there,' Rose pointed to the house, 'is not my business. You can sort out these county lines in whatever way you see fit. Frankly, you'd be doing everyone around here a favour.' Greenwood watched the house. 'I just want Redman and Hill.'

'You'll need to catch them red-handed,' said Greenwood.

'Which is why I'm here,' Rose replied. 'I don't have access to the things I'll need to find on them.'

Greenwood laughed, showing off great teeth. 'You mean drugs?'

'And money. Dirty as you like.' The downstairs windows of the house were shattered, but there was a light burning upstairs. Someone was definitely at home, and Greenwood's body language told Rose she was straining to get inside. 'And, of course, Hill's territory will be yours for the taking.'

'I never wanted his patch.'

'Might as well have it,' said Rose. 'Make everything neat and tidy.'

Greenwood moved the bat from one hand to the other, banged it against her leg. 'If I do this for you, we're even.'

Rose had anticipated this. It was a shame to let Greenwood off the hook, but she knew that, however this ended, she would have to move on. She didn't mind too much: she'd had plenty of practice and, if she was honest, this place was bloody terrible. 'Agreed,' said Rose, and walked away.

'Do you ever get sick of using people?' Greenwood called after her.

Rose pointed to the car. 'You're dragging a sixteen-year-old with you to take out the competition and you want to lecture me?'

Sol drove like a demon through the Crosshills. 'Up here?' he barked at Mads. She bounced around in her seat as he took a corner at forty, the wheels screeching. 'Answer me.'

Mads looked out of the window, blinking. 'It's pitch-black, Sol, and I'm not even from round here.'

A Citroën C1 pulled out ahead, a green P plate flapping on the bumper, barely held in place by string and Sellotape. The driver bunny-hopped as he ground through the gears. Sol hit his horn.

'You were just there,' he shouted. 'How far from here is it?' Mads shook her head, tears spilling down her cheeks. She was terrified, but Sol couldn't worry about her feelings right now. 'Was there anything unusual about it?'

'Like what?'

'I don't know! Just something you noticed so I can find it.'

'It's a house, on an estate.' Mads sobbed now, shoulders shuddering. 'The windows were smashed in.'

As they came to a crossroads, the Citroën stalled, red brake-lights flashing into the night. Sol roared in frustration and overtook the little car, clipping the wing mirror with a bang that made Mads scream. 'I want to get out,' she shouted, snot coursing down her mouth. 'Let me out.'

Sol hit central locking. 'As soon as we find Liberty.'

Liberty watched Angel walk away and pulled out her phone. It made sense to bring Hill down and get Angel off her back at the same time. Her first port of call for a job like this would have been Frankie, of course. Her chest tightened at that thought. Crystal hadn't been in touch, which must mean he was still in theatre. Her next instinct was to call on Crystal, who had no love for Hill or the police, but she decided against that. Right now, Crystal needed protecting from everything, including herself. Her finger hovered over Jay's name in her contacts. He'd know exactly what to do, but if it went tits up, he was the one with a record as long as his arm.

She called Mel.

'Everything okay?' Mel asked, the music in the Black Cherry deafening.

'I need your help, Mel.'

'You've got it.'

'You don't know what I want yet,' said Liberty.

'Doesn't matter.' In the background Liberty heard breaking glass. 'Hold up, Lib.' There was the distinct and recognisable sound of someone getting an ear-bashing. 'Right. Tell me the story.'

Liberty told Mel what Rose had proposed and Mel simply listened. 'You'll need to get Redman and Hill together with the gear, then let Angel know,' said Liberty.

'Fine,' Mel replied. 'Just so we're clear this is the first and last time I will ever be a grass.'

'Amen.'

With Mel taking care of the Angel side of things, Liberty rapped on Tia's window and the pair of them crossed the road, in step.

'You don't have to do this,' Liberty said. 'If you'd rather not.'

Regardless of what Angel had said, she didn't feel guilty about using people, but she accepted that this was probably not the wisest idea she'd ever had. There were two men inside, both with guns, and she'd seen what a mess a bullet could make.

Tia pulled out her own weapon and nodded at the house. When they reached the gate for the second time, Liberty put a finger to her lips, and they crept around the side of the house to the back. The garden was overgrown and there was a kennel on a small patio. A discarded dog bowl was full of rainwater and brown leaves.

Silently, Liberty tried the door. Locked. A couple of panes of glass were broken. Tia unwound her scarf, tied it around her hand and pushed the glass through. There was a tinkle as it hit the floor inside and both women waited. When it was clear that the noise hadn't alerted anyone, Tia stuck her hand through the now empty panel and unlocked the door.

Liberty stepped inside what had been the kitchen. The white goods had long since gone and even the work surfaces had been ripped out so that she could see into the top drawers. Most were empty, apart from the odd battery and leaflet for pizza delivery. Black damp spores covered the walls and a thick layer of green-blue mould was thriving in the sink.

Tia followed Liberty into the house, trainers crunching the shards of glass. Liberty threw her a glare and the kid mouthed, 'Sorry.' When she saw the mould in the sink, she gave a silent gag.

227

They inched through the kitchen to the room beyond and bare floorboards creaked. There was no furniture, apart from an old leather sofa, peeling strips of gaffer tape failing to cover gaping holes.

A noise from above made them whip up their heads and check the ceiling. Footsteps upstairs. Liberty gulped and gripped the handle of her bat with both hands. Tia held her gun at chest height, eyes following the progress of whoever was above them. Liberty slid to the doorway that led to the stairs, stood to the right-hand side, bat ready above her head. Tia took her place on the left and pressed herself into the wall.

Blood banged in Liberty's ears as they waited in the darkness.

When nothing happened, Tia opened her arms in a what-now gesture, but Liberty put up her hand that they should wait. Despite the cold, a bead of sweat trickled down the back of her neck.

At last they heard feet coming down the stairs. Thud, thud, thud, thud. Moving towards them. It would be seconds before their owner entered the room. Liberty planted hers apart, ready and waiting.

He walked through the doorway and Liberty immediately saw it was the younger. Seventeen or eighteen. At least six foot, lanky as Jay had been at that age. He saw Liberty first, eyes wide at the bat. 'What the actual—'

Tia pressed the barrel of her gun against the back of his head and hissed, 'Shut up.'

Chapter 19

21 September 1990

I've got my back to the skip outside the club, my feet paddling about in what look like carrot peelings. Matt's still right up in my face, sweat pouring off him. I nod to Red that I'm not in any trouble and he keeps his distance.

'You can't prove owt,' I tell Matt. 'If Kitty hasn't said our Jay gave her the gear, then how are you going to prove it?'

'I don't need to,' he says. 'I can call the police anytime and they'll find him and his mates wandering around in there with pockets full of drugs and money.'

I laugh at him. 'Do you think the police don't already know what goes on in there? Do you think they give a shit?'

'And what about you? Your brother is a dealer. Do you give a shit?' I can't believe he's asked me that. I mean, does he think I don't even care? 'How does it make you feel, Lib?'

I'm shaking hard. 'How does it make me feel? It makes me terrified, Matt. Absolutely terrified. And do you know what else? It makes me angry.' I push him in the chest. 'It makes me fucking angry that there's people like you and Kitty and Tobias with everything. A mansion with a pool – that no one can be arsed to even use, by the way – and your own rooms and cars and the whole lot handed to you on a plate with lashings of frigging coleslaw.' I push him again and he staggers backwards. 'And then there's Jay who's got nothing. No mam or dad, nowhere to live, no money. All he's got is me and I'm not enough.'

Red comes over.

'I'm fine,' I spit at him. 'He might be a dick, but he won't hurt me.'

'He might not,' says Red, and turns towards a massive gang of lads striding down the street towards the club.

It's the Cheetham Hill lot. Tooled up to the back teeth, like an army on the move.

I race inside to find our Jay, but I can't find him anywhere. At last I spot Sean at the bar, chatting up Steph. 'Where's my brother?'

'Bogs, I think.'

I dive into the Gents and three lads in a row at the urinals turn to me. 'All right, Lib?'

'Cheetham Hill are here.'

They stop mid-flow and run out, doing up their flies as they go. Another lad jumps out of the cubicle. But no sign of Jay.

I cross to the Ladies, shouting, 'Jay, are you in here?'

There's a lass at the sink, filling empty plastic bottles from the tap. Christ, it's no wonder Steph's never busy.

The locks are always broken so I push open the first door and the girl on the pot just waves at me. I kick the next door and find our Jay, his tongue down some lass's throat and her hand down the front of his jeans. 'We've gotta go,' I tell him, and drag him out.

'What the fuck are you talking about?'

'The Cheetham Hill lot are here and it's all about to kick off,' I say. 'We'll get out through the fire escape at the back.'

'Lib, I can't—'

A bottle flies through the air and hits the girl at the sink. She slumps, blood everywhere. Jay pushes me into the cubicle with the lass he was necking seconds before. 'Stay here.'

'Jay, you're not going out there.'

He shuts the door. 'I said stay here.'

Present Day

Rose received a call from an unknown number. 'Yes.'

'Tell me Redman's address,' said a woman's voice that she didn't recognise.

'Thirty-three St Stephen's Street.'

'Meet me there in ten minutes,' said the woman.

'Hill's got a goon in his car,' said Rose.

'Then we'll have to deal with it.'

Rose was about to ask how, but the woman had already hung up. She dropped her mobile onto the passenger seat and took a deep breath. Was she doing the right thing? Or did the others have the measure of her? A game player and user?

She popped the boot of her car and got out to collect her baton, pepper spray and Kevlar vest. She pulled off her waterproof and pulled on the stab vest. It was heavy, like strapping five kilos of sugar to her body, and it smelt like a pair of old trainers that saw the treadmill regularly but never the washing machine. Her jacket barely fitted over it, the zip straining at the seams, but there was no way she was tackling Hill and Redman without it.

She grabbed the baton and pepper spray and threw them into the car next to her phone. No more time for questioning herself.

'Let's do this,' she said, and drove away in the direction of Redman's place.

The younger didn't move, caught between Liberty in front of him, bat held aloft, and Tia behind, a pistol pressed into the back of his skull. His eyes locked on Liberty's as Tia passed her free hand around his waistband. She found what she was looking for and held it up for Liberty to see. What looked like a starting pistol, modified for street use. Liberty took it from Tia and wedged it at the base of her spine between jeans and belt.

A bang came from upstairs and all three looked to the ceiling.

231

Liberty reached over to the younger and put a finger on his lips, then pointed back to the kitchen, the thick end of the bat still inches from the top of his skull. 'Move,' she whispered.

He turned slowly and Tia went with him in an intricate dance, gun still at his head, a handful of his hoodie in her other fist in case he tried to leg it. They crunched through the fragments of glass in the kitchen to the back garden and moved as one around the side of the house.

When they reached Frankie's car, Liberty opened the boot and reached in for a roll of silver gaffer tape. She needed both hands for what she was about to do so let go of the bat. The younger's eyes fell on it.

'Don't think about it,' Liberty told him. 'We both know she'll blow your head off before you even get your fingers to it.'

'Truth,' said Tia, and pushed the gun even harder into the younger's scalp so that he had to bend forward.

Liberty pulled out a six-inch length of tape and used her teeth to separate it from the roll. She held it by each end and smoothed it across the younger's mouth. He inhaled heavily and quickly through his nose.

'Don't panic,' Liberty said. 'Keep your breathing calm and you'll be fine.'

She pressed her wrists together to show him what to do next, then wrapped tape around them several times, before biting the end. From experience she knew that this hurt, but with any luck they could let the kid go soon enough.

The boy's nostrils flared as he tried to regulate his breathing and Liberty nodded in encouragement. 'Now,' she said, 'get in the boot.' The younger shifted back instinctively but the gun at his head stopped him going more than a few inches. 'In.'

He shook his head wildly, tried to speak around the tape but gagged, eyes wide in fear.

'For fuck's sake, get in,' hissed Tia, 'because, let me tell you,

I'm not interested in keeping you safe. That's her idea.' She jabbed
the gun, making him wince. 'I really don't mind offing you right
here and now.'

Liberty picked up the bat and prodded the lad in the stomach.
'Quick as you can.' Tears welled in his eyes. 'Try not to cry. It'll
just block up your nose.'

Tia leaned in to his ear. 'Which will mean you can't breathe,
fool.'

The younger sniffed in an attempt to quell his tears and Liberty
patted the bottom of the boot with her bat. He took a step forward
and stooped, his head under the boot lid.

'That's right,' said Liberty, and pushed down on his back.

He dropped his head as far as he could, belly touching the
metal, right knee bent and raised, so that he was half in and half
out. He grunted as he tried to shuffle in.

'It would have been much quicker if you'd just let me kill him,'
said Tia.

Liberty rolled her eyes and helped him with the other leg. Then
she rolled him on his side, so that he wouldn't choke if he threw
up. Hopefully. She stooped so that he could look into her face. He
was petrified, of course, the fear lashing off him like sweat.

'I'm going to do your feet then shut you in,' said Liberty, one
hand on top of the boot lid.

The younger rolled his head from side to side and shouted.
Even with the tape it was clear he was saying, 'No.' The tape had
done a number on Liberty, like Sellotape at Christmas, and she
had to pick at the end with her nail. At last she managed to free
it and went to wind it around the lad's feet, but he shocked her
by kicking out. The smack of his trainer in her mouth sent her
reeling and she landed on her arse in the road.

Tia roared and Liberty scrambled to get up, fingernails scraping
against the wet tarmac. The pain in her mouth was white-hot
and she could taste blood, but she needed to get back to the boot

before Tia killed him. 'Tia,' she warned, through lips that felt twice their size. 'Don't.'

In one leap she reached the car. Tia had the younger by the hair, head dragged backwards, gun under his chin.

'Do. Not. Kill. Him.'

Tia's shoulders heaved but she didn't pull the trigger. Liberty nodded at her and yanked off the boy's trainers, threw them to the back of the boot. Then she wound tape around his bare ankles, blood from her mouth dripping onto his jogging bottoms. There was no way she could bite the tape, so she left the roll attached to him and stood back.

Tia kept the gun under the younger's chin for a second and slammed the lid shut. 'You okay?' she asked.

Liberty pulled her hand from her mouth, checked the blood in the palm. She ran her tongue around her teeth. Nothing broken.

Tia peered at her lips. 'I think you need a stitch in that.'

Sol swung the car into a street where every other house was unoccupied. 'Is this it?'

'I think so,' Mads replied.

'Which one?'

Mads checked out the houses, with their boarded windows and graffitied doors. 'I'm not sure.'

Sol passed a black Mercedes and slammed on his brakes. Mads shot forward like a rag doll and screamed. Sol ignored her and jammed the car into reverse, barrelling backwards until he was parallel with the Mercedes. He was almost certain it was Frankie's car, and since Frankie was otherwise engaged, it must mean Liberty was there.

He shot the car to the kerb, hitting it hard, and jumped out. Mads stumbled from the passenger side and took her chance to run away. Sol didn't try to stop her, too intent on checking Frankie's car. No one in the front or back. He scanned the houses. Which one would it be? Not one on the same side of the road as the car. Liberty was too smart to park outside. She'd score a space close enough but on the opposite side where she could do a recce undetected.

He checked out the two houses directly to his right, both derelict. He'd take bets that the one he wanted was either of them. Both looked unfit for human habitation, yet flickering candlelight told him humans were holed up in both.

There was nothing he could do but check them in turn, choosing order at random. An eeny-meeny moment he could have done without. He stepped into the road and heard a sound, like a muffled shout followed by a bang. He turned and saw Frankie's car rock. He looked in the windows again, but the car was definitely empty. This time the noises were louder and the rocking more insistent. He stared at the boot. No. Fucking. Way.

The woman Rose met near Redman's house was not what she'd been expecting. At least sixty, in an outfit her stepfather would have called 'cheap and nasty', she introduced herself as Mel and threw a nylon holdall at Rose's feet.

Rose unzipped it and checked the contents. Around a kilo of heroin, three thousand pounds in used notes and a knife.

'Will that do you?' Mel asked.

Rose zipped the bag and nodded. 'What about the muscle in the car?'

'Let's put him out of his misery.'

'I'm not killing anyone,' Rose protested.

Mel curled her lip and pulled out a Taser gun from her purple fun-fur coat. 'He's just going to have a little kip.' Was it possible that this tiny woman, with more wrinkles than an apple at

Christmas, was going to Taser someone? 'Let's crack on, love. Paul Hill isn't going to be in there all night.'

She tottered towards the car and knocked on the driver's window. It lowered slowly in an electric whir, revealing Hill's right-hand man. Ed Sheeran spilled from the speakers.

'He's got a nice voice,' said Mel, 'but it does my head in when he raps.'

'Mel?' said the man.

She smiled at him, all yellow teeth, and reached into the car. There was a sizzle, a gurgle, and the man slumped onto the steering wheel.

'Help me move him,' said Mel.

'Where?'

Mel looked around and pointed at a bus stop a hundred feet away. 'We'll stick him behind that.' She opened the Range Rover door, pulled the man's arm and let gravity do the rest. He landed on the pavement with a sickening thump. She grabbed a foot. 'Well, don't just stand there, princess.'

Rose grasped the other foot, shin huge and hairy where his trousers rode up. Redman had hairy ankles, she remembered. Was it a thing on men that she'd never noticed? Together they dragged him down the pavement, his head bumping and banging on every crack and crevice.

They were both out of breath by the time they'd hauled his carcass the short distance to the bus shelter.

'He'll wake up soon, so let's get this done,' said Mel. They tried to push him behind, but he was too big, and his shoulders got wedged between the shelter and the wall behind it. 'Hold up.' Mel dropped his foot and strutted to the other end of the shelter, squeezed behind it and grabbed his head. She pulled with all her might and Rose pushed but he was still half in, half out.

Someone wandered up the street towards them, so Rose stood in front of the pair of fat legs on the ground.

'All right, Rose?' said Salty.

'Fine.'

He stared at the legs for a long moment, and said, 'Need a hand?'

Between the three of them they managed to stuff most of the man out of sight. His feet still poked out, so Mel took off his shoes and covered his socked feet with leaves and rubbish.

'Here.' She handed Salty the shoes. 'Now fuck off.'

'I think it's worth a twenty at least,' he said to Rose.

'I haven't got any money on me.'

Salty scowled. 'You scratch my back and I'll scratch yours.'

The man behind the bus shelter opened his eyes and moaned.

'Chuffing hell,' Mel shouted, and gave him another blast of the Taser, then turned to Salty. 'I'll scratch your back with this, sunshine, if you don't do one.' He didn't need asking twice. 'Junkies. Always worth a bob on.'

They rushed back to Hill's car, popped the boot and threw the holdall inside.

'You got something with the copper's prints on it?' Mel asked. Rose produced a couple of baggies that Redman had confiscated during the operation. She stowed them in the bag. 'The knife's got Hill's prints. And the brown.'

'How?'

'Let's just say some of his people can see which way the wind's blowing and fancy working for the Greenwoods.'

Rose closed the boot. 'Now what?'

'Over to you, love.' Mel handed Rose the Taser and leaned on the horn before scurrying away.

Sol used a screwdriver to open the boot.

No. Fucking. Way.

The young lad looked up at him with terrified eyes, hands

and feet bound, mouth taped, wriggling like a worm on a hook. Sol leaned over and tore the tape from the lad's mouth. He took greedy gulps of air.

'You okay?' Sol asked.

'Help me,' the boy pleaded. Sol reached for the tape on his wrists and began sawing with the screwdriver. Then he stopped. 'Get me out of here,' the boy screeched.

Sol bit his lip. 'Which house are they in?'

'You've got to get me out.'

'I will,' said Sol. 'But I need to know which house.'

'What?'

'Which house is Caleb Clarke in?'

The lad opened and closed his mouth. 'Forty-one.'

'I'll be back.'

'No,' the boy shouted, at the top of his lungs. 'You can't leave me in here.'

Sol pushed the tape back onto the boy's mouth, ignoring his groans. 'Sorry.' He went to shut the boot lid. 'I will come back, I promise.'

Liberty checked the chamber of the younger's gun as she crept through the deserted kitchen. It was loaded. Tia grimaced at the sink for a second time.

They paused at the kitchen door and listened. Nothing. Liberty held up three fingers to Tia and, on the count of three, strode into the sitting room, gun outstretched. Empty. She exhaled and pointed it at the door to the stairs.

Tia slipped past her and tiptoed to the door, waiting to the side, her own gun ready. Liberty joined her and they stood, listening intently. There were two of them now, and Liberty knew Clarke was already injured, but he was a dangerous man. They couldn't underestimate him.

Liberty tapped Tia's hand and pointed a finger to the ceiling. She was going up. Tia patted a hand to her chest, *Me first*, but Liberty shook her head.

She slid her foot along the floorboards and went through the door, gun first. It was as heavy as the bottles of milk Mam used to buy where the cream had always settled at the top. Her arm was already tired. If Clarke appeared at the top of the stairs, she'd be an easy target. She needed to get up to the landing as quietly as was humanly possible.

She scanned above, one last time, and started her ascent.

The first step was solid, and Liberty swallowed in relief. Behind her, Tia took up position, heat radiating from her. Liberty knew Tia would have her gun trained at the top of the stairs. She pressed her toe on the second step, feeling for any movement, but once again she found a rigid piece of wood.

She took step after step like that, squinting into the shadows for any movement at the top, ears pricked for the slightest sound.

At the halfway point, her foot found a loose board, and she knew that any weight on it would give her away. Holding her breath, she stepped over it, grateful for another firm plank.

Almost at the summit, she heard a sound and froze. Then it came again. A low murmur. She risked a look at Tia, who nodded that she'd also caught it. Then a figure, large and dark, moved across the landing, feet grating on wood, and making a guttural noise with each step.

Liberty leaned to her left and flattened herself against the wall with gritted teeth. Tia followed suit. The plaster was cold and damp against the skin of her neck as they waited. At last the noise moved away, then stopped altogether. Tia nudged Liberty and they climbed the final few steps, though kept their backs to the wall, ascending like crabs.

At the top, Liberty surveyed the scene. Narrow landing with mouse droppings. Four doors. All ajar. Beyond the doors, three rooms in blackness, one with the pale-yellow glow of a candle. Surely that must be the one where Clarke was holed up. She lifted her finger as if testing the wind, then pointed it at the door in question.

It was time to do the job.

Chapter 20

21 September 1990

There's a riot on the dance floor. Lads fighting it out with fists and iron bars and bats. One of the Cheetham Hill lot pulls out a machete but Red slams him in the ribs with a fire extinguisher before he can carve anyone up.

I catch sight of our Jay as he knocks out some kid in a Stone Roses top. He's got a right punch on him, I'll give him that. But then another lad jumps off a podium onto his back. Jay spins around trying to get him off, but the lad digs his fingers into his eyes, making Jay howl.

I race to the bar and grab a bottle of Johnnie Walker that's never been opened. Not even when Tony tried a three-doubles-for-a-tenner night. I hold it above my head in both hands and whack the lad on our Jay. First on his shoulder blade, then the base of his spine. He yelps and falls off. As he goes down, I hit him on the head and the bottle breaks.

There's a lot of blood and the lad doesn't move. Jay and I stare at him on the floor.

Then Matt's at my side and he takes the broken bottle from me. 'Move.'

I can hardly breathe as I follow him out of the club. Jay tags along, too shocked to argue, plus his right eye is a mess, all scratched and bleeding. He must be in agony.

Matt throws the bottle into the skip and leads us to his car. When we're inside, he grinds the gears and we're away. No one speaks until he pulls into the hospital car park.

'I'm fine,' says Jay.

'You're not,' Matt replies.

We wait on a row of metal chairs, side by side, while our Jay gets stitched up. A doctor tells us he's lucky not to have lost his sight.

'Here we are again,' says Matt.

I smile into my lap. 'I promise you I'll take him away from here and you'll never see us again.'

'You don't have to do that,' he says. 'I won't tell anyone.'

'It's not just that,' I say. 'I have to keep him safe and I can't do that if he's serving up.'

'Where will you go?'

'Home,' I say. 'They'll have to take him back into care.'

Matt's eyes open wide. 'I've got a feeling he'll never agree to that.'

'He will if I go with him.'

Matt grabs my hand and this time I don't pull away. He kisses my fingers and I let him. Then he gets up to leave. 'If you ever need anything, you know where I am.'

Present Day

Liberty and Tia stood outside the bedroom and waited a final few seconds. Liberty put up three fingers and mouthed the countdown. Three. Two. One.

She kicked open the door, arms outstretched, gun aimed.

The flames of two candles danced as the man on the bed struggled to sit. Even in the gloom, his head wounds were visible. A red gash to the side of his head, ear a pulped jellyfish.

He pointed his gun at Liberty, but Tia was already in the room and his eyes flitted between the two women.

'Drop it,' said Liberty. Clarke smirked. Yellow eyes in the yellow light. 'Drop it now, or we'll both shoot you. And that's gonna sting.'

He weighed up his chances. He might manage to get one, but he'd be dead before he could witness it. He dropped the weapon in the V-shaped space between his legs and Liberty moved to grab it. But before her hands could touch the metal, there was the sound of feet running up the stairs. Surely the kid couldn't have freed himself. Tia turned to the noise and Clarke retrieved his gun. Liberty could do nothing but bat away the gun as he fired. It fell from his hand, but not before a bullet whizzed through the air and hit the person who had just stormed the room.

'Sol!' Liberty screamed, as he slumped to the floor.

It felt as though he'd been hit with the force of a speeding car and crashed onto his back. Liberty's screams filled the air as a sickening heat washed over his shoulder and neck. Then the sound of metal hitting flesh and a groan.

Sol thought his arm must be on fire and tried to lift it, but it was glued to the floor.

'Sol.' Liberty's face was above him but fuzzy around the edges. Like she'd been rubbed with Vaseline. 'Sol, can you speak?'

He tried to lift his arm again and an electric shock ran through the entire side of his body. He shuddered and felt suddenly cold. Tia hovered above him now, unravelling a scarf from her neck. The room began to spin, and Sol closed his eyes.

The next thing he knew, he was outside. Wind and rain whipped around him, but the fire had rekindled as if his shoulder had been plunged into a furnace. Liberty and Tia were still above him, Liberty speaking like a Gatling gun into her phone.

He attempted to orient himself. Legs outstretched in front of him, boots smeared with blood. Hard wet pavement under his arse. Metal at his back. He was sitting on the ground with his back to a car.

A firework went off in his neck as he moved it to look at his arm. A black scarf was tied around his shoulder, the wool threaded under his armpit. His sleeve was completely red.

Tia crouched in front of him. 'You're not dead, then? That's a result.'

'I've been shot,' Sol said.

'Bet you made a fucking great detective.'

He laughed and instantly regretted it. 'What happened to Clarke? Tell me you didn't kill him.'

'We didn't kill him,' she dead-panned.

'Oh, shit.'

Tia winked. 'We didn't. Your missus knocked him out, but he's not dead.' Sol looked up at Liberty, who was still talking frantically. 'She's sorting a doctor for you.'

'Wouldn't it be easier to just take me to hospital?'

'And say what?' Tia pulled out a packet of tobacco and built a rollie. 'We were just dealing with the scumbag who done Frankie when you turned up uninvited.' She popped the roll-up into Sol's mouth and lit it for him. He took a grateful puff. 'What the hell were you doing, Sol?'

Good question. 'I didn't want Lib getting hurt.'

Tia plucked the fag from his lips so he could blow out the smoke. 'Lib had it all under control, don't you worry about that.'

A car pulled up and the passenger window lowered. Mel stared out at Sol, face like nettle juice.

'Cheers for this,' said Liberty.

'Get him in the back, then,' said Mel. 'And don't expect me to help you. The last one nearly gave me a chuffing prolapse.'

Rose filmed the door to Redman's house on her iPhone. Her heart leaped when it opened and Hill stepped out, still speaking to Redman, who stood in his doorway.

When Hill reached his car, he noticed that the driver was missing and checked up and down the road.

'What's up?' Redman asked.

Hill ignored him and pulled out his phone. A moment later, the muffled sound of 'Macarena' escaped.

Redman padded out into the street in his trainer socks. 'Is he not answering?'

Hill nodded at the boot where the chorus was in full swing and reached into the car. He pressed the pressure pad and the boot opened. Chucking the muscle's phone in on top of the gear had been Mel's idea. The woman was a certified genius.

When Redman and Hill went to the boot and peered inside, Rose jumped into action. In a split second, she was at their side, pepper spray in hand.

Hill growled at her, but she just gave him half a can right in the eyes.

As Hill fell to the ground, Redman went to grab Rose, but she nailed him with the second half of the can. With them both on the floor, blind and writhing, she pulled out the cuffs and got them both secured.

'I'm going to rip you, limb from limb,' Hill roared.

Rose patted his head and went for her radio. 'Officer in need of urgent assistance.'

Forty-five minutes later, Rose convinced the custody sarge to let her into Redman's cell. His eyes were still red and watering, and he was on the floor, knees up, so that those hairy ankles were on full display. His socks were wet.

'You set me up,' he said. Rose noticed that someone had scratched the words *Fuck the Police* into the wall. Which was pretty funny in the circumstances, she had to admit. 'You put all that stuff in the boot.'

'And where would I get so much heroin and cash?'

Redman swiped at a tear that coursed down his cheek. 'Liberty Greenwood.'

'Liberty Greenwood the solicitor?'

'Liberty Greenwood the gangster.'

Rose leaned against the door. 'And why would she help me? Not so long ago I had her sent down.'

Redman pulled his sleeve over his hand and wiped his nose, checked the smears of snot on the cuff. 'You're holding the Delaney murder over her. Don't think I won't spill it all.'

'We've got absolutely nothing on her, though, have we, Joel?' Rose said. 'No statement from Garcia. Nothing.' She smiled at him. 'So, save your breath.'

'You're evil.'

'I'm not the one taking backhanders from Paul Hill.'

Redman looked right at her with red-rimmed eyes. 'It was never about the money. Never.'

'Bet you didn't refuse it.'

'Then you lost your bet,' he said. 'When Hill first came to me, I told him where to go.'

Rose crossed her arms. 'What changed?'

'I might have left the Peabody, but my family are all still there.' He lowered his head and pushed his hair flat. Flecks of grey were showing at the roots. 'That RTA with the lorry? That was my uncle who had his head knocked off. The kids in the back were my sister's. Happened two weeks after I turned Hill down.'

'You should have told someone,' said Rose.

He sniffed and she didn't know if it was the spray or if he was crying. 'You're not from round here so you've no idea what you're talking about.'

Jay sipped a bottle of Bud and rapped his hand on top of a box of butt plugs in the back office at the Black Cherry. 'So, Clarke's in the boot of your car?'

'Sol's car,' Liberty replied.

'How the hell did you manage that?' Jay asked.

'I knocked him out and we carried him. The younger's in

mine. Well, Frankie's, actually.' She reached across, grabbed the bottle from her brother and took a gulp. 'I'm fucking knackered.'

'And Sol's been shot?' Jay asked.

'Mel's sorting that.' Liberty passed back the bottle. 'Apparently, Clarke's boss is on his way to show us what's what.'

Jay finished the beer and dropped the empty into his bin. 'That might be his plan, but he hasn't bargained on the Greenwoods.'

Liberty stepped forward and put her arms around Jay's neck. He smelt of cologne and something musky. 'Are you shagging one of the dancers?'

'I'm offended you even think that,' he said. Liberty gave him a look. 'Okay, okay. It was just a one-off.'

'The new girl with the lip ring?'

He kissed her cheek. 'I'm not made of stone, Lib.'

'You lot will be the death of me,' she said.

'Nah. You'd be lost without us.' He grabbed his coat. 'Even Crystal.'

'Now you're just being daft.'

It was foggy in the kitchen. Sol wondered how it could be foggy inside. When the mist cleared, he could see the ceiling above him. He counted the spotlights. Nine. Three rows of three. The bulb had gone in one.

'I've given you something for the pain,' said the doctor.

Well, Sol assumed he was a doctor – could be a vet for all he knew. He turned his head to the sound of metal clanking against metal and wished he hadn't. A scalpel in a silver kidney dish and no getting away from how sharp it looked.

If he'd been in a proper hospital, they'd put him to sleep for this bit, but presumably the hopefully-doctor couldn't administer an anaesthetic in the kitchen of his 1970s semi. Sol would put good money on the fact that Frankie was having anaesthetic on tap.

The stuff would be gurgling into his veins. The thought made him laugh. Frankie Greenwood, the gangster who had never paid a penny in tax in his entire life, was receiving the very best the NHS had to offer, while a copper – a good public servant – had to have his bullet removed by some dodgy bloke who couldn't change a light bulb.

There was a sharp sting, like a needle piercing his skin, then a sensation of wetness. Sol closed his eyes tight, until he heard a ping and saw the bloodied slug sitting in the metal dish.

'The bone's not broken,' said the doctor. 'There's muscle damage, obviously.'

'Obviously.'

'It'll be a while before you're playing cricket again.'

Sol smiled politely and hoped he'd get another shot of gear.

The grey of the warehouse floor and walls was punctuated by swathes of green where moss was growing in the cold and damp. Puddles formed around the base of the concrete pillars in orderly lines.

Liberty made her way up a metal staircase to the second floor. She could see a couple of stars through the skylights above. Or maybe they were planes. Two chairs had been placed at the far end and two people had been tied to them. Clarke and his younger.

Jay's men nodded at Liberty and left her alone with her brother and their prisoners.

Clarke's head hung on his chest, T-shirt covered with vomit and blood. He was no longer unconscious but was clearly feeling the effects of his earlier battering. The younger still had his mouth taped and looked around him in wild terror. A stain on his crotch told its own tale.

'He might not know anything,' said Liberty.

Jay shrugged. 'Only one way to find out.'

He reached forward and ripped off the gaffer tape.

'She's right,' the kid squealed. 'I don't know nothing.'

'About what?' Jay asked. The kid's lips quivered. 'You say you don't know nothing, but about what exactly?'

'Anything. I don't know nothing about anything.'

Jay looked at Liberty. 'That's fairly conclusive.' He grabbed the lad's chin, squeezing hard, so that his mouth became a grotesque pout. 'But let's just make sure, eh?'

He pulled out a knife, held it up so the younger could see it, waited for the whimper, then released his chin.

'Honest. I don't know anything at all.'

Liberty nudged her brother's arm. 'I'll tell you what I want to know.'

'Go on,' said Jay.

'When did we get this place?' she asked. Jay's laughter rang around the building, the echo reverberating. 'Because I'm thinking we could do it up as luxury flats.' She smiled at the younger. 'What do you think? Urban living?' His eyes went wide, and he looked from Liberty to Jay, panting at the sight of the knife. He tried to smile back at Liberty. 'You know the sort of thing, all stainless-steel kitchens and high ceilings,' she said.

'Like our Crystal's,' said Jay.

'Exactly.'

Jay shook his head. 'All feels a bit clinical to me. Not a place to bring up kids.'

Liberty fixed him with a stare. 'You know?'

'I'm not stupid, Lib.'

'She might not want to keep it,' said Liberty.

Clarke raised his broken head. Blood from where Liberty had smashed him with her gun had run down his face and dried. It made the whites of his eyes pop. 'Fucking get on with it.' His voice was slurred. 'Yap, yap, fucking yap.'

'He's all manners this one,' said Liberty.

249

Clarke grinned and spat at her feet. In spite of herself, she jumped back to avoid the blob of snot and blood. Clarke gave a cackle and Jay pounced on him, slicing his cheek with the blade. Clarke sucked down a loud intake of breath as his flesh opened and fresh blood poured down his face.

The younger began to cry. 'Please, please, please.'

'Shut up,' Clarke roared at him. 'They're going to kill us anyway so don't give them the fucking satisfaction.'

Liberty watched the lad's tears. She'd never killed anyone. She'd done things she wasn't proud of and she'd given the order to have Delaney removed, but she'd never killed anyone. There was no way she'd ever be able to do that. Jay probably had. Maybe Crystal too. She doubted Frankie had. He liked to play the hard man but he was the baby, always the baby. In a different life he'd have a wife and two kids. He'd run the Sunday football team, handing out oranges at half-time, giving his players a hug when they lost eleven–nil.

She smiled again at the shivering kid. 'What's the plan with Vine?'

'I don't—'

Jay approached with the knife and the younger screamed.

'Just tell us what Vine's planning,' said Liberty. 'Then all this stops.'

'I don't know.'

Liberty crouched in front of him. There was some blood from her mouth on his white towelling sock. 'I think you do. And I think you want to tell me before my brother makes a right old mess of your face.' There was a hissing sound as he wet himself again. 'How many men and where are they heading?'

'Say nothing,' Clarke growled.

Liberty patted the younger's knee. 'Come on, mate, you know you want to tell me.'

'I think he said Carter Street.'

PLAYING DIRTY

Clarke screamed at the top of his lungs, rocking violently in his chair until it tipped, and fell backwards. Liberty ignored his shouts and smiled at her brother, but his face was white as he looked to the top of the stairs. Crystal stood there, motionless.

'You were meant to stay with Frankie,' he shouted.

Crystal shook her head. 'He's . . .'

'Don't say it,' Liberty begged. 'Just don't say it.'

Crystal closed her perfect lips and blinked at Liberty. The air left the building and Liberty's chest burned. She could see Jay thrashing, hands on his head, but she couldn't hear anything except rain beating down on the skylights above her.

She could see him then. Little Frankie in his shitty nappy, sucking on a baby bottle of purple pop, giggling as he watched Crystal and Jay play Operation on the first step of the stairs. The batteries were dead, and they had to shout, 'Buzz,' when someone touched the sides, which made Frankie double up with laughter.

She reached behind her, pulled the gun from her belt and shot Clarke in the head.

Chapter 21

24 September 1990

We're a bit early when we get to the train station, so our Jay goes off to buy some sandwiches for the journey. He keeps fiddling with his eye patch, so it's got really grubby. But the doctor said he's got to protect his eye for at least a week so there's no way I'm letting him take it off.

'Are you sure about this, Lib?' Rob asks.

I'm not sure at all. I mean, I know for certain that I don't want to go back into care. And although I've convinced our Jay that they'll put us together, I can't swear they will. But what I am sure about is that if he stays here he'll end up back in jail or worse.

'You're doing so well in college and that,' says Rob.

'They've got colleges on the other side of the Pennines,' I tell him.

He laughs because he told me that when he was trying to convince me to come and live with him in Manchester.

I open my rucksack and take out my 'Feed Your Head' hoodie. 'I want you to have this.'

'I don't think it'll fit us, Lib.'

'Then cut the arms off and customise that jacket,' I say.

He takes it from me and gives it a sniff. 'Could do with a wash.'

'Like your hair.'

He ties it around his waist. 'I'll hang on to it in case you come back.'

Our Jay appears with two cheese-and-onion pasties. Christ, the other passengers are going to love us. We check our tickets one last time and go

through the barrier. When we're at the train door, I turn. Rob's still there
watching us.

'I love you, Lib,' he shouts.

'I love you too,' I yell back.

When we're in our seats, Jay gives me a look.

'What?' I say.

'I thought you two were just mates.'

I grab my pasty and open it. 'We are.'

Then the train sets out and we're on our way back to Yorkshire.

Present Day

Mel opened her door to Liberty with a grave look that didn't
match her dusky pink Ugg slippers as they squeaked along the
plastic sheeting that covered the hallway and the kitchen floor.
There was a glass of vodka pre-poured on the draining board,
which Mel pressed into her hand.

'I can't think about it yet,' Liberty said.

'I know.' Mel nudged the glass to Liberty's mouth. The first
sip made her split lip sting like a bitch. 'Get it down you.' Liberty
drained the glass and Mel tipped out another finger into it. 'That's
it for now. You need a clear head.'

'Is Sol okay?'

Mel popped the bottle of Absolut back into her fridge and
raised her chin to the ceiling. 'Resting.' She took the glass from
Liberty, rinsed it under the tap and dried it with a sunflower-print
tea towel. 'Time to clean up, I think.'

Liberty glanced down at her clothes, spattered with blood.
Some of it her own, most of it Clarke's. She slipped off her boots
and socks, and the plastic sheeting crunched as she wiggled her
toes. Then she dropped her trousers, rolled them into a ball and
placed them on top of her boots. Soon she was standing in only
her underwear.

253

'Shame about those knickers.' Sol smiled at her from the doorway. He was deathly white, arm bandaged and in a sling. 'I always liked 'em.'

'Avert your eyes, you,' she said.

'Isn't it a bit late for that?' Mel asked, and handed her a fluffy robe covered with pink stars and hearts.

Liberty ditched her bra and pants and slid into the robe, putting up the hood with bunny ears.

'Good look,' said Sol.

They went up the stairs to the bathroom, leaving Mel on her hands and knees, rolling Liberty's clothes into the plastic sheeting. 'Don't mind me. I'm just an old lady who has to do all the bleeding work round here.'

'You're fitter than all of us, Mel,' said Sol.

'Well, I'm in better nick than you, that's for sure.' She parcelled up the sheeting with an expert hand and sniffed at Liberty. 'Mind clean the shower after you.'

Wrapped in a towel, Liberty spritzed Mr Muscle across the shower door and scrubbed.

Sol sat on the side of the bath, checking a dish of mini soaps. He held up a yellow one in the shape of a duck. 'Why?' He smelt it and dropped it back among a handful of roses, apples and what looked like a soap-based Marge Simpson. 'What happens now?'

'I meet Ricky Vine.'

'And do what?'

She rinsed the cloth under the tap and checked her reflection in the mirror of the bathroom cabinet. Tia had been right: her lip *did* need a stitch. She sighed, reached for a wide-toothed comb and began to untangle her wet hair. 'If I had any way to make him leave here and never come back, I would,' she said. 'But I don't have any leverage. So, that leaves me with one option.'

Sol held out some clothes that Mel had left for her. 'Get dressed.'
'Where are we going?'
'You want leverage,' he said. 'I'll give you leverage.'

Sol jimmied the lock on the nail-bar door with a short iron bar. He'd taken the chance that the alarm box outside was just a dummy and been proved right. The air was still thick with the smell of varnish, and the dust from a thousand acrylic nails had settled on the work stations. No wonder the staff all wore masks – the stuff was probably more lethal than asbestos.

Liberty tailed him through the shop to the CDU office door, hair still wet and pinned into a bun. He hid a smile at her outfit. Mel's leather trousers and leopard-print PVC jacket weren't Liberty's usual style.

'Stop laughing,' she said.

'I'm not.'

The office door gave way on the second jam of the bar with a crackle of wood, and the lock actually fell out, landing inches from Sol's toe. He kicked it into the office. 'Welcome to Mission Control.'

She scanned the wall, decorated with pictures of Clarke and Vine. 'What is this place?'

'Long story.' He pulled the photos down with his one good hand. 'I'll tell you on the way to Carter Street.' She reached out to help, the coat falling open to reveal a neon pink sweater, the V-neck so low, he could see the top of her bra. 'Nice top.'

She looked down at her boobs. 'I'm thinking of working in the Cherry for a bit of extra dosh.'

Jay was waiting in his car a few streets away from Scottish Tony's. Crystal was in the passenger seat. Liberty slid into the back.

'What the fuck are you wearing?' Jay asked. He pinched the shoulder of Crystal's denim jacket. 'Give her this.'

'Unfortunately, I'm not a size zero,' said Liberty.

'Four, actually,' said Crystal.

'Yeah, well, I haven't been a size four since I *was* four.' She shrugged off the leopard-print coat. 'Give me yours, Jay.'

He unzipped his leather bomber and handed it to her. She did it up to her chin and rolled the cuffs. It smelt of sweet-and-sour chicken.

'Vine's in the café.' Crystal unwound her scarf and tossed it at Liberty. 'He's brought a lot of people with him.'

'What about us?' Liberty asked.

'Tia's done a great job of rounding up the troops. A lot of Hill's people have already jumped over to our side.'

Liberty emptied Jay's pockets. A roll of twenty-pound notes, two lollies, a gun. And a business card for Liberty Chapman that she'd given him when they'd first reunited. Had he kept it in his pocket all this time? 'Well, they're not stupid, are they?' she said. 'Hill won't be weighing anyone in for a long time.'

'He's finished, whatever happens,' said Crystal.

Liberty glanced at the photographs of Clarke and Vine once more. 'Do we think he'll go for this?'

'He's lost one and we've lost one,' said Jay.

Liberty stacked the photos on her lap, patting the edges with her palm so they made a neat pile. She couldn't think about who and what she'd lost. Not yet.

'Right, let's get on with it.' She wound Crystal's scarf around her neck. 'And just hope he doesn't kill me.'

The street outside Scottish Tony's was busy. Both sides of the pavement were lined with cars and vans, men milling around the doorway to the café. Youngers cycled up and down the middle of the road. Liberty's mouth went dry. If she couldn't sort this, a lot of people were going to get hurt on both sides.

Jay pulled up and she got out with a nod. A whistle went up from one of the youngers, three short blasts, and the doors to other cars opened, people ready to protect her.

Inside there was standing room only, every seat taken, and several men were leaning against the counter. The windows were steamed up with hot breath and tea.

Liberty spotted Vine at a table at the back, flanked by some serious muscle. She lifted her chin and marched over with as much authority as she could muster while wearing skin-tight leather pants a size too small and her six-foot brother's bomber jacket.

'Can we talk?'

Vine looked her up and down. He had chubby pink cheeks and there was a glossy sheen across his forehead that could be sweat or grease or a mixture of the two. He gave a minute gesture with his head and the muscle evaporated.

Liberty took a seat. 'I think it's time we called it a day.' Vine rested his tongue on top of his bottom lip. It was as pink as his cheeks, like a plump, raw worm. 'Take your people and move on,' she said. Vine turned to the men at the counter and laughed. They all joined in. Liberty knew they'd be armed but was assuming that they wouldn't be stupid enough to gun her down in public. 'Leave tonight and we'll compensate you for your loss of earnings.'

Vine smiled at her. 'Trouble is, we like it here.'

With so many people squeezed into the café, the air was still and hot. Liberty wished she could take off her jacket but there was no way she was displaying her cleavage to this moron. 'Leave tonight and no one else needs to get hurt. You won't be out of pocket.'

'And if we don't want to do that?' Vine asked.

Liberty produced the pile of photographs from inside the jacket and placed the first on the table so that it faced Vine. Then she took out her phone. 'Your place, I believe. Very nice.' Then she set down each photograph in turn. The girlfriend's house, his nan's house, the boxing gym. 'Your pride and joy, I'm told.'

Vine narrowed his eyes at the pictures, fingered the corner of the one of the gym. She'd got his attention now. Her mobile vibrated on the table with an incoming FaceTime call. She pressed accept and slid it next to the picture so that Vine could see the screen. Someone in a black balaclava held something up. Vine leaned closer to get a better look. The vein throbbing at his temple confirmed he could make out the bottle of petrol with a rag stuffed in the top.

Then the screen spun 180 degrees so that they could both see a white building. There was the rustle of a nylon Puffa jacket as the caller moved closer and the sign came into view: '24/7 Boxing Gym'.

'Don't even think about it,' said Vine.

Liberty leaned back in her chair, arms crossed. This was the moment she had to keep her nerve. With every cell in her body telling her to run away from there as fast as she could, she needed to nail herself to the seat.

Vine flicked the photographs back at Liberty and one fell off the table. 'If you do anything to my gym, I will rip you apart.'

Liberty tapped the photograph with her shoe. It was the one of Vine's nan's house. Vine was stood at the door, a bunch of chrysanthemums in his arms. Mam had always hated them, said they were for cheapskates.

'You can leave tonight without even being taxed,' she said. 'Or my people will torch the lot.' She put her head on one side. 'I know everything about you, Ricky Vine. I know where you go for a drink. I know where your kids go to school. I know where your nan plays bingo on a Thursday.' She dropped her voice. 'And I will burn it all.'

The phone vibrated again, and Liberty accepted the call. She checked the screen. 'Isn't that your girlfriend's place?' A younger came into view wearing a red ski mask. He held up a bottle in one hand and a lighter in the other. 'Is she in?' Liberty asked. 'I can't see any lights.'

Vine jumped to his feet and upturned the table. Liberty's people reached for their weapons, but she stayed exactly where she was, glued to her seat. Vine kicked the table with a roar and sent it skidding across the café floor until it crashed into a wall. Still Liberty stayed in her chair. He stood over her, sweating and panting, shiny face grimacing at her. He could have killed her in a second, but she stayed put.

He pointed a shaking finger at her. 'Don't ever set foot in Manchester.'

'No intentions,' she replied. 'I've heard it's a shithole.'

They let themselves into Frankie's flat with the key he'd given Liberty and laughed at the tip he'd left behind. Phone chargers, cups, half-full cans of Diet Coke. There was even a piece of toast, with his teeth-marks in it.

Liberty ran her finger across a line of socks hanging over the radiator, now dried to hard cardboard.

'What shall we do with all his stuff?' Jay asked. 'Can't just chuck it, can we?'

Crystal picked up a hoodie from the sofa and held it to her cheek. 'We should donate it to a rehab centre.'

Liberty and Jay stared at her, It was such an un-Crystal thing to suggest, yet totally perfect.

Jay shook his head. 'I can't do this right now. Need to see the boys, you know?'

'Give them a kiss from me.' Liberty turned to Crystal. 'And you should go and see Harry.'

Jay hugged her tightly and left with Crystal. Liberty waited until she heard the door close before falling to her knees. She let the tears come, tasting the salt in her throat. She cried for hours until she was exhausted. She cried for Mam and Dad. She cried for four little kids. She cried for the clever one, the funny one and the pretty one. But most of all she cried for the baby. And when there were no more tears left to cry, she crawled to Frankie's bed and let herself black out.

Chapter 22

Two weeks later

Sol took the train to Birmingham because his arm was still in a sling and he couldn't drive. He pulled the scrap of paper from his pocket and checked the address he'd scribbled down. A taxi ride later he met Hutch and Gianni outside the CDU headquarters.

'It's a bit nicer than the nail bar,' said Sol.

'Oh, don't get used to it,' Hutch replied. 'We've already got a satellite office up and running in the back of a pawn shop in Handsworth.'

'Who have you got in your sights this time?' Sol asked.

Hutch took his bags. 'A group of traffickers at the top of the chain.'

'Informant?'

Hutch smiled. 'Let's just say we've got someone in mind.'

Buckman was already on her feet, when Rose slipped into the back of the courtroom. The prosecutor had dyed her hair jet black, like a magnificent Cleopatra.

'I'm assuming we're looking at a transfer to the Crown Court today,' said the magistrate.

'Indeed,' Buckman replied.

Rose watched Hill and Redman in the dock. Hill stared dead

ahead, looking every one of his years. Redman's hair was now peppered with grey.

'What's the position on bail?' the magistrate asked.

'The applications are exhausted for the time being, so the defendants will be on remand.'

Rose smiled at the thought of the pair of them doing time and left them to it.

Liberty met Crystal outside the hospital, and they walked in silence to the lift.

When the doors closed, Crystal brought out a bag of raisins, popped two into her mouth. Liberty stared dead ahead and hid her smile.

In the antenatal unit, they waited their turn, Crystal scowling at the other expectant mothers. 'I'm too old for this shit,' she growled. 'I don't even like kids.'

When her name was called, Liberty virtually had to drag Crystal into the sonographer's room and force her onto the bed. 'Undo your jeans, then,' she told her.

Crystal lifted her jumper and Liberty could see that her sister's belly was already bursting out of her skinnies. When she undid the zip, the sides parted with a sigh of relief.

The sonographer squirted gel over Crystal's stomach and moved a probe over the pale skin. The ultrasound screen showed black and white patches but nothing resembling a baby.

'Maybe it's a mistake,' said Crystal.

'So, what's that in there?' Liberty asked, pointing to the round mound of Crystal's belly.

'A tumour? You'd be sorry if I was dying.'

'At least we'd all get some peace.'

The sonographer continued to slide the probe from side to side, until she stopped with a smile. 'There we go.' Liberty's jaw dropped at the sight of a kidney bean on the screen. 'There's the head and the heart, all looking good.'

'Is it a boy or a girl?' Liberty asked.

The sonographer turned to Crystal. 'Does Mum want to know?'

Crystal shook her head as she stared at the screen.

'How will you choose a name?' Liberty asked her.

'Already got one,' Crystal replied. 'It'll work either way.'

Liberty grabbed her sister's hand. The Greenwoods were going to have a new baby.

Acknowledgements

Many years ago, I set about writing my first novel for a bit of fun. Little did I know that I'd still be going strong with this, book number ten. I've told everyone I want a commemorative bench so in that expectation I need to thank all the usual suspects. To the Buckmans, for plucking that first book from the slush pile – spelling mistakes and all – and Krystyna and everyone at Constable for their continued support. And finally, as ever, my gratitude to my fabulous family. Who else would I want to share my bench with?